MURDER AT THE CHESTNUT WIG

CAPE MAY HISTORICAL MYSTERY COLLECTION
BOOK FOUR

A.M. READE

PAU HANA PUBLISHING

Pau Hana Publishing

Print ISBN: 978-1-968697-00-6

Ebook ISBN: 979-8-9872901-9-4

Printed in the United States of America

For the General Lafayette Chapter
National Society and New Jersey State Society
Daughters of the American Revolution

ACKNOWLEDGMENTS

As always, I wish to thank my first reader, John Reade. His insight is always invaluable as I craft the final version of the manuscript. But he's not the only one.

Holly Bolicki has been of great help to me and I thank her for eagle-eyed input. I would also like to thank my editor, Jeni Chappelle, for her expert guidance and advice. This book would not exist without her. If you're looking for an editor who's easy to work with, who understands your voice and your vision for a story, I encourage you to contact Jeni at jenichappelleeditorial.com.

I am grateful for the three highly skilled and totally delightful authors in my critique group who have provided me with endless support, suggestions, and feedback on this book. I urge readers to check out Susan Cory (the Iris Reid Mysteries), M.R. Dimond (the Black Orchid Mysteries), and Millicent Eidson (the MayaVerse Microbial Mysteries). I have the pleasure of working with them on their own stories, too, and I thoroughly enjoy them.

There are two other important people whom I'd like to recognize. I often contribute to charity auctions by offering the opportunity to name characters in my books. Mary Louise Holt and Frank Blough both won auctions to support the New Jersey Society Daughters of the American Revolution and the Cape May MAC, respectively, and I humbly thank them for their donations. Mary Louise chose the name Jeannine Holt. Frank

Blough chose the name Chloe Cooper. I very much enjoyed getting to know both characters as the story evolved.

I would also like to thank the women of the New Jersey Society Daughters of the American Revolution and, in particular, the General Lafayette Chapter, for their support and friendship. I am proud to count myself among their ranks. Their passion for history and the sharing of stories from the past inspire me all the time.

CHAPTER 1

I don't know if I could have prepared myself for what was about to happen that Saturday night. I don't believe so. One can hardly anticipate something like that.

My gaze swept across the dining room, taking in each detail. Everything was in place. Gaslit wall sconces cast a soft glow on the polished sideboard and buffet. Delicate lace curtains swayed gently in every window to allow the desultory breeze indoors while providing the privacy my clients valued. The imported carpet, arranged so only the perimeter of the glossy wooden floorboards beneath it was visible, swallowed loud voices and heavy footfalls. Damask-covered tables were arranged throughout the large room to promote quiet conversation.

My eyes rested at last on the looking glass hanging on the wall. The mirror reflected my solemn demeanor, from the top of my head to the waist of my gown. I reached up to tuck in a tendril of wayward hair. I had chosen my new gown specifically to complement the wig I wore. The gown was the soft color of a ripe summer peach. The fashionable sloping shoulders, wide neckline, and voluminous skirt accentuated my waist, which had thankfully not thickened over the past eighteen years since

Daniel and I married in 1834. The gown was becoming, though I longed to discard the corset and petticoats. The corset made it hard to breathe and the petticoats were the last things I wanted to wear on a July evening when the fickle wind hadn't yet dissipated the heat of the day.

I took as deep a breath as I could and let it out slowly. Wearing a wig again, this gown, these uncomfortable silk slippers, seemed an affront to Daniel's memory. He had been gone three years and a day, though, and it was time for me to publicly claim my place as the owner, proprietress, and hostess of The Chestnut Wig, the most popular gambling salon in the region. It would be strange to greet clients again without Daniel at my side. At least I would no longer have to pay another hostess for her services, as I had done during the entire duration of my mourning.

Soft footsteps approached from the rear of the house and I turned around, leaving my reflection behind.

"Jeannine, it's nearly six o'clock. Are you ready?" Chloe, my cousin, gave me a concerned look. I knew she worried that I would be nervous on my first night back in the public eye without Daniel. Dressed in a long black gown, she held in one hand the leather-bound journal in which she maintained meticulous notes about our food and beverages, menus, staff schedules, and supplies of crockery, serving dishes, and extra utensils. As she was now in first mourning, her husband having passed fewer than six months previously, she stayed in the summer kitchen as much as possible during our hours of business. It would be improper for our clients to see her, and she was not one to buck customs. Though I had occasionally deviated from the rigidity of mourning rules after Daniel's passing, particularly in the sweltering heat of summer, Chloe showed no sign of doing likewise.

"The girls in the summer kitchen are finishing the meal

preparations. The waiters are lined up, ready to bring the trays into the house," Chloe said.

"Thank you. Have them wait until the clients start to arrive."

Chloe nodded, then scrutinized my face for several seconds. "You have been out of the public eye for three years. Are you worried about this evening?"

I tried smiling, but it probably looked like more of a wince. "If I had closed the salon when Daniel died, I would worry that people wouldn't return to a gambling parlor run by a woman. But it was common knowledge that I ran the salon behind the scenes during my mourning, and patrons continued to visit."

I looked down and twisted the gold wedding band on my left hand while I spoke. "Likewise, I would be worried if I had delegated all my Chestnut Wig responsibilities during mourning and only returned to work tonight. Since serving as hostess was the only duty I delegated, I expect it to be much the same way it was when Daniel was alive. If anything, I confess to being a bit restless. I want this evening to be successfully behind us."

"You'll be wonderful." Chloe shifted the journal under her arm and took both my hands in hers. "Daniel would be so proud of you." My cousin may have been six years my junior, but she felt more like an older sister.

Chloe had plunged into despair when her husband died, and though I had no need for an assistant, I had hired her in order to give meaning and routine to her days. When she became my assistant, I also invited her to live in the Chestnut Wig with me. Our mothers had been sisters, so Chloe had been a good friend since we were children. I couldn't bear to see her suffering from loneliness and despondency. I recalled my first six months of widowhood—the smallest inconveniences reduced me to tears, my concentration wandered, and I was utterly crushed in spirit. I wanted to help Chloe through such dark times as much as I could.

Widowhood can be a lonely time, particularly in the first few years, as I had learned. What with the long period of mourning, as well as the restrictions about leaving the house, the rules about speaking to others, and wearing a full veil when out-of-doors, a new widow could feel as if she had no business being happy or spending frivolous time with others. Chloe was still early in her widowhood, and it was important to me that she have someone living with her who understood what she was experiencing. If Chloe needed private time to mourn, she could have as much time as she wanted. But if she needed company, she could have that, too.

My dear cousin gave me a knowing smile and led the way to the back of the house. I gave each of the gaming rooms on the first floor a cursory glance as we passed. Together we walked along the winding path leading from the back door to the summer kitchen, where the sounds of food preparation filled our ears.

The summer kitchen was a luxury not everyone could afford. It was a stone building situated behind the main house, used during the summer so the heat generated by cooking did not make the house any warmer than necessary. We had another kitchen inside the house for use when the weather grew colder. An attic over the summer kitchen was empty now, though it provided extra storage space if necessary. Outdoor shutters over the tall windows downstairs provided privacy when needed.

Stepping inside the stone building, I inhaled the scent of grilled meat, roasted vegetables, watermelon soup, and a mingling of other luscious aromas. Several negro women worked efficiently and in tandem, talking among themselves and laughing liberally. One of them looked up and saw me. "Good evening, Mizz Holt." Then she nodded at Chloe. "And Mizz Cooper. Food's almost ready. Smells good, don't it?"

"It does. I'd love to taste all of it, but I'm afraid this corset won't allow it," I said with a chuckle. I hoped there would be food left over, for I would certainly eat some after I removed the infernal stays. I turned to the waiters lined up along one wall of the kitchen. "Ready, gentlemen?"

All the men, like the women who worked in the kitchen, had varying degrees of dark skin. The captain, Solomon Sanders, smiled and stood even taller. "We are, Mizz Holt. And good luck tonight."

I smiled broadly at him. He had been with Daniel and me longer than any other waiter and he was my personal favorite. "You'll help me if I need it, correct, Solomon?"

He grinned. "You know I will, ma'am."

I turned to Chloe. "It looks like everything out here is ready. I'll unlock the front door and let you know when to send in the waiters."

Chloe nodded once and consulted her journal. "We have extra pear brandy tonight, so try to get folks to drink that."

"I will," I assured her. "If I know our clients, they do love their pear brandy."

Leaving all the staff and activity and noise behind me, I retraced my steps back to the house. A lone blackbird cawed, unseen, as a light breeze ruffled the treetops. To my right was a shaded alcove where Chloe and I would breakfast on warm mornings or read on Sunday afternoons. Our little wrought iron table for two nestled in the thick grass beside a red maple tree, surrounded by a bounty of summer flowers in riotous colors. I longed to be at that table now, wigless, wearing a simple day gown and reading a book, but The Chestnut Wig came first. Our gambling salon was, after all, the reason I could afford the staff and the lovely furnishings and the very food we ate.

I hastened my steps and entered the house. All was quiet, but that would end soon. I glanced out one of the front windows and noted the men already assembling in front of Congress Hall, a large hotel up the block a bit and across the street.

In just a few moments they would make their way to The Chestnut Wig for an evening of civilized gaming, conversation, and plentiful and delicious food and drink. Glancing again at the mirror in the dining room, I checked my reflection one last time. The lustrous russet wig I always wore over my mouse-brown hair while I worked gave me a feeling of strength and constancy. It was the very thing I needed tonight.

I had begun wearing a variety of chestnut wigs when Daniel and I married. He named our salon after them in tribute to me, and I intended to continue the tradition in his beloved memory.

I unlocked the door and stepped into the shade of the wide veranda. I didn't even have time to sit in one of the wooden rocking chairs before the men in front of Congress Hall began to make their way to the house. I stood at the top of the front steps, a wide smile on my face.

"Jeannine Holt!" The first man to reach the steps bounded toward me and took each of my hands in his. "What a privilege for us to be here at The Chestnut Wig tonight. We've been looking forward to your public debut as the proprietress, haven't we, gentlemen?" He turned toward the men ascending the steps behind him. Wearing solicitous smiles, they responded with a chorus of agreement. He turned back to me. "There are several others whom I know will be here this evening. I'm sure they'll arrive shortly."

A number of my clients were annual summer-long guests at Congress Hall. I had become acquainted with many of them over the years, though I hadn't seen them much since Daniel passed.

I thanked him and gave the men a gracious nod before directing them through the foyer and into the dining room, where they would begin their evening with a sumptuous buffet before continuing to the gaming rooms on the first and second floors of the house. The card dealers and croupiers I employed were already in place.

In the doorway, I touched a small button on the wall. It would ring a bell in the summer kitchen to summon the waiters to the dining room.

As the minutes ticked by, more and more people arrived. I recognized businessmen from town, as well as summer visitors who stayed in lodgings smaller than Congress Hall. Daniel had been friends with many of them. My shoulders relaxed and my jaw unclenched a bit as I surveyed the room. This evening would not be so bad.

CHAPTER 2

The men in attendance, all dressed in black or brown frock coats with trousers of tan, white, and even plaid, chose seats and tables while the waiters arrived bearing trays of food. My staff placed the food on the sideboard and buffet, beside tall stacks of our fine porcelain dishes. The guests knew to help themselves. There was a general shuffling as they stood and mingled around the food. As they returned to their tables, I walked around the dining room carrying a crystal carafe of caramel-colored pear brandy, proffering it to anyone who wished to imbibe. That task complete for the time being, I turned my attention to the clients who preferred wine. It was the hostess' duty to serve the beverages, though if I were in conversation with a guest or otherwise occupied, the waiters would make sure the guests had enough to drink throughout the evening.

Presently I heard the front door open and close. Two late-comers appeared in the dining room doorway. Gideon Welch and Isaac Campbell didn't frequent The Chestnut Wig as often as many of the other men in the room because they were busi-ness owners themselves and often busy with their own enterprises. Isaac owned a steamboat company. His small but highly profitable fleet of steamboats carried travelers between Cape May and points south. His office was located along the docks on Cape May's inner bay. Gideon owned the very popular Seaside Hotel, an elegant inn catering to the wealthiest of travelers.

When my Daniel was alive, he and Gideon had fallen out over Gideon's attempt to woo our cooks to his hotel's kitchen. Gideon's ploy had been unsuccessful because he had a disreputable tendency to disparage and denigrate his employees, whereas we have always treated our staff with respect. He had never forgiven Daniel for referring to his behavior as "cunning" and "unscrupulous."

Since Daniel's passing, however, Gideon had returned to The Chestnut Wig on several occasions. He and I maintained a civil attitude toward one another during the few instances I had seen him during my mourning period. I had a hunch he preferred to frequent a different gaming salon, but The Chestnut Wig had become a status symbol of sorts, so he liked to be seen at my establishment.

There was another reason I did not care for Gideon. Solomon Sanders, the captain of my waiters, was a former employee of his. Solomon had related several stories of Gideon mistreating his negro staff, from striking them to belittling them in front of guests, to withholding pay if they made mistakes.

After obtaining plates of food, Gideon and Isaac chose a table near the perimeter of the room, next to a window. With their heads together and voices low, they appeared to be in earnest conversation.

I approached their table and offered red wine. Both men nodded and thanked me, clearly eager to return to their exchange.

I did not intend to eavesdrop. However, I caught a snippet of their conversation as I stepped close to the window to adjust a curtain that had blown outward and become snagged on the shrubbery.

"There must have been a mistake," Isaac said. "I'm sure Mr. Shaw will look into it on Monday morning. If the bank were open on Sundays, he would no doubt do it tomorrow. He naturally wouldn't want any misinformation to reflect poorly upon the bank."

Mr. Shaw was the president of the bank in Cape May. Not being a fan of games of chance, he never visited The Chestnut Wig, but I knew him from our salon's long association with the bank.

"I'm sure you're correct," came Gideon's reply. "I am most eager for Mr. Shaw to shed some light on the situation. Dr. Jonathan Pitney has practiced medicine on Absecon Island for several years now and he is quite familiar with the health benefits of the sea air and abundant sunshine. I daresay you and I experience those same benefits ourselves, living as we do so close to the ocean. His plan for a health resort is an excellent opportunity for me and other business owners to expand our ventures northward. And a railroad is the most efficient way to drive those ventures into the future."

I fetched the brandy decanter and moved to the table closest to Gideon and Isaac, keeping one ear tuned to their conversation and the other ear trained on the rest of the room. "Like you, I have invested a significant amount of money in the railroad. I agree with your analysis of the project," Isaac said.

"I assume Mr. Shaw will be able to resolve the issue immediately," Gideon said. "However, if he can't, I will have to take further steps to safeguard my investment."

This was not the first time I had heard talk of the proposed railroad to Absecon Island from Camden, just outside Philadelphia. I had even done some research into it myself, and I was always interested to hear others' opinions about it. Though I did not care for Gideon, I maintained a grudging admiration for his business judgment. And I respected Isaac, though I knew little about him personally.

I stoppered the brandy decanter and stepped back toward the wall so I could survey the entire room. So far the evening was a success.

The waiters moved soundlessly among the patrons, bringing plates of food if requested, clearing used plates and utensils. I was proud of my employees. Several of them had shared stories of callous, wicked treatment at the hands of former employers and I was pleased they had found a happier place to work at The Chestnut Wig. Carrying on Daniel's custom, Chloe and I provided our staff with impeccably laundered and pressed uniforms to wear while working in the dining room and gaming rooms. It was a great source of satisfaction, and the men and women who worked for us appreciated the care we took in providing them with well-fitting, well-made clothing. Watching them glide among our guests, I knew we had the neatest and best-presented employees at any establishment on the New Jersey cape.

I smiled when two women, dressed in resplendent silks, entered the dining room. Mrs. Violet Curtis and Mrs. Ada Miller, both widows, were acquaintances of mine. They occasionally came to The Chestnut Wig to play at cards, and they were quite excellent strategists. It was not uncommon for their collective winnings to outstrip the collective winnings of the men. As they were above me in social standing, I would never dare to address them by their Christian names, but I thought of them as Violet and Ada.

"Welcome," I said, walking toward them.

"Mrs. Holt, how lovely to see you," Violet said. The younger of the two women, she was approximately my age, well-dressed and adorned with glittering jewelry. "Your gown is simply stunning. How are you faring on your first night back as hostess?"

"It is lovely to see you, too, Mrs. Curtis. My first night back is going very well. And thank you for the kind compliment, though all the credit for the gown goes to my seamstress."

Violet's older companion, Ada, had been a widow for two decades. She leaned in close to me. "I couldn't wait to get out of those dreadful widow's weeds. Especially in the summertime, wearing black all the time was simply too hot. And decidedly unbecoming. And you, having to wear them first for Daniel and then in half mourning for your cousin's husband. Thankfully you can now wear what you wish. And I must say, you look fetching in peach."

I grinned at Ada. I hoped I would be like her in twenty years.

"Please, ladies, enjoy some refreshment." I gestured toward the buffet, where one of the waiters was replacing a tray of meat cakes. "What is your preference for a beverage? I'll bring it to you. We have a delightful pear brandy this evening."

Both women indicated they would have the brandy and walked to the buffet. When they were seated with their food, I went to their table to pour their beverages. As I did so, a loud oath came from across the room. I stopped pouring midstream, turning to see who was angry and what was causing the trouble.

Gideon Welch's eyes bulged as his jowly face turned every shade of pink. I scanned the room quickly to determine the cause of his anger, and my heart sank when I saw Solomon stand from a kneeling position near Gideon's table. He kept his eyes focused on the floor while Gideon launched into a tirade.

"Solomon, you clumsy old oaf! 'Tis bad enough I have to look upon your disagreeable negro face when I come in here, but now you've gone and spilt my drink. Get out of my sight, you filthy cur."

Every voice stilled, every person froze. Gideon's abuse was outrageous and unacceptable. Sudden, red-hot anger flooded my body.

I set the brandy on the ladies' table with a *thunk* and hurried to Solomon's side. I would not tolerate Gideon speaking to him in such a manner. Solomon no longer worked for Gideon—he worked for me and he was a fine man. I spoke to him in a low voice. "You go out to the kitchen. I will speak to Gideon."

But my words came too late. The noise from the fracas had attracted the notice of the other waiters who were tending to guests in the adjoining game rooms. They streamed into the dining room at once, their faces betraying a startling depth of rage. And though Gideon's words were shameful and wrong, I hoped the men's fury would not boil over.

I thought back to the stories my staff told about past injustices, insults, and mistreatment, and I realized what I was seeing. It was the release of a long pent-up anger, anger that had been simmering toward abusers, wealthy white men in particular, for ages. It was an anger that only took one spark, the ignorant comment of a foolish man, to ignite into a conflagration.

I knew this would not end well.

I demanded they turn around and leave the room at once, but they seemed not to hear me in their rage. My guests in the dining room, except Ada and Violet, were already pushing their chairs back and making their way to Gideon's side, as if choosing battle positions. The thirty-five or so white men far outnumbered the six negro waiters. Everyone was shouting simultaneously. I tried clapping my hands for order, but no one listened.

I do not know who started the violence, but before I could even make my way safely to the doorway of the dining room, a melee had broken out. Fists swung, elbows jabbed, glass broke, food flew, white and black men pushed and shoved each other, and the shouting grew louder.

Solomon was in the thick of the fray. He appeared to be fending off blows from some of the white men. Several waiters came to his aid and succeeded in dragging him away from the brawl. He leaned against the wall, his chest heaving from exertion. His eyes met mine, then he looked quickly away. The back door slammed and Chloe rushed toward the dining room, stopping short in the doorway as she took in the scene, her mouth hanging open in astonishment.

"This is bedlam! What's happening?" she cried. "I could hear the noise all the way in the summer kitchen."

"Gideon Welch started a fight between the guests and the waiters by insulting Solomon. Someone needs to run for the sheriff." I searched the room for Violet and Ada. They were shouting at the men to stop fighting. I waved my arms until Violet caught sight of me. I beckoned her to me, and Ada followed.

"Do either of you have a coachman waiting outside?" I asked.

Violet nodded. "I brought Ada tonight in my carriage."

"Have the coachman fetch the sheriff, please. And tell him to hurry!"

Violet flew toward the front door.

By the time she returned only a few moments later, the fight was waning. Disheveled men, many with bloodied noses and lips, were becoming exhausted. One by one, they staggered away from the knot of people at the center of the skirmish. Neither my waiters nor my guests were particularly young men —I was surprised they had been able to fight as long as they had.

As the noise died, I moved swiftly to the center of the room. I stood with my hands on my hips, scolding everyone. "I am sickened that all of you would engage in such barbaric behavior. How dare you bring your fisticuffs to my salon? What were you—"

As I spoke, I glanced at the floor, where a large red stain appeared to be seeping from behind the circular table nearest the buffet. I froze, hoping it was wine. Everyone was silent, staring at me. I hesitated a moment, then stepped closer.

Gideon Welch, his face turned toward me and his eyes wide open, lay prone behind the table, his back covered in blood. I screamed.

CHAPTER 3

$\mathcal{A}$s shouts of alarm erupted and people pressed forward to see the carnage, Solomon rushed to my aid.

"What is it, Mizz Holt?"

I pointed toward Gideon. Blood pooled on the carpet beneath him. A gaping hole had been ripped into his fine white shirt and the blood appeared to have come from a wound in his torso.

Solomon faltered for a moment, then grabbed my elbow and led me to the table farthest from Gideon. He pulled out a chair for me and I sat, feeling woozy. Violet rushed toward Gideon while Ada poured me a large measure of brandy. With the exception of one guest, Bert Branson, the men in the room remained glued to the places where they stood.

Bert, who had been injured in an accident many years previously, limped forward with the help of his cane. "I will fetch the doctor."

Another man spoke up, offering to go in Bert's stead. Before he could do so, Violet knelt beside Gideon and reached for his wrist. She had nursed her husband through the illness that led to his death, so she was quite capable.

As Bert and all the others looked on, Violet held Gideon's wrist for a full minute, then shook her head as she stood. "He's dead," she announced.

I covered my mouth with both hands. The men, white and black alike, answered with a chorus of gasps and cries. Isaac, Gideon's dinner companion, inhaled sharply as his hands flew to his chest and he sat down heavily on the nearest chair. Several men made to leave and fled toward the dining room door, but Violet caught Ada's eye and nodded toward the doorway. Ada moved to block anyone from entering or leaving. Her ample size and somewhat advanced age would prevent anyone from trying to force their way from the room. I was still in shock, grateful for someone else to be taking charge of the situation.

Violet spoke up. "Every one of you will stay exactly where you are until the sheriff gets here. My coachman has already gone for him and will get the doctor the moment the sheriff arrives," she said in a loud voice. She glowered at the waiters, muttering words like "savage" and "brutes" and "infantile." I frowned, but said nothing, not wishing to rouse everyone's passions again. They were not the ones who had started the fight, but they were the ones who would surely bear the consequences.

From where I sat in the dining room I glanced up to see Chloe, white with shock, sitting on the stairs leading to the floors above. I had forgotten about her in the skirmish. I fortified myself with a long sip of brandy. Ada moved out of the way briefly so I could leave the room. I sat on the step below hers.

"How are you doing?" I asked quietly. At the moment, the best way for me to keep my own feelings of horror and dread at bay was to focus on someone else.

She looked up, her eyes blank. She swallowed. "I can't believe this."

I motioned for her to move over and I squeezed onto the

narrow step beside her. I whispered, "Gideon Welch is a clot. If he had kept his mouth shut, none of this would have happened."

She shook her head. "And this started because he insulted Solomon, you say? Poor Solomon, having to endure such abuse." She gave a start, her eyes widening. "Where is Solomon? Is he injured?"

"He is not seriously hurt, but he did sustain some bumps and bruises, from the look of him. He's still in the dining room." I glanced through the doorway and saw the waiters along one wall and the guests seated haphazardly among the tables. No one was speaking—Violet and Ada were thankfully making sure of that. Chloe returned to the summer kitchen to explain to the women out there what had happened. I waited on the stair in silence until I heard the distinctive sounds of a horse racing toward the house. Thank heaven, the sheriff had arrived. I went outside and waited for him on the porch. He ran up the front steps and jerked to a stop when he saw me.

I called out to Violet's coachman, instructing him to fetch Doc Parsons.

"Rouse my deputy, too," the sheriff shouted.

I gave the sheriff a brief summary of what had happened and escorted him quickly to the dining room. He took in the entire room with a sharp glance as he walked straight to Gideon's body. Like Violet, he knelt beside Gideon and felt for a pulse. Finding none, he stood up and turned in a circle, taking in the details around him. He told me to fetch two of my croupiers.

Curious, I went upstairs to one of the gaming rooms and summoned two card dealers. They accompanied me downstairs and waited, eyes wide with confusion, for the sheriff to address them.

"I need you to keep watch over the men who were in this room at the time of the murder," the sheriff told them. He deputized the croupiers and ordered them to take up their posts in the adjoining game room. That room had emptied quickly when the fight began—the men in there had run into the dining room to see what was causing the ruckus. That made them potential witnesses, so the sheriff would have to question each of them.

I led everyone from the dining room into the game room. The sheriff ordered the croupiers-turned-deputies to prevent them from talking to each other or leaving. Violet and Ada sat stiffly on straight-backed chairs in the hallway.

It was not long before the doctor and the sheriff's deputy arrived. The doctor hastily inspected Gideon's body, then asked the deputy to assist him in moving the body to his wagon. He said he would make a more thorough examination at first light. After he departed, the sheriff turned to me.

"I need a place to interview everyone," he said. I showed him to the private parlor across the hall where Chloe and I often gathered to chat after the close of business. It was a beautiful room. Two grandfather chairs and matching ottomans sat on a thick, luxurious carpet covered with blue and pink roses. Its wide gold border lent a sunny warmth to the room. Between the two grandfather chairs sat an occasional table displaying our favorite curios. There was a pink horsehair sofa and a polished secretary in one corner. Along the back wall was a marble fireplace. It seemed a shame to sully our calm, exquisite sanctuary with the sordid details of a murder investigation.

The sheriff asked me to sit and tell him everything that had transpired since our guests began arriving earlier in the evening. I related everything I could recall, then he asked me a series of questions.

"Did you see anyone attack Gideon Welch?"

"No."

He gave me a hard stare. "It sounds like no one saw the assault. How is that possible?"

I refused to squirm under his brash question. "Given the noise and chaos erupting all over the room, I'm not surprised no one noticed it."

"Did you see Gideon attack anyone?"

"Verbally, yes. Physically, no."

"And you said one of your waiters was the cause of the fight ..." He glanced at piece of paper in his hand. "... Solomon Sanders? How long has he been working for you?"

I gave the sheriff a stern glance. "I said nothing of the sort. Solomon was not the cause of the fight. Gideon's rudeness was the cause of the fight. Gideon became unnecessarily enraged at Solomon for some reason I do not know. The waiters who became involved in the commotion were simply defending Solomon. But to answer your question, Solomon began working here when Daniel was still alive."

The sheriff knew Daniel well, as they had grown up not far from each other. Like me, Daniel had not been fond of him. "It has been many years. I don't know how long, exactly."

"What do you know about him? Personally, I mean. Away from work."

"He and his wife and their four daughters live on the outskirts of town. They are a lovely family. Sheriff, Solomon did not do this. I know him well and he would never do such a thing."

The sheriff stared at me for a moment. I wished I knew what was running through his mind, though I could venture a guess and it was not a charitable one. "That's enough for now, Mrs. Holt, but I may have more questions for you."

He held the door open and I swept past him. He walked into the hallway, where he gestured toward Violet. "I would like to speak with you next, Mrs. Curtis."

After he interviewed Violet, he called Ada. When she emerged from the parlor several minutes later, she and Violet left immediately in Violet's carriage. Though Violet lived just around the corner, Ada lived farther away. I was sure both women wanted nothing more than to be in safety of their own homes.

The sheriff interviewed Chloe next, since she had witnessed part of the clash in the dining room. Her interview only lasted a few minutes, then she returned straightaway to the summer kitchen. The sheriff strode into the game room and nodded toward Isaac Campbell. "Please come with me, Mr. Campbell."

Isaac, whose color had almost returned, stood up on shaky legs and followed the sheriff from the room. His shirt front was speckled with blood, but that was no different from many of the other men waiting to be interviewed. Several long minutes passed before Isaac emerged from the parlor. I was standing in the doorway to the game room, next to the dining room. He nodded toward me, bid me good evening, and left. The sheriff came to stand near me and pointed to the closest white man. "You're next. Come with me. The rest of you keep quiet and wait here."

One by one, the sheriff interviewed every white man in the room, allowing them all to go home as he finished questioning them. I was surprised at how little time the interviews took but soon realized the sheriff had no intention of letting the negroes go so quickly.

The youngest waiter was the first to be interviewed. He followed the sheriff from the room, his eyes wide and his hands fidgeting. The silence was almost unbearable while the rest of us waited for the interview to end. When he returned to the dining room, I sent him home. The sheriff interviewed the rest of the waiters and as they finished, they departed one by one. Normally they would stay to clean up from the evening's activities, but just this once, the cleanup could wait.

Solomon was the last waiter to be interviewed, and he was gone an eternity. It was long past midnight when he and the sheriff emerged from the parlor. I discreetly gestured for Solomon to wait for me on the porch while the sheriff joined his deputy in the dining room. The deputy had been combing the room for clues to the murder while the sheriff interviewed suspects, and now the sheriff asked the deputy for a summary of his thoughts.

I joined Solomon on the porch while the lawmen were occupied. "How are you?" I asked. The sheen of sweat on his face shone in the darkness.

"He thinks I did it. I'm sure of it," he replied. I could hear his breathing, shallow and hurried.

I laid my hand on his arm. "I know you didn't do it and I told him so. You go home to Lydia and your daughters and get some rest. It's been a long night."

"Yes'm." He descended the stairs quickly. I stood on the porch listening until his footsteps died away.

The sheriff and deputy came outside a few minutes later. "I'll be in contact with you as necessary, Mrs. Holt. I think this investigation should not take long," the sheriff said.

Though I couldn't be certain whom he suspected, my stomach roiled as if my body sensed the answer already.

CHAPTER 4

An hour later, Chloe and I sat in our private parlor, dressed in our nightclothes. It wasn't our normal practice to wear nightclothes in the parlor, of course, but nothing about the evening had been normal.

"We are going to be exhausted when the sun comes up," I said. It was past two o'clock already.

"Hmh," Chloe said distractedly. A moment later she spoke again. "Who do you think killed Gideon?"

"I haven't the faintest idea. He was not a good man. Heaven only knows how many people in that room may have reason to dislike him."

"But to attack him like that … that was the work of someone who harbored far more than dislike." Chloe shifted in her chair and tucked her knees under her, covering them with her long nightgown. "What did Solomon do that made Gideon so angry?"

I shook my head. "He spilled a beverage. Red wine, I believe."

Chloe grimaced. "There will be an overwhelming amount of cleaning to do before we can open Monday."

I sighed. "I know. There is blood all over the carpet where Gideon died, and that will have to be removed and cleaned, if not discarded. I have never seen a room in such a state. Spilled food, spilled drinks, broken glass, chipped china, and that's just the floor. We shall have to clean the tables and the sideboard and even the walls."

Chloe shook her head. "Do you want to start now?"

"The sheriff and his deputy may want to examine the dining room again for clues to the murder. Perhaps we should wait until tomorrow. If he doesn't come in the morning, I shall go to his office and tell him we'd like to start cleaning. Right now I think we should try to get some sleep."

Chloe followed me up the stairs to my rooms, which were on the third floor, then continued to her own suite of rooms on the fourth floor.

To my surprise, I was able to fall asleep and I didn't awaken until late in the morning. After dressing in my day gown, I hurried downstairs and into the dining room. I stopped short in the doorway and let out a gasp.

In the light of day, the scale of destruction looked even worse. I stood, stunned, ticking off in my head the tasks that needed completing before we could reopen our gaming salon. It would take every free minute until Monday evening to clean up the mess. *If only Gideon had kept his own counsel,* I thought, *I would not be spending the next two days cleaning up the damage he caused.*

A few minutes later Chloe found me in the dining room leaning against the wall and gazing around the room in dismay. She was holding a cup of tea.

"Come along, Jeannine. I've been in the summer kitchen tidying things up since the sun rose." She handed me a cup of tea. "This will do you good." I forced myself to look away from the disarray, then followed her to our oasis of calm in the yard behind the house. We descended the stone steps at the back door and wound our way along the path to the little wrought iron table under the red maple tree. Our yard never failed to bring me a feeling of peace, and a faint sense of hope began to rise. I would fortify myself with some tea, then a bit of food. The day would look brighter after that.

Chloe fetched her own cup of tea from the summer kitchen and sat across from me at the table. Her eyes held a faraway look as she gazed over my shoulder. We were both lost in our own thoughts until she spoke. "How long do you think it'll be before the sheriff makes an arrest?"

I stared into my tea as if it might hold the answer, then met her gaze. "I wish I knew. I assume he'll be back this morning to investigate the dining room in the daylight. There were so many people in the house last night, and they're all either witnesses or suspects. I suppose the women are the only ones who aren't considered suspects at this point—you, me, Violet, Ada, and the cooks. I truly do not believe any of the waiters would do such a thing, but I do worry that one of them will be arrested."

"Solomon was employed by Gideon Welch a long time ago, wasn't he?"

I scoffed. "If by 'employed' you mean mistreated and paid barely enough to survive, then yes, Solomon was employed by Gideon."

Chloe was silent for a moment. I suspected what was going through her mind, and her next words confirmed it.

"Solomon must hate Gideon for the treatment he received during that time," she finally said. As much as I loved Chloe, I bristled inwardly at her unspoken suggestion. She had not lived under my roof long enough to know Solomon like I did.

"I don't believe Solomon hates anyone," I replied evenly. "I've known him longer than you have, and I feel quite confident that he feels holding on to hatred is akin to withering one's own soul."

"I believe you. Forgive me if my words gave you offense. I was merely thinking aloud." Chloe said.

"If Solomon killed Gideon, there could be no one under heaven more surprised than I," I said.

A rustling along the garden path caused us to turn our heads. A moment later the sheriff rounded a bend in the path and came upon us. He removed his hat. "When there was no answer to my knock, I assumed you were in the summer kitchen. I was on my way there when I heard your voices."

"Good morning," I greeted him. "Would you care for a cup of tea?"

"No, thank you, Mrs. Holt." He held up a knife, its sharp blade covered in a dull, dark red crust. "I found this in the bushes under one of your dining room windows. It is caked with blood, clearly the murder weapon." Chloe and I stared at the knife. It was a gruesome sight. Anyone could have used it to kill Gideon—every table was set with knives and there were extras on the sideboard.

The sheriff cleared his throat. "I thought you would both want to know. I have arrested Solomon Sanders for the murder of Gideon Welch."

CHAPTER 5

Upon hearing of Solomon's arrest, I dropped my teacup onto the table. Warm tea splashed over my day gown and the cup shattered, several of its broken fragments scattering about my feet. Chloe gaped at the sheriff.

"How is that possible? On what grounds?" I sputtered. "You haven't even seen the dining room in daylight." I rose to my feet and Chloe followed suit. "May I ask what evidence you have found to incriminate Solomon? What about all the other men who were fighting alongside Gideon?"

"I can't share any information related to my investigation. Suffice it to say I have determined the other men in the room did not commit the murder. I will be taking Solomon to see the magistrate in Cape May Court House after I leave here. I thought it appropriate to inform you he will not be coming to work today. Or ever again."

My throat seized. Murder was punishable by hanging, and when the defendant was a negro, the hanging was sure to be preceded by unspeakable beatings and torture. I straightened my shoulders and clasped my hands in front of me so the sheriff would not see them shaking. Somehow I managed to sound firm when I spoke. "Sheriff, this is simply deplorable. I know Solomon did not kill Gideon Welch. You cannot possibly have completed a full investigation of everyone who was in the house last night."

The sheriff glared at me, probably wondering where I found the audacity to challenge his procedures. I stood even straighter, knowing my Daniel would have offered the very same objection.

"Mrs. Holt is right," Chloe chimed in. "Solomon is a kind, gentle man. He would never hurt Gideon Welch. Or anyone else." I glanced at her, relieved at her support for Solomon.

"I shall go see Solomon at once," I said, lifting my chin.

The sheriff shook his head. "Can't. No visitors allowed for a capital offense."

I stared at him, dumbfounded. He grinned, seeming to take joy in my expression. "Good day, ladies." He jammed his hat on his head, turned on his heel, and departed down the garden path. Chloe and I were stunned into silence. To give myself time to think and calm down, I bent to pick up the broken pieces of china on the ground. My hands trembled as I gathered them into my apron. I took a deep breath to steady myself. Chloe was staring after the sheriff as if unable to move.

"Let me dispose of this." I nodded toward the small pile in my apron. Chloe followed me to the midden, where I placed the broken china with the other rubbish, then we walked the few steps to the summer kitchen. It was empty of cooks this morning. When we had crossed the threshold and closed the door behind us, Chloe spoke first. "Solomon's poor wife must be frantic with worry."

"My heart breaks for her. But if I know Lydia, she will work doubly hard to make sure she and the children have what they need to survive. If I thought she would accept charity, I would give her all the money she needs. But I know she wouldn't hear of that. Since she takes in laundry, we'll be sure to give her a few extra dresses and underthings to wash. Not too many, mind you. We don't want to overwork the poor woman."

"That may help Lydia, but what about Solomon?"

"To help Solomon, I shall have to do the sheriff's job for him. It is clear he's not going to do it himself." I crossed my arms over my chest. Before Chloe could ask any questions or break the disapproving stare she fixed on me, I spoke again. "And time is of the essence. Since you are still in mourning you cannot leave the house. But I can. I will do everything possible to prove to the sheriff that Solomon did not kill anyone."

"Jeannine, you are a business proprietress, not a detective. You don't know the first thing about solving a crime. And not just any crime—a murder! I beg of you not to do it. You will surely get yourself hurt or killed. And then what would I do without you?" Her eyes took on the familiar shine of unshed tears as she blinked rapidly.

I spoke in what I hoped was a soothing voice. "I'll be careful. I wouldn't do anything to jeopardize our safety. Or the other work we do here." I glanced over my shoulder as if there were someone in the summer kitchen who might overhear us.

I referred, of course, to the clandestine rescue work we rarely spoke about. Our activities, and those of everyone else who worked as stationmasters and conductors along the underground railroad, were in direct contravention of the federal Fugitive Slave Act. Keeping them secret could mean the difference between life and death for the fugitive slaves we sheltered.

And the difference between imprisonment and liberty for those of us caught harboring them.

While I oversaw the care of the fugitives who came to stay with us, Chloe's job was to gather information about escapees from the men and women who worked for us. Being part of the free negro community, they would often hear gossip and rumors of runaways making their way north. The market where farmers sold produce, meat, and other foodstuffs was a good place to exchange such information. I sent my staff there for many reasons, not the least of which was to swap recipes, household hints, gossip, and other information, but often they would receive early word that a fugitive was headed toward Cape May. They would share that information with Chloe and she, in turn, would relay it to me. We told our staff that we passed along the information to people who could help the slaves. That was untrue, but doing so was safer for them and for the fugitives we sheltered—the less they knew about our activities, the lower the chance they could be arrested for aiding fugitives and the lower the chance the fugitives would be discovered on our property.

We did not do the work alone, of course. There was a network of people throughout the north, and even some in the south, who did their part to help. Cape May's proximity to the Delaware Bay and its sea routes to the south made it an attractive place through which to transport fugitive slaves. There was a cook at Congress Hall, Araminta Ross, who would be available to help us throughout the summer. We knew her to be a staunch friend to freedom seekers.

At various times over the years, I had become aware of infrequent and quiet rumors that Daniel and I harbored runaway slaves. There was no proof, of course, since we kept our activities well concealed, so no one had ever made any overt accusations.

"I need you to keep doing your job for the railroad. Let me worry about Solomon."

Chloe sighed. "Very well."

"I need to change out of this gown. The tea has stained it." I nodded to myself. *Good,* I thought. *That means we already have one extra dress for Lydia Sanders to launder.*

By the time I changed out of my frock and donned a fresh one, it was too late to attend Sunday services. Before I did anything else, I saddled one of the horses and went to call on

Solomon's family. If I couldn't visit Solomon in jail, I could at least check on Lydia and the girls.

No one was home. A neighbor told me they were staying with Lydia's brother nearby until Lydia recovered from the shock of Solomon's arrest. I went home under a cloud of worry.

Despite it being the Lord's Day, Chloe had started cleaning the dining room. Since I needed something to stay busy, I joined her. We spent the entire day scrubbing the walls and the cleaning up the broken crockery and wine glasses. When we finally tumbled into our beds late that night, we had made a sizable dent in the mess.

The next day our staff arrived early to help clean up the debris. Armed with rags and buckets of soapy water, Chloe and I and our helpers went to work. Two of the waiters took up the bloody rug and laid it outside on the ground between the house and the summer kitchen. I told them I would like to clean it, if possible. I hoped the blood would come out with a vigorous scrubbing. It was an expensive rug and I did not want to discard it unless absolutely necessary.

Three of the cooks volunteered to scour it with hard-bristled brushes and soap. I thanked the women and sat on my heels to rest my back as they left the dining room. I noticed one cook, Eliza, watching Chloe out of the corner of her eye as she worked. I knew Eliza to be a reliable source of information and gossip, and I suspected she had learned something at the market that she wished to tell Chloe. I touched Chloe's arm. "I think you and Eliza should fetch us some water to drink," I said in a low voice.

Chloe gave me a knowing look and beckoned Eliza to follow her.

They returned several minutes later bearing a large pitcher of water and a tray of cups. "We brought water for everyone," Chloe announced. I caught her eye and she nodded ever so slightly. She would tell me later what Eliza had said.

By late afternoon we finished scrubbing off all the food that had been stuck to the floorboards. Spilt red wine had stained some of the wood, but there was little to be done about it. At least it wasn't blood. I fetched my reticule and handed money to everyone who had helped clean up. I gave them a bit extra, too, out of sincere appreciation for their efforts.

When everyone had left, Chloe and I went outside to examine the rug on the ground. It was nearly dry from spending the afternoon in the hot sunshine, and we were pleased that almost no blood was visible. We decided to keep the rug and to situate the tables in the dining room so that any small stains remaining would not be visible to patrons. Together we dragged the rug into the summer kitchen to continue drying. We dared not leave it outside overnight and allow the dew to soak it.

After a light supper, we retired to our sitting room. Chloe lit two gas lamps while I made myself comfortable on the sofa. When she sat in the chair opposite me, I leaned forward intently.

"Tell me what you learned from Eliza."

CHAPTER 6

Chloe spoke in a low voice, despite there being nobody about to overhear us talking.

"Eliza heard something at the market."

I looked at her expectantly.

Chloe continued. "I'm quite sure most of the people in Cape May are talking about Gideon and the horrible way he died, but Eliza said the negroes are all talking about Solomon. She said Lydia was inconsolable when the sheriff came to take him away just before sunrise Sunday morning." She shook her head. "I feel so sorry for his family."

"I do, too, but we are going to help them, as I told you earlier. And I'm going to try to figure out who is really responsible for Gideon's death. Did Eliza say anything else?"

"She said there's been talk of a fugitive trying to escape from a master at Congress Hall."

"Male or female?"

Chloe shook her head. "She didn't know, but she did hear that the person is unwell."

It was unusual to receive specific details about fugitives until they arrived, since it was safer for everyone involved if that information was not widely known. If Eliza knew the truth about our activities, she had never given any indication of it.

"Is the attic above the summer kitchen ready to receive a visitor?"

Chloe nodded. "I freshened the sleeping mat just last week and took a chamber pot up there today. The attic is clean."

"Thank you," I said. It was helpful to know the fugitive might be arriving from Congress Hall. We were not the only people in Cape May who helped move cargo along the underground railroad. We did not know the identities of the others, thereby exposing fewer people to danger. However, since the runaway was coming from the hotel just across the street, it was almost certain Araminta would be involved in the escape and would bring the runaway to our house.

Chloe opened her mouth to speak but closed it again.

"What is it?" I asked.

She hesitated before answering. "This is getting more dangerous all the time, Jeannine. I have read that a growing number of people are earning lucrative wages under the Fugitive Slave Act. Do you think it is wise to continue the work?"

"I agree, it is becoming more dangerous. But we have to help. I promised Daniel I would continue the work we began together."

"But things are different now. Neither of us has a husband to rely upon for protection. Do you worry about your own safety?"

"I worry more about the safety of the people we shelter here. They have the most to lose. And the most to gain if we do what we know is right."

"You are correct, of course. But I worry sometimes."

A flutter of concern danced through my stomach. Was Chloe having second thoughts about our work along the underground railroad? The idea made me nervous.

I rose and patted her hand on the arm of the chair. I did not wish her to know her words troubled me. "We are doing good works."

I went upstairs to change into my nightclothes.

THE NEXT DAY found Chloe and me gathering the heavy table linens from the dining room and placing them in a wickerwork basket. I hefted the basket through the trees behind the house to the stable where I kept our two horses and the carriage, a bright yellow conveyance with blue trim.

Our former coachman was a delightful man who had worked for us for many years. Since Daniel died, the poor old gentleman had become ill himself, and eventually he could no longer work. I could not visit him and his wife while I was in mourning, but as the mourning period grew longer and my restrictions eased somewhat over time, I had been able to visit them on occasion. His health had not improved, and I could no longer pretend he might return to work for me.

I employed a neighborhood boy to come twice per day to care for our two horses and keep the stable tidy, but he was too small to prepare the carriage when I needed it.

I needed to look for another coachman. I was tiring of doing the arduous work myself every time I needed to hitch a horse to the carriage. I didn't mind driving the carriage—in fact, I rather enjoyed it. Most wealthy women would not dream of driving their own conveyance, but though I was wealthy, I wasn't at the same social level as most affluent women. As a mere businesswoman and not a lady of leisure, I was their social inferior.

I hitched one of the horses to the carriage and drove to Lydia Sanders' house with the cumbersome load of linens, hoping she would be home from her brother's house.

She was home but in obvious distress. When she opened the

door, she was wiping tears from her eyes. She caught her breath on seeing me.

"Mizz Holt, thank the Lord it's you. I was afraid someone was comin' to tell me Solomon was hanged." Her shoulders shook as she sobbed.

I put my arm around her and led her to the table in the kitchen. I held her hand in silence, and after several minutes her tears slowed. She hiccupped.

"I'm tryin' to do the wash, but I can't stop cryin'," she said.

Lydia operated her laundry business from the back door, where she accepted linens and garments from many people and establishments in town, including at least two small hotels. She was busy and would be even busier now that she had missed a day because of her grief over Solomon, but I always believed it was better to be busy than to brood.

"I can't get used to the idea of him being gone." She twisted a handkerchief in her fingers.

"Solomon is innocent. I am going to do everything in my power to figure out who killed Gideon Welch so Solomon can come home," I said.

"I hope you can do that before they hang him." Lydia's tears started again.

I hoped so, too. "If there is anything I or my cousin can do for you, please let one of us know. Send a message with one of the cooks." Many of the cooks and waiters lived in the same part of Cape Island, and everyone knew everyone else … and their business. I was sure all the neighbors would band together to help Lydia's family any way they could.

"There's nothin' we need. I promised Solomon I would take good care of our girls."

I told Lydia to take all the time she needed to launder the linens I brought, then left with a promise to do everything in my power to help Solomon. When I returned to my house with the empty basket it took me a long while to unhitch the carriage and groom the horse. By the time I went into the house I was sweltering and breathless.

Chloe had a pitcher of water ready for me when I set the wash basket on the floor with a sigh. "It is time to hire another coachman," I said, wiping the perspiration from my hairline.

"I should have come out to help you with the carriage. How is Lydia faring?"

"As one might expect. She's afraid Solomon will hang for Gideon's murder but determined to keep busy and provide for her family."

I felt better after having a glass of water. I picked up the basket again, placed it in the closet where we kept it, and went straight to the dining room. Chloe followed me.

"Do we know of anyone looking for a coachman position?" she asked.

"I do not, but I shall ask Violet or Ada next time I see them." I looked around the dining room, satisfied with the cleanup process. I would ask a couple of the waiters to move the clean rug from the summer kitchen, where it was almost dry, back into the dining room. "They know everyone, so if someone is looking for a job, they will have heard about it, I am sure."

Chloe's eyes followed my gaze around the room. "When do you plan to open for gaming again?"

"I think if we open tomorrow evening, that should give the cooks enough time to gather the ingredients from the market and prepare food."

Chloe nodded. "I agree. The sooner we get back to business, the sooner life will take on a semblance of normality."

"I look forward to it," I said.

That afternoon two waiters and three cooks arrived to help us. I gave the waiters instructions for replacing the rug in the dining room, and while they worked Chloe and I talked to the cooks. The women were relieved to hear we would be opening The Chestnut Wig for business the following evening, as they and their families depended upon the wages they earned from the job. They expressed concern that the salon might lose business after the murder, but I assured them their jobs were secure. I had faith my clients would return.

We discussed what foods would be served and what ingredients they should procure at the market the next morning. After the rug was in its proper place and the waiters had arranged the tables to cover any faint stains that remained, they and the cooks left. Chloe and I spent the evening preparing the room for clients. Just before we retired, I went out to the summer kitchen to ensure the outdoor shutters were closed over the windows. Chloe disliked the job, so I often did it for her. By the time we went upstairs to our rooms, it was late and we were tired, but the dining room looked as if nothing had gone wrong inside its stately and comfortable walls.

CHAPTER 7

The faint sound of scratching awakened me after I had been asleep for some time. I leapt out of bed and reached for my peignoir. I tied it around my waist and hurried first to the windows overlooking the street below. Seeing nothing and no one, I crossed the room to the windows overlooking the yard behind the house. The large trees shrouded the area in darkness, but there was enough silver light from a waning moon to barely make out two figures standing flat against the back of the house on either side of the door.

Based on Eliza's information, I suspected who it was.

I hurried down the stairs and through the darkened house to the back door. Solomon had greased the hinges several days previously, so it opened without a sound. Somewhere to my left a bird, having been awakened by the presence of three people in the middle of the night, scolded us with an annoyed caw.

I stood aside and allowed my two visitors to enter. The first, Araminta Ross, was a diminutive negro woman, dressed in black and wearing an enormous scarf around her head. The second was a much younger negro woman. She was as thin as a bean vine and wore a dress, but it looked more like a flour sack. She carried a small sewing basket.

Somehow the furtive nature of our activity lent itself to silence. Even in the safety of the house, we spoke in low voices and moved as quietly as possible.

"I am glad to see you again, Araminta," I whispered to the older woman. I squeezed her hand. "I heard you were coming."

Araminta Ross nodded toward her young companion. "She's been stayin' with her master at the big hotel. Her master don't know she's gone. She knows she's free here in New Jersey, but that don't mean she's safe. There'll be people lookin' for her. And she's hurt. You'll take care of her until she's strong enough to get to her next stop?"

"Yes, of course." I placed my hand on the young woman's bony arm.

We were interrupted by the sound of a soft tread on the stairs behind me. Araminta gave a start and put her hand on the doorknob. The young woman gasped softly.

"There's no need to worry." I addressed the younger one. "My cousin, Chloe Cooper, lives and works here with me." In the faint light from the moon coming through the back door, Araminta nodded.

Chloe appeared at the bottom of the stairs. "I thought I heard scratching at the door."

"Chloe, you remember Araminta Ross. And this is ..." I glanced at the young woman. Sometimes the people who came to The Chestnut Wig for shelter did not want to provide their real names. I didn't know how this woman wished to be known.

"Emeline." Her voice was so weak I had to lean close to hear.

Chloe smiled at Emeline. "Let me show you where you'll be staying."

Emeline looked toward Araminta, who nodded again. Emeline followed Chloe out the back door and through the darkness to the summer kitchen.

"How long will it be before anyone knows she's missing?" I asked Araminta.

"They'll know at first light. I have to go. Send a message when she's well enough to travel."

"I will. Thank you, Araminta."

She said nothing, but opened the back door and slipped into the night. I watched her go, but within seconds I lost her. She was invisible against the trees.

I stood in the rear entryway waiting for Chloe to return. I didn't have to wait long, for presently she came hurrying along the path from the summer kitchen.

"How is she?" I closed and locked the door behind her.

"Quite weak," Chloe said. "I gave her a bit of bread and butter and settled her in the attic. It's awfully dark up there, but she didn't want me to light a candle. I told her I would bring break-fast to her in the morning. I do believe she was asleep by the time I descended the stairs into the kitchen."

"Thank you. Do you think she'll need a doctor?"

"I think we should have someone look at her." Chloe frowned. "She was wincing with every breath."

"I'll send for the negro doctor in the morning. Let's try to get back to sleep."

Chloe followed me up the stairs, then continued to the fourth floor after I closed my bedroom door. I tossed and turned the rest of the night. I never slept well after the arrival of a fugitive. There were too many things that could go awry, and I worried about this particular woman. She would have to stay at The Chestnut Wig until she regained her strength and I had no idea how long that would be. Sheltering a fugitive for even a night or two was dangerous enough for both the fugitive and for Chloe and me. It looked as though Emeline might be here a good bit longer than that.

I was awakened before dawn the next morning by birdsong

in the back of the house, and it brought a smile to my face. Bird-song was a comfort—if the birds felt safe enough to be at my house, then I knew no one lurked in the shadows. The lilting tweets and trills assured me no one was searching for Emeline on my property. Yet.

Since I planned to open the house to guests that evening, there was much to accomplish that day. But first I had to speak to Emeline. In the summer kitchen I set the water to boil for tea. While it heated, I knocked on the door to the attic and opened it slowly. I called Emeline's name quietly in case she was still sleeping, then identified myself immediately so she wouldn't be afraid. She answered me with a croaking rasp. I made my way up the stairs.

"How are you feeling this morning?" I asked. As I pulled a stool closer to the pallet where she lay, she struggled to push herself up using her elbows. "Lie still, dear. I can see you're no stronger than you were last night. Were you able to sleep?"

Emeline nodded. "Yes'm."

"I'm preparing tea downstairs in the kitchen. Would you like a cup?"

"Yes'm. I'll get it."

"You will not. You will stay right where you are until you feel stronger. I will bring your tea to you. Your only task right now is to rest and regain your health and your strength. I'm going to send for a doctor to examine you this morning. How did you become injured?"

"My master beat me."

I winced. The poor woman.

"What if my master comes lookin' for me?" she asked.

I had wondered the same thing since learning that Emeline's master was staying at Congress Hall. But I didn't wish to worry her. I had helped other people caught in worse circumstances and Chloe and I would succeed in helping Emeline, too.

"That man is no longer your master. But if we receive word that someone is looking for you, we will take care of you. Do not concern yourself with that."

I returned to the kitchen, poured tea for Emeline, and delivered it to her. By the time I descended the attic stairs again, she appeared less frightened.

CHAPTER 8

*L*ater that morning, with the help of my stable boy, I sent a message to the negro doctor asking him to come and evaluate Emeline. He arrived shortly thereafter and I showed him to the attic.

I knew the doctor to be a fine man, but I nonetheless wished to keep Emeline's identity as a fugitive slave a secret. I had advised her to provide the doctor with an alias and to tell him she was employed as a cook at The Chestnut Wig. I also asked her to concoct a plausible story about how she had gotten hurt. She devised a simple, yet credible, story about being waylaid on her walk to work. If the doctor thought she was lying, he said nothing about it. He cleaned and bandaged her numerous blood-encrusted wounds, did his best to splint two broken bones, wrapped her torso to stabilize several broken ribs, and prescribed rest. He gave her some laudanum and assured us the young woman would recover in time.

With the help of our employees, Chloe and I readied the dining rooms for the guests who would arrive later that evening. After polishing the candlesticks and the silver, we prepared each table with linens, utensils, and beverage glasses.

Chloe collected a large bouquet of pink hydrangeas from the back garden and arranged them in a lovely crystal vase which she placed on the sideboard.

As six o'clock drew near, I found myself in quite a state of agitation. I knew Chloe was anxious, too. She twisted a black handkerchief around and through her fingers until I feared she might never untangle it. Several times I saw her peer through the curtains to the street outside. Finally I went to her side and took her hands in mine.

"I didn't think anyone could be as highly strung as I am, but I was wrong." I smiled.

She took a deep breath. "Have I made it that plain?"

I nodded. "My own nerves are as taut as a wire, too."

"Do you think anyone will come tonight, or will the shadow of a murder scandal keep them away?"

"I believe people will come, if for no other reason than simple human curiosity. Macabre as it may be, they'll want to see where Gideon died. My job will be to prove to them that The Chestnut Wig is worthy of their time and money. Your job will be to prove that the food and beverages here, as well as the impeccable service, are as good as ever." I squeezed her hands and let them go.

"So what's causing your anxiety? Do you fear someone will guess that we're harboring someone in the summer kitchen?" Chloe asked.

I experienced a frisson of anxiety. I shook my head slightly and lowered my voice. "We should not speak of that in the open." I glanced around, even though I knew no one was nearby to hear us. "I'm not afraid of that. My concern comes from turning over and over in my mind what happened the last time people gathered here. I don't want anything of that nature to occur here ever again."

"Nor do I." Chloe exhaled with a quiver, tucked her handkerchief into the sleeve of her mourning gown, and nodded. "I'll make sure everything is ready in the kitchen. I've also given Emeline plenty to eat in the attic."

"Thank you, dear."

At the appointed hour I unlocked the front door and stepped onto the porch. It was a lovely evening—warm but not hot, breezy but not gusty. The scent from the blue cloud catmint planted in the front flower beds floated on the air. I breathed deeply and watched with relief as men and women from Congress Hall, all dressed in their evening finery, made their way through the big hotel's massive gardens toward The Chestnut Wig. They talked in low voices, not the exuberant tones I was accustomed to hearing from people coming to the gambling salon, but I supposed they, too, were experiencing some trepidation.

I stood at the top of the porch steps and greeted the guests as they arrived. I recognized several of the men, as they had been in attendance when Gideon Welch died. Bert Branson, the gentleman who walked with a limp and a cane, was not in attendance. Nor was Isaac Campbell, who had been Gideon's supper companion.

To be frank, I was pleased to note Bert Branson's absence, as he was in debt to The Chestnut Wig. The food and drink were provided to clients at no cost to them, but I charged a handsome rate to gamble and of course the house won more often than not. I extended credit to my clients, and most of them paid promptly when I presented them with a bill each month. The reason was simple: most of my clients gambled for fun, not for income. They were easily able to afford the pastime I provided them. According to my ledger, Bert had not paid his last two bills. Unfortunately, I hadn't yet discussed it with him, so I had no one to blame but myself. That did not mean, however, that I intended to continue extending him endless credit.

I went indoors when the influx of customers slowed. Clients were milling about the dining room, chatting and already sipping wine and apéritifs. I invited them to choose places to sit and to help themselves to the delicious array of foods set out by the waiters on the buffet. The cooks had outdone themselves this evening with plates of beef, duck, and pork. There were three fruit compotes and a great many rolls and buns, as well as potatoes, string beans flavored with lard, and any number of summer vegetables roasted in a sweet glaze.

Talk was subdued in the dining room that evening. I noted several people looking surreptitiously at the floor, no doubt in search of the blood stains my staff had washed out. Not for the first time, I breathed a sigh of thanks for the people who worked at The Chestnut Wig.

I was pleased to see Violet Curtis and Ada Miller come through the front door an hour after we opened for the evening.

"How are you coping, Mrs. Holt?" Ada asked, taking my hand in hers.

"I'm doing well, all things considered."

Ada and Violet exchanged glances. Violet leaned closer to me and said in a low voice, "We heard your head waiter has been arrested for the murder of Gideon Welch. That must be dreadful for you."

"Not half as dreadful as it is for Solomon and his family, I daresay." A note of acidity crept into my voice.

"One never knows what to expect when one hires these people," Violet continued with a significant look toward my waiters, standing at attention against a far wall. She lowered her voice. "And, of course, on top of that you have to handle the, erm, *rumors* about your house."

It took all my powers of diplomacy to tamp down the unease that threatened to paralyze me with fear. "I don't understand what you mean," I lied.

"You know," Violet said, leaning even closer. "There are rumors around town that you harbor certain ... individuals ... I'm sure you know what I mean. I don't put any stock in such rumors, of course. I only mention it because it's just one more thing that you unfortunately have to handle."

My eyes widened into what I hoped looked like surprise. "Truly? I wasn't aware of such rumors." My tone dripped with innocence.

Violet straightened and gave a little cough. "I expect your waiter will go on trial."

"I expect so. Will you excuse me? I should make sure everyone has sufficient food and drink. Please help yourselves to anything you wish." I gestured toward the dining room, then followed them stiffly, holding my anger in check, as they made their way into the already-crowded room.

I took up a carafe of wine and made my way among the tables, then among the patrons already in the other gaming rooms, offering it to anyone whose glass was nearly empty. As Daniel always said, though it cost a good deal of money to slake the thirst of all the people who came to The Chestnut Wig to gamble, it more than paid for itself when one considered how much those people went on to spend as each evening lengthened.

The night, thankfully, was uneventful. When all the guests had left, Chloe oversaw the tidying of the summer kitchen while I directed the cleaning of the dining and gaming rooms. When all the staff had left, Chloe and I looked in on Emeline.

CHAPTER 9

$\mathcal{I}$ lit a candle and went up the attic stairs ahead of Chloe. "Emeline?" I called quietly. The tiny flame did almost nothing to dispel the darkness.

"Yes'm," came the soft reply.

"How are you feeling?"

"A little bit better." Emeline paused and I could hear her shifting on her sleeping mat. "Do you know what'll happen to me next?"

"It's best that I not have that information. Araminta, the woman who brought you here, will make the decision when the time comes. Either she or someone else will direct you to the next place of shelter."

"Has anyone come lookin' for me?"

"I'm not aware than anyone has."

"Even my master?"

"What is his name?"

"Mr. Cowan."

"I don't recognize the name, and I saw nothing suspicious." Indeed, I had noticed no one asking strange questions, no one taking any interest in the rest of the house besides the gaming rooms. "Chloe, did any of the staff mention anything unusual this evening?"

"No. Everything seemed to run quite normally."

Emeline released a sigh of relief.

"Don't worry, my dear. We have ways to keep you safe and hidden apart from this attic. If necessary, we can move you."

"To where?" Emeline asked in a nervous voice.

"Somewhere very near. Now you get some rest. One of us will come see you in the morning."

After Emeline lay down again on the sleeping mat, I followed Chloe down the attic steps. We stepped out of the summer kitchen, locking it behind us, and made our way to the house in silence.

Once inside our private parlor, Chloe spoke. "I fear Emeline's master will come here and make trouble."

"I do, too. Perhaps we can find out more about Mr. Cowan. Maybe Solomon's wife or one of the other women will have heard something about him. It would be strange if he were not searching for Emeline. A woman her age is too valuable to leave behind without some significant effort made to find her."

"Even if she's hurt?" Chloe asked.

I nodded. "As the doctor told us, she is not so badly injured that she is in danger of dying. It's only a matter of time before she regains her strength."

There was an easy silence between us while we were lost in our separate thoughts. After a few moments I moved across the room and sat down at the walnut secretary. I pulled a piece of paper from one drawer and took the pen from the inkwell on top of the desk, then commenced a detailed list of the things I needed to do the following day. While I was making my notes, Chloe bid me goodnight and went upstairs.

Without Chloe to keep me company, our private parlor was utterly silent. Even when we were engaged in our own reflections, Chloe's presence lent comfort to the room. Now that she had gone to bed, my own worries crowded my mind, causing my nerves to jangle and become disquieted. I took my list and went upstairs to my own rooms.

THE MORNING DAWNED rainy and gray, with a cool wind driving from the west. By the time I went downstairs Chloe was up and had closed the windows to prevent the rain from coming in. I held my list in my hand.

Chloe nodded toward it. "Is that what you were composing last night?"

"Yes. I have so many things to do, I feared I would forget some if I didn't write them down."

"What is on this list of yours?" She asked with a smile.

"As a matter of fact, the first thing on the list is to talk to you about hiring a coachman."

"Talk to me about it?"

"Yes. I'd like you to mention it to the cooks this evening. See if any of them know of a family member or friend looking for a job. I will ask the waiters. If we can hire a family member or a friend of one of our employees, I would prefer that to hiring a stranger."

"Very well. What else is on the list?"

"I need to—"

There was a knock at the back door. "I'll answer it," I said. Chloe ducked into a gaming room while I went to the back door and opened it.

Lysander Greaves, who supplied us with the best brandy in West Jersey, greeted me with a warm smile, his white teeth standing out against his smooth, deep brown skin. It never ceased to amaze me that someone so young—he was no older than twenty-five, still unmarried and as much a gentleman as any man in Cape May—could have such a solid reputation as a distiller of spirits. His late father had taught him well.

"Good morning, Lysander. Please come in." I stood back as he entered. "What brings you here this morning? Before you leave, I must talk to you about procuring more of your wonderful apple brandy."

"That's why I'm here, Mizz Holt. I've made an extra-smooth batch and I thought of you first. I know how your customers prefer their brandy."

"I'll take the entire batch, if you're willing to sell all of it to The Chestnut Wig."

Lysander's grin widened. "I sure will, Mizz Holt. I can bring it by in a few days. Same terms as usual?"

I nodded. "Chloe or I will pay you when you drop it off." Then I had a thought. "Lysander, do you by any chance know of someone looking for a position? My cousin and I need a coachman."

He looked up as if he might find the answer on the ceiling. Finally he spoke. "No, I can't say as I know of anyone. If I hear, I'll certainly tell you."

"Thank you. We shall see you soon."

Lysander bade me a good day and left. I found Chloe in the gaming room. "Now I can cross brandy off my list." We chatted about the other errands and tasks for several minutes but were interrupted by another knock at the back door. I opened it to find the boy we hired to look after our horses and clean the stable.

"Good day, Miss Holt," he said. "I finished my chores early this morning. I'll be back later today to feed and water the horses again."

While he waited, I fetched my purse and plucked out two coins, which I dropped into his hand. "Thank you, young man. I wish you were old enough to be our coachman. You would make a fine one."

"Maybe someday I will!"

He thanked me, then turned and ran off, waving goodbye. I gave him a fond smile, which he did not see in his haste to get home.

Chloe emerged from the gaming room and joined me in the hallway. "I do despair of wearing black all the time and of not being able to see anyone but the people who work here," she said.

"It does get tiresome, I know. But it doesn't last forever. And it always helped me to remember that my discomfort honored Daniel's memory." I knew Chloe missed her husband as much as I missed mine. My pain had dulled a bit after three years, however, and she was still in the throes of hers.

A short time later I left to see the sheriff to discuss Solomon's situation. He was not in his office, so I went to his house. His wife answered my knock and raised her eyebrows in question upon seeing me.

"Good day, Mrs. Holt. How are you?"

"I am fine, thank you. I'm here to see your husband, if you please."

"He's in the parlor. Please come in." She stood aside to allow me to enter the hall, then closed the door behind me. I followed her to the parlor, where the sheriff sat reading a broadsheet. He set the paper aside and stood, eyeing me warily.

"Good day, Mrs. Holt. What brings you here this morning?"

"I am despairing because my longest-serving employee is in Cape May Court House under suspicion of a murder he did not commit. I am here to learn what progress you have made with the case."

The sheriff's wife left the room quietly.

"I told you the case is closed, Mrs. Holt. I know who killed Gideon Welch. I arrested him Sunday morning, as you are aware."

"What proof do you have that Solomon killed Gideon?"

"That information is confidential."

"And why is that? You leave me with no choice other than to assume you have no proof."

The sheriff bristled. "We have all the proof we need, and it does not concern you. My advice is to find a replacement for Solomon Sanders because he won't be coming back to work."

I had a feeling his "proof" was nothing more than hearsay and speculation—not that it mattered when it was a negro's life at stake. "You are aware, of course, that his family depends upon his income in addition to the laundry his wife takes in."

"It's a shame he didn't think of that before killing Gideon Welch."

I needed to change tack, so I smiled as sweetly as I could manage, batting my eyelashes several times. Perhaps I would catch more flies with honey than vinegar.

"Sheriff, I'm afraid I have gone about this in the wrong way. You see, I can never replace Solomon Sanders because he has been an invaluable employee for many years, first to my husband and now to me. I simply don't know what I shall do without him. Is there nothing I can say that will convince you of his innocence? I know you're a man of the law—you must understand that the real murderer is still out there somewhere."

"Mrs. Holt, there is no murderer running around town. I have done my own investigation, and Solomon is the person who killed Mr. Welch."

"Have you any idea when his trial might be?"

"The magistrate is ill. The trial has been postponed until he's well enough to get back to work."

"Thank you for your time, Sheriff. I will see myself out."

I left the room, pretending not to notice his wife peering around the corner to the kitchen. Once outside, I took a deep breath. My errand had been an utter failure, but I held my head high as I walked down the street away from the sheriff's house. I only looked back over my shoulder once, to see him standing on his front porch, watching me depart.

I had worked myself into quite a stew by the time I arrived at my house, and it took all my strength of will not to slam the door behind me when I went indoors. Chloe came down the stairs as I stood in the front hallway attempting to collect myself.

"Why, Jeannine, what happened? You look as if you're about to burst."

"That sheriff is the most irksome man. He refused to listen to me."

"What happened?"

"He declined to discuss Solomon's case with me, saying only that he investigated it himself and is convinced he has the right man in custody. His investigation, I'm sure, is nothing but falsehoods. But because Solomon is negro, that won't matter to the court."

"Don't fret, Jeannine. We shall find something to clear Solomon's name, I am sure of it."

I was sure Chloe meant well, but telling me not to fret only angered me.

CHAPTER 10

*L*ate that evening after our guests departed, I directed the waiters as they tidied the gaming rooms while Chloe supervised the women in the kitchen. I knew the wait staff preferred to talk among themselves when I was not within earshot, so I often tried to stay in a different room to allow them the freedom to speak their minds. But this night I watched with growing unease as they whispered to each other, casting wary glances in my direction. Each time they noticed me watching them, they looked away.

Finally I marched up to the second most senior man. "What is it you don't wish to tell me?" I asked.

He looked at me with poorly feigned surprise. "What do you mean, Mizz Holt?"

"You know very well what I mean. You have all been making it quite obvious that you are trying to avoid telling me something and I would like to know what it is."

He looked down, then around at his fellow waiters, who had stopped their work to stare at us.

"Well?" I prompted.

"See, Mizz Holt, we don't want to be the ones to bring you bad news, but there's somethin' you oughtta know about Solomon."

A pit opened inside my stomach. "What is it?"

"Now, I'm not sayin' this is true. I'm just sayin' this is what we've heard tell."

"Please just tell me what it is. I shall make my own judgment."

He shuffled his feet. "Well, ma'am, there's talk that Solomon was convicted of a crime and spent some time in jail before coming to Cape May."

I gaped at my staff in a most unladylike manner until I remembered to close my mouth. I blinked several times, trying to grasp what I was hearing. Finally I regained my ability to form words. "What kind of crime?"

"I dunno." He looked around and the other staff members nodded, murmuring in low voices.

"And the rest of you have heard this, too?" I asked.

My question was greeted with a chorus of "Yes'm."

"And you believe this rumor?"

This time, they darted glances at each other and said nothing. Their silence spoke volumes.

This was a worrying development, and one I needed to learn more about. Solomon a convicted criminal? It was unthinkable. I shook myself out of my darkening thoughts and took a deep breath. I addressed everyone present. "Let us finish our work for the night so you can all go home. It's very late."

Only a few minutes later, their tasks were complete. The waiters left, accompanied by the women from the kitchen. Chloe followed me into our private parlor and poured herself a glass of sherry from a crystal decanter on a small table. She offered me one, but I declined. I paced the room several times while she settled comfortably with her beverage.

"You shall wear a hole in the carpet," she said lightly. "That furrowed brow means you are deep in thought about something. Would you care to share what it is? Is it Solomon? Or Emeline?"

I sighed. "Tonight while we were readying the rooms for tomorrow evening, one of the men said there is a rumor Solomon has been convicted of a crime."

Chloe's eyes widened. "What crime?"

"No one seemed to know. And even more disheartening, the other men seemed to believe it. I intend to find out more about it."

THE NEXT MORNING Chloe and I were walking together to the summer kitchen when I remembered our earlier discussion. "Did you speak to the cooks about a coachman?"

"Yes, and unfortunately none of them know of anyone looking for a situation."

I nodded briskly. "Very well. I will ask Violet or Ada the next time one of them is here. One or the other may know someone looking for employment."

We stepped into the relative cool of the stone summer kitchen. "Would you care for tea?" I asked. "I'm going to set the water to boil."

Chloe nodded and busied herself taking an inventory of two cupboards against one wall. After putting the kettle on I went upstairs to the attic. I smiled to see Emeline sitting up on her sleeping mat.

"Good morning, Emeline," I said. "How are you feeling?"

"Better, ma'am. I thought there might be something I could do downstairs. I'm a good worker."

Indeed, the young woman looked improved. She was not as

gaunt as when she arrived, and her eyes were less hollow. She still wore bandages, but she seemed better able to move around. And, I reflected, she must be terribly bored up in the attic by herself. I motioned for her to follow me downstairs, where I addressed Chloe.

"Is there something Emeline could do in the kitchen? All the chores in the house are already done. Besides, I would rather not have her traversing the yard between the kitchen and the house. It's best to keep her in here."

Chloe nodded. "Yes, we can find a task for you, Emeline." She looked around. "I know just the thing. I have been planning to have one of the cooks scald all the wooden mixing bowls to cleanse them thoroughly. You can start with the smallest ones today. You need to scald them in boiling water and wait for them to cool. Then you'll dissolve potash in warm water, add a bit of lime, and scrub the insides of the bowls. Lastly you'll scald them again, then rinse them in cold water. If you finish those today, I'll have you work on the larger bowls tomorrow and the next day."

"Thank you, ma'am. I've done that before for Master Cowan."

I frowned. "You need not refer to Mr. Cowan as 'Master' any longer. You do not have a master as long as you are here."

Emeline nodded, her eyes wide, and a smile flitted across her face.

"Cleaning the bowls will be a good task for you, and it can be completed before the rest of our employees arrive," I said. "I would like you to go back up in the attic before they get here. Not that I distrust them—I simply think it's better if they don't know about you."

"Thank you, ma'am." She hesitated. "Mizz Holt, ma'am, have you gotten any word from Mizz Ross? I was wonderin' what'll happen to me next."

Naturally she would be anxious about Araminta Ross' plans for her future. "I have not heard from her, but that isn't unusual.

As I told you, she has to wait until the time is right to move people to new stops along the railroad. She must be very careful not to attract any unwanted attention. As soon as I get word from her, I will let you know."

"I understand, ma'am." She nodded happily, an eager light shining in her dark eyes.

CHAPTER 11

Neither Violet Curtis nor Ada Miller came to The Chestnut Wig that evening, so I could not speak to either woman about hiring a coachman. But it was just as well, since I was busy with a great number of guests who crowded the game rooms. Both men and women came over from Congress Hall, and I recognized several of them as returning clients. A recent murder in my place of business was not keeping patrons away.

Isaac Campbell, who had been dining with Gideon Welch before Gideon's death, arrived early in the evening. He asked me for a brandy as he moved into the dining room. I took the decanter to his table, where he sat alone, and poured the rich amber liquid while he lamented Gideon's death.

"I can't believe he's gone," he said in a subdued voice.

I nodded. "It happened so quickly."

"I visited his wife and sons. They are bereft, of course."

"Having lost my own husband three years ago, I can imagine how his wife is feeling right now."

He sighed, then spoke in a low voice. "I hear someone has been arrested for the crime."

"That is correct."

Do you know who it is?"

"Yes, though I'm convinced the sheriff has the wrong person in custody."

Isaac waited, not saying anything.

"Solomon Sanders," I said after a moment. I tightened my grip on the neck of the decanter.

His eyes widened. "The waiter? That cannot be. He seems a fine fellow."

"He is."

Isaac set his glass down and shook his head. "If only I had seen what happened. The moment the brawl began, my attention was diverted in all directions. Obviously the killer took advantage of that."

I nodded. I didn't wish to discuss Gideon's murder any longer, nor Solomon's arrest. I changed the subject rather abruptly. "Mr. Campbell, I understand you are somewhat familiar with the railroad being proposed between Camden and Absecon Island. If you have a few minutes some evening, I would like to discuss it with you."

His eyes betrayed his surprise. "I would be happy to discuss it with you, Mrs. Holt. May I ask how you learned about that?"

"I like to stay abreast of affairs that affect my business."

"Do you wish to talk this evening?"

"If you are able, yes. If not, I can wait."

"I would be happy to talk to you about it after you close up tonight." He lifted his glass and I moved away to let him dine in peace.

I had been greeting and mingling with guests for at least two hours when a portly man with a fleshy red face sauntered into the foyer. His clothing reflected his status as a wealthy man—I suspected his tailor was a favorite with fabric merchants, given the man's huge girth. He wore the latest evening fashions, including black trousers and tailcoat, a high top hat, and a white shirt paired with a white cravat. Though many men in the house wore similar styles, this man stood out. Perhaps because of his size.

I greeted him with a smile, offering him my hand. He bent over it gallantly, then straightened and cast his eyes about the foyer and down the hall toward the dining and gaming rooms.

"Welcome, sir. May I escort you to the dining room? You will find plenty of food and drink that I daresay rival any in Cape May."

"Thank you," he said. His southern drawl was softer than I expected. It was not unusual for hotel patrons, especially the southern planters, to spend exorbitant sums of money on games of chance at The Chestnut Wig. It was, it seemed, a favorite pastime of theirs. Indeed, if they wished to lose their money in my establishment, that was fine with me.

"Is this your first time here?" I asked. "I don't believe we have had the pleasure of your company."

"I have been visiting your charming town, but it's my first time in The Chestnut Wig." As he spoke I walked ahead of him into the dining room and looked about for an empty chair. Finding one at the table where Bert Branson sat with two of his friends, I beckoned the man to follow me.

"If I may interrupt, gentlemen," I began. Bert reached for his cane. He and the other men stood cordially. I gestured toward the man beside me. "This is ..." I turned toward the guest to allow him to introduce himself.

He bowed slightly. "Jasper Cowan, at your service."

I managed to suppress a gasp of surprise. It was Emeline's master. My mind reeled with questions. Was his appearance at The Chestnut Wig a coincidence, or was it something more nefarious?

The men around the table introduced themselves in turn. "Mr. Branson, I trust you will show Mr. Cowan around the other rooms this evening," I said. I turned to Mr. Cowan. "Sir, please help yourself to the food on the sideboard. Would you care for brandy? I have some very rich pear brandy that is a favorite among my guests."

"Thank you very much."

I glided slowly away from the table, looking around the room to make sure other guests had sufficient food and drink. I picked up the carafe of brandy from the sideboard, noting with consternation that my hand shook ever so slightly. One of the waiters standing next to the sideboard stepped forward.

"You all right, Mizz Holt? You're mighty pale," he said in a soft whisper.

I managed a smile and took a deep breath. "I am fine. Thank you." I contemplated asking him to pour the brandy for Mr. Cowan but quickly discarded that thought. If there was one thing I wanted to avoid, it was sending a negro to serve him. He did not need any more negroes waiting on his every whim. The very idea of the man's ownership of another human being made my blood boil, and that ire was just what I needed to steady myself enough to pour his brandy.

That task complete, I made my way through the other rooms downstairs to make sure everything was running smoothly. The low murmur of voices, the glasses clinking, and the familiar sound of chips moving around the tables calmed me.

I returned to the foyer. I stood across and catty-corner from the dining room doorway, from where I was able to see a segment of the room without anyone observing me. I kept my eye on Mr. Cowan. It was with no small amount of apprehension that I noticed his eyes roving surreptitiously about. When he pushed his chair back and stood, excusing himself from the table, I moved quickly and quietly into the private parlor I shared with Chloe. I kept the door ajar a sliver to watch him.

He approached one of the waiters and looked him up and down through narrowed eyes before asking a question I could not hear. The young man pointed in the direction of the privy attached to the side of the house. Having a privy that did not require one to leave the house was a luxury, and I know my guests appreciated it.

To reach the privy, one had to walk down the hallway leading from the front door to the back door, turn left through the butler's pantry and continue down a short corridor. I caught my breath when I saw Mr. Cowan reach the back door, glance over his shoulder, and place his hand on the doorknob.

I did not even think about my next move. I left the parlor at once and walked toward him with swift strides. "Mr. Cowan."

He turned around with a startled look but quickly recovered himself, gracing me with a thin smile.

"Please accept my apologies if one of my employees provided you with the wrong directions to the privy. I trust that's what you are trying to find?"

"Yes, yes it is. Where might it be?" His red face darkened.

I gestured to my left. "You will find it through the pantry and down the short passage. Please do not hesitate to ask for anything while you are here." I hoped my voice was convincingly pleasant.

I watched him until he disappeared into the privy.

CHAPTER 12

I waited in the foyer, trying to look busy by arranging a vase of fresh flowers on a console table, until Mr. Cowan emerged from the privy. He offered me a courteous nod before returning to his table in the dining room. I turned on my heel and hurried out the back door, through the yard, and into the summer kitchen. The large room was abuzz with activity. I spied Chloe near a sink, talking to one of the cooks.

"Chloe," I called. She looked up in surprise.

"Is anything wrong?" she asked. She pointed at something in the sink and the cook turned her attention to it. Chloe hastened toward me.

"Where is Emeline?" I asked in a whisper. Several cooks glanced toward us as we huddled with our heads together.

"In the attic. Why?"

"Make sure she stays up there. Do any of the women in the kitchen know she's up there?"

"I don't believe so. Jeannine, you're worrying me. Whatever is the matter?"

"Emeline's master, Mr. Cowan, is in the dining room. I think he suspects she might be here."

Chloe gasped softly. "What makes you think that?"

I told her what I had witnessed.

"What did you do?"

"I interrupted him and showed him where the privy is located."

Chloe took a shaky breath. "He must know Emeline is here."

"He may be just guessing, hoping to find her. As long as she stays in the attic during business hours, she should be safe enough for now. I must get back to the house. Don't leave the kitchen for any reason."

"I shall stay right here. Be careful. Those southern masters will stop at nothing to retrieve what they consider to be their property." Chloe's eyes held a worried look. I squeezed her hand and returned to my guests.

When I glanced through the dining room doorway, Mr. Cowan was engaged in a lively conversation with Isaac Campbell. They were discussing the proposed railroad to Absecon Island and, as usual, Isaac was expressing his enthusiasm for the idea.

"Do I think it will affect my steamboat business?" Isaac was saying. "No. My boats travel mainly between Cape May and southern port cities, and business is booming. As long as there is no railroad planned from the south, I don't foresee a conflict with my own customers."

Mr. Cowan laughed and said something in response, but I couldn't hear it.

There were no incidents of concern for the rest of the evening, though I did tell Isaac Campbell we would have to postpone our discussion of the railroad. I needed to get everyone out of the house so Chloe and I could talk about Mr. Cowan and what his presence might mean for Emeline's safety.

When it was time to close the games and send the guests on their way, I stood on the porch and bid them all goodnight as they departed. One by one the men bent over my hand and thanked me for another enjoyable evening of cards, dice, and congeniality. Even Mr. Cowan's smile seemed genuine when he wished me a pleasant evening. He was deep in discourse with another guest as they left the parlor, so if he hoped to take another look around the first floor of The Chestnut Wig, he was thwarted.

When the staff had gone for the night, I leaned against the dining room doorway and closed my eyes. I had helped Daniel run The Chestnut Wig all those years, but I had never realized how tiring it could all be until I had to do it myself. Alone in the house, I moved through each gaming room, tidying here and there so it would be easy to set up the next day. Finally I turned down all the gas jets to dim the lights.

I locked the back door behind me as a precaution, then hurried across the yard to the summer kitchen. I typically enjoyed being out-of-doors in the nighttime, with just the hum of the insects and the moonlight for company, but given Mr. Cowan's earlier appearance, on this night I did not wish to tarry. I did not even bother to go around the outside of the summer kitchen to close the shutters as I usually did. I found Chloe seated at a small table in the corner, writing in a ledger. Gas lamps lit the large room, giving it a homey air.

I locked the door behind me and sat across from Chloe. I leaned close to her and spoke in a low voice. I didn't want Emeline to overhear us. "I trust no one said anything about Emeline this evening? And that she stayed in the attic?"

Chloe nodded. "After she finished cleaning the wooden bowls, but before any staff or guests arrived, I sent her up to the attic with tea and a plate of bread, cheese, and fruit for her supper. She did an excellent job, I might add. She is a fast worker. "

I leaned back in my chair. "Mr. Cowan did no more snooping, but he seemed engrossed in the various discussions going on all around him for the rest of the evening. If he wanted to take a look around, he was foiled by the other men who can talk of nothing but economics and such."

"Do you think he'll return?" Chloe asked.

I didn't answer right away. I was thinking about what could happen to Emeline if Mr. Cowan found her or heard from someone that we were sheltering her in the attic of the summer kitchen.

As I mused to myself, I happened to glance out one of the windowpanes at the other end of the kitchen. I was shocked by a pale face peering through the glass.

CHAPTER 13

I gasped and stood so quickly my chair toppled backward onto the floor.

"What's wrong?" Chloe cried, leaping from her seat.

Without answering, I ran to the door, unlocked it, and yanked it open. With Chloe in my wake, I stumbled over the threshold and toppled onto the ground, entangling my feet in my skirt. I hoped our ruckus hadn't disturbed Emeline, and I hoped even more fervently that if she heard us, she didn't descend from the attic to figure out what was causing all the noise. What if the person at the window was Mr. Cowan and he saw her?

I scrambled to my feet and ran around the corner of the kitchen, but it was completely dark. I didn't see anyone. The trees growing thickly between the kitchen and the back of the property loomed over me. An intense feeling of being watched, of malice itself, swept over my body. When I stopped short, Chloe ran straight into me.

"What are you doing?" she demanded breathlessly.

"I saw someone in the window," I whispered.

She grabbed my arm and pulled me toward the kitchen door. "Then why are we out here? We need to get inside right now!"

The foolishness of my actions struck me like a bolt of lightning. Why, indeed, had I chased that person? I turned on my heel and followed her as fast as my feet could go back to the summer kitchen, slamming the door and locking it behind us.

Chloe was trembling. Her face was white and her eyes flashed with anger. "Jeannine, you must think—think!—before doing something like that again. You nearly scared me witless. What would we have done if that person had still been out there, bent on harming us? Or robbing us? Was it a man? Did you recognize him?"

I shook my head. "I have no idea who it was. Please accept my apology. It was silly of me to go running off into the darkness like that."

Chloe's tone softened. "Of course I accept your apology. Do you suppose it was Mr. Cowan?" She whispered, as if he could hear us talking.

"Since he considers Emeline his chattel, it wouldn't surprise me if he were out there. Or perhaps someone in his hire." I moved toward the attic door and pressed my ear to it. I could hear nothing from upstairs. "I think we should warn Emeline to be especially vigilant."

Chloe's eyes widened. "Surely you're not going to tell her that Mr. Cowan was at the gaming tables earlier."

"I believe we have to tell her. If she gets a notion to leave here or even to light a candle in the attic, she must know the danger she'll be in. We have a duty to protect her. I couldn't live with myself if we put her in the path of danger."

"Very well." Chloe's voice belied her anxiety. She opened her mouth as if to say something, then closed it and looked down at her feet, hesitating. I waited for her to tell me what was on her mind. She lifted her gaze to meet my eyes. "Jeannine, I am not so sure hiding Emeline is a good idea."

I took her hands in mine, ignoring the prick of unease I felt in my stomach. "I will go upstairs to talk to her. I hope Araminta will be quick in arranging her escape from this area. She will be much safer in Philadelphia, where there are more people to protect her and many more places to hide from the slave catchers until she can get to Canada. Do not fear, cousin. We are doing the right thing by sheltering Emeline. After I talk to her, we'll lock her into the summer kitchen, lock ourselves into the house, and all of us will be safe."

Chloe sat at the small table downstairs while I ascended the attic stairs. "Emeline?" I called into the darkness. "It is I, Mrs. Holt."

"Yes'm?" came a tiny voice from the far reaches of the attic.

"There's no need to be afraid, my dear. Come and sit with me for a moment. There's something we must discuss."

I could hear her making her way slowly toward me. Chloe had placed two straight-backed chairs in the attic, so I sat in one and invited Emeline to sit in the other. She sat silent as a stone waiting for me to speak.

"Now I don't want you to fret, but I think it's important for you to know that Mr. Cowan was in the gaming house tonight," I began.

She gasped. "He found me."

"I'm not so sure of that. He was looking for you, certainly, but the important thing is that he did not find you."

"How did you know he was looking for me?"

"I caught him supposedly searching for the privy." I paused, debating whether to tell her about the face in the window. I was loath to tell her but, I reflected, it was important for her to understand she could not reveal herself unless it was to people I trusted completely.

"There is one more thing," I said. Emeline's clothes rustled as her knee bounced up and down incessantly. The entire wooden floor shook with the force of it.

"My dear, you must get hold of yourself. I have one more thing to tell you, but it won't do to have you falling apart with nerves."

The young woman's knee stilled. I took a deep breath. "Did you hear the commotion downstairs just a short while ago?"

"Yes'm."

"That was Chloe and me. I saw someone peering in through one of the kitchen windows and we ran out to see who it was."

Emeline let out a soft gasp. "Who was it?" she asked.

"I don't know. Whoever it was must have run off when we chased him."

She swallowed, a very loud sound in the otherwise silent attic. "Do you think it was Mr. Cowan?"

"I can't be sure, of course, but it is possible. My aim in telling you this is not to scare you, but to emphasize the potentially dangerous situation we are all in. If it was Mr. Cowan, I hope he has finally concluded that you are not on my property and will conduct his searches elsewhere. If it was not Mr. Cowan, there may be a prowler on the loose and I don't want you exposing your whereabouts to him, either. Do you understand?"

"Yes'm. Do you think anyone'll be looking for me during daylight? Because I'd sure like to help downstairs. I don't like doin' nothin' for my keep."

"I understand, Emeline. Let me think about it. Tell me, does Mr. Cowan have any friends or business associates at Congress Hall that you know of? We need to be aware of any people he might send here on his behalf. People who mean you harm."

"No, ma'am. Not anyone that I know of, and I was with Master Cowan most of his waking hours."

I nodded. "Very well. We will keep our eyes open, but it seems our main concern is Mr. Cowan." *Or a slave catcher,* I thought. "Is he married?"

"Yes. His wife is here with him. Mistress Cowan is a mean one."

"I can imagine. I have heard the stories about mistresses being worse than their husbands."

"That's the truth."

"Goodnight, my dear, and try to sleep well. I will see you tomorrow."

"Goodnight, ma'am."

A moment later Chloe and I left the summer kitchen and locked the door behind us. We did the same upon going into our house. I confess I did not sleep well that night, and I know Chloe did not, either. I could hear her pacing the floor above me well into the wee hours of the morning.

CHAPTER 14

The next day I went visiting. Since Solomon could not have visitors and I didn't want to intrude on Lydia again, I decided to make other calls.

My first visit was a somber one, to Gideon Welch's house. The family would be in mourning, but as Gideon died at The Chestnut Wig, it would be unseemly if I did not offer my condolences. A week had passed since his death, so it would not be improper for me to pay a call. I worried I would be somehow blamed for his death, but his wife and sons were quite gracious. Mrs. Welch looked tired, from her pallid face to her slippered feet, which rested on a hassock.

"I hope you'll tell me if there is any way I can be of assistance," I said at the close of my visit.

Caleb, the eldest of Gideon's three sons, nodded and placed a hand on his mother's shoulder. "Thank you. We will."

I bid them goodbye. My next visit was to my friend Eunice, who lived nearby in a large, comfortable home. She had just returned from a trip and I was eager to hear about it.

Upon arriving at Eunice's house, I stood outside the front

door as her manservant took my card to present to her, then he returned and asked me to follow him. I found I was not the only one looking forward to hearing about her trip—when I walked into the parlor Eunice sat conversing with another woman. She stood and walked toward me with her hands outstretched.

"Mrs. Holt, how lovely of you to come see me," she said. When we were alone we addressed each other by our Christian names, but in front of others we used more formal address. She turned to the other woman. "Mrs. Branson, I believe you know Mrs. Holt. Please join us, Mrs. Holt." Eunice gestured toward a chair near her.

I bowed courteously to Mrs. Branson, who inclined her head toward me. I knew her vaguely. She was a seamstress. I did not use her services, as I preferred my own dressmaker, but I heard she was of tolerable skill. I also knew her husband to be the Mr. Bert Branson who frequented The Chestnut Wig. In truth, it was somewhat embarrassing to meet Mrs. Branson socially, given her husband's indebtedness to me.

I could not know for certain whether Mrs. Branson knew of her husband's penchant for gambling, but I had a suspicion, based on the glowering look she bestowed upon me when Eunice was not looking.

"I was just telling Mrs. Branson about my trip to Charleston," Eunice said. "We traveled on one of Isaac Campbell's steamboats. A delightful trip and such an inspiring city! And there were a great many people. It was very exciting, of course. My husband and I attended the theater on several occasions, and the gardens must be seen to be believed. But oh, the heat in South Carolina is oppressive."

Eunice regaled us with stories of the people she met and the places she visited. After thirty minutes of lively talk, Mrs. Branson and I took our leave. Eunice saw us to the doorway of the parlor, and her manservant showed us out. When he closed the front door quietly behind us, I pulled on my gloves and was about to descend the steps when Mrs. Branson spoke.

"It would have been impolite of me to say anything in there," she began, tilting her head toward Eunice's front door, "but I know exactly who you are."

I was taken aback by her biting tone, though after seeing the way she looked at me in the parlor, I should not have been surprised. In my experience, there is nothing worse than a wife who blames her husband's shortcomings on someone other than her husband.

I quickly determined that my wisest course of action would be to treat Mrs. Branson with the utmost politeness.

"You know me?" I questioned, all innocence.

"You are the owner of that den of vice, The Chestnut Wig."

"Why, yes. That's correct, though I wouldn't refer to it that way, of course. To me, it is my business and my livelihood."

"Your livelihood," she sneered. "I should say! A livelihood based on the veritable theft of other people's hard-earned wages."

I imagine she would not mind quite so much if her husband were making money rather than losing it, I thought.

Aloud I said, "I fear I do not know what you are talking about, Mrs. Branson. I have never committed a theft in my life and I would be loath to do so. Heaven forbid it."

"How else would you describe your 'business,' as you so shamelessly put it?"

"I beg your forgiveness, Mrs. Branson, but my business is no different from any other business where people go to purchase goods and services. I simply provide my clients with entertainment. It is quite legal, I can assure you."

I struggled to keep a knowing smile from my face. Propriety dictated that Mrs. Branson not be more forthright with her accusations, but I knew she was aching to do so. And my refusal to engage her in a debate was enraging her—I could tell from the high spots of color in her cheeks and her occasional spluttering when she spoke.

"Pray allow me to express my views this way," Mrs. Branson said. "There are certain business establishments that redound to the public good, and certain establishments that contribute to society's ruination. Your enterprise does not belong in the former category."

"Thank you for your concern for The Chestnut Wig," I said. "Good day, Mrs. Branson." I bestowed my brightest smile on her. I made believe I was searching for an item in my reticule while Mrs. Branson descended the front steps of Eunice's house with rather more "harrumphing" than necessary. When she had turned the corner and was out of sight, I knocked on Eunice's door again.

The manservant answered the door with a hint of surprise. "How may I be of service, Mrs. Holt?" he asked.

"Could you please tell your mistress I'm here?"

"Yes, ma'am. Please wait a moment." He closed the door and I only had to wait a few moments before he opened it again and ushered me to Eunice's parlor a second time.

"This is a delightful surprise, Jeannine," she exclaimed with a smile. "Did you forget something?"

"No, but I was just talking to Mrs. Branson on the porch, or rather, I was receiving a talking-to from her. I was hoping you could tell me a little bit about her."

Eunice drew me down beside her onto the horsehair sofa. "What do you mean by 'talking-to'?" she asked.

I smiled. "Mrs. Branson wanted me to know what she thinks of my running The Chestnut Wig. And I will say that her thoughts about it are not at all charitable."

Eunice giggled. "And if I know you, you did nothing to make it easy for her to share her thoughts."

"You *do* know me. I certainly did no such thing. If she thinks she is the first person to disapprove of a gaming house, she should have another think."

Eunice sat back and smoothed her skirt. "It doesn't surprise me to hear Mrs. Branson has such strong feelings about The Chestnut Wig. She has strong feelings about everything. Did she say why she is so opposed to it? Or does she simply think *you* should not be the one running it?"

"I believe she does not approve of any aspect of it, be it my ownership or its very existence."

"She has been especially peevish lately. She calls here about twice per month, and when she does I can always expect to hear endless complaints about something. I was determined not to allow her to derail the conversation today." She gave me an impish grin.

"Do you know what has made her so irritable?" I asked.

Eunice's delicate brow furrowed. "She hasn't said anything that would explain it, but I heard they recently had to let a house girl go."

That was interesting news. It hinted at possible financial issues in the Branson household. I would have to keep an eye on Bert's account.

"And now that I think about it," Eunice continued, "Mrs. Branson has worn the same dress the last three times she has called on me." She frowned. "Other callers wear the same day gowns occasionally, of course, but Mrs. Branson has always prided herself on rarely wearing the same thing twice to the same place. I suppose it's easy enough for her to make herself a new gown if necessary, or at least alter an older one. That is, as long as there is money to buy the fabric and notions to do it."

The thought that the Bransons might not even be able to afford fabric for Mrs. Branson to make her own gowns was a bit disconcerting. "Perhaps she's too busy making clothing for other people to make new frocks for herself," I suggested.

Eunice smirked. "If I know her, she would sew all night long in order to avoid wearing the same gown twice to the same place. No, I'm beginning to suspect the Bransons have overspent themselves."

I was barely listening, instead reflecting whether I might discuss Bert's debts with him privately before allowing him to continue to play at The Chestnut Wig. I had assumed his indebtedness was merely an oversight or forgetfulness on his part, but now I was beginning to wonder whether that were indeed the case. Better to require him to pay his arrearage, I thought, than to continue extending him credit if he couldn't repay me.

Eunice and I moved on to other topics of interest, and I left again after a quarter of an hour. I was eager to get home and share with Chloe what I had learned. If my suspicions were correct that Bert Branson had gotten himself into financial troubles, I needed to think first about my business and the people who relied on me for their income every week.

Chloe's eyes widened when I told her about the Bransons' alleged lack of financial resources. She saw our ledgers and knew how much he owed The Chestnut Wig. "I, too, thought he had merely forgotten to pay the money he owes," she said. "But I think you should talk to him regarding the debt. We can't risk his default."

"If he comes this evening, I will take him aside and speak to him," I said.

"Do you think that's the best way to address the problem? He might take offense. Would it be better to call on him at home? It wouldn't do to embarrass him in the presence of the other people in the house."

Chloe was right. It would reflect poorly upon my business judgment if I brought up the subject of debt with a client in the gaming salon. I checked my watch. It was too late to call on Bert that day, so I would have to wait until the following morning. I didn't relish the thought of seeing his wife again, so I was content to put it off.

The rest of the afternoon was taken up with the various tasks of preparing the food and rooms for the clients who would be arriving in mere hours. Chloe retreated to the summer kitchen while I dressed and donned one of my chestnut wigs for another evening of business.

CHAPTER 15

It was simply a dearth of luck that Bert Branson should be the first person through the door that evening, followed by the circle of friends with whom he normally played at cards. I greeted him politely, though I struggled to avoid alerting him in some way, perhaps with a stern expression or a timely raised eyebrow, that I wished him to avoid gambling. I could not bring myself to make any kind of insinuation while he was surrounded by fond acquaintances.

Instead, I gave my attention to the other guests, who arrived singly and in small groups ready to spend their evening playing the various games at The Chestnut Wig. I kept a close watch for Emeline's former master, Mr. Cowan, but he did not make an appearance. I wondered if that meant he had given up looking for Emeline at our house, or was merely biding his time until he could return. The thought of him brought to mind the face I saw in the kitchen window, and I shuddered involuntarily.

"Are you catching a chill, Mrs. Holt?"

The inquisitive voice startled me, as I was standing with my back to the door and had not noticed anyone coming up the front steps. I turned quickly.

"Good evening, Mrs. Curtis. Thank you for your concern. Perhaps I should wear a shawl. Good evening, Mrs. Miller. Welcome."

Ada Miller smiled and made her way into the parlor. Violet Curtis lingered next to me, giving me the distinct feeling she wanted to discuss something. I gave her an encouraging smile.

"I hope you don't mind my interfering," Violet began, "but I have heard a rumor that you're looking to employ a coachman."

"You are not interfering in the least. Yes, I am looking for a coachman. The one who served us for so long has become too ill to work. Do you know of someone?"

"I do. The woman who makes my gloves mentioned her husband is looking for work. His name is Benjamin Graham. He is a fine hand with horses and a hard worker. I thought you might appreciate knowing about him. I have taken the liberty of composing a letter of introduction for you to give him." She lifted her reticule and pulled out an envelope with her wax seal. I accepted it gratefully.

"I appreciate this very much. Where might I find Mr. Graham?"

Violet told me where the man lived. I intended to go to his home to speak with him first thing Monday morning.

For the rest of the evening, I kept an eye whenever possible on Bert Branson's activities at the gaming tables. From what I could gather without speaking to my waiters or croupiers, he was winning and losing in equal amounts, meaning that the amount of money owing to The Chestnut Wig remained at a steady figure.

Later that evening after the guests had left and the staff had all gone home, I made my way out the back door and across the yard to the summer kitchen for a snack. I was pleased to see the shutters were already closed. As I stepped through the doorway, the first thing I saw was Chloe, wringing her hands as she paced the floor of the summer kitchen.

"Why are you so agitated?" I asked. "Is something wrong?"

"Jeannine, Araminta came back tonight."

"While the salon was open? Whatever for? Why would she dare such a thing?" My mind galloped at a furious pace—there could be no good reason for Araminta to appear at our house during business hours.

"She brought a severely injured woman." Chloe lowered her voice. "I helped her up to the attic, where Emeline is currently ministering to her injuries."

I gasped and snatched up a candle from the table. Hastening toward the attic steps, I spoke over my shoulder. "Lock the door. Tell me exactly what Araminta said. But be quick, because I must see the woman for myself." I paused with my hand on the attic doorknob.

Chloe hurried to join me. "The woman was badly beaten by her master, who caught her trying to escape. The proprietor of the hotel told Araminta to take the woman to see the doctor, but Araminta brought her here instead because the negro doctor is in Philadelphia."

"The poor woman. And Araminta, taking a risk like that! Did any of the cooks here see the injured woman?"

"I do not believe so. Araminta came to the door and asked for me. If anyone thought it was odd, they said nothing. When I joined her, she beckoned me outside. The woman was slumped against the back wall of the summer kitchen. We decided we would try to make her comfortable out there and I would help her up to the attic as soon as the cooks left."

"I hope it wasn't a long time. Leaving her outside in the damp cannot have been good for her."

"Certainly not, but there was no other choice."

"You did the right thing." I thought for a moment. "I wonder if her owner expects her to return tonight after she supposedly sees the doctor."

Chloe lowered her voice to a whisper. "Jeannine, I trust you won't keep her here. It is too dangerous. Araminta should not have brought her here, knowing we're already sheltering one escaped slave. Not to mention the foolhardiness of bringing someone here during our hours of business."

"But what else could she do? There was no doctor who could see her."

"Jeannine, her very presence puts us in further danger." There was a steady determination to the set of Chloe's mouth.

"I am sure Araminta is working to arrange the next location for both Emeline and the woman in the attic. And speaking of her, I think we need to go tend to her right now."

I opened the door to the attic and made my way upstairs. The first thing I noticed was a low moaning coming from the corner of the large space. I stepped toward the sound, holding my candle low so it would not be visible from the window.

"Oh, Mizz Holt, she ain't doin' well at all," Emeline greeted me.

I knelt beside her and the woman. "She's just a girl," I said. I leaned close to her. "You are safe here."

The girl's eyelids fluttered, then closed again. Her face was bruised and a large gash on the side of her head was sticky with congealed blood. One of her arms was at an unnatural angle. "Have you been able to do anything for her?" I asked Emeline.

"I cleaned up some of the blood with a handkerchief," she said, gazing at the girl. "She's got scars on the back of her head, too. This ain't the first time she been beaten so bad."

I closed my eyes in disbelief. How could someone treat a child so?

"Do you know how old she is?" I asked.

"She say she's twelve."

"Did you ever see her while you were at Congress Hall?"

Emeline shook her head. "She musta got there after I left. You gonna keep her, right?"

"We'll keep her as long as we can. Until Araminta can make other arrangements for her." I refused to look at Chloe.

But as it happened, there was no need for Araminta to do that.

CHAPTER 16

I hurried to the summer kitchen early the next morning to check on Emeline and the girl in the attic. I put the kettle on to boil for tea and sliced bread for toast before ascending the attic steps. I was unprepared for what I saw. The anonymous girl lay motionless on the floor, her bruised and maimed face covered with a linen cloth. I inhaled sharply.

"Mizz Holt, thank the Lord you're here. She's gone to her reward!" Emeline was on her knees, rocking to and fro, weeping quietly into her hands. "I tried everything I could think of to save her, but nothin' worked!" Emeline's voice rose as she cried, and presently Chloe appeared at the top of the attic steps.

"Shush!" she cried. "We don't want anyone to know you're in the attic." Then her eyes drifted to the stiffening body lying on the floor, and her hands flew to her mouth. "Is she ...?"

"Yes," Emeline sobbed.

It was difficult to keep my own emotions under control. I swallowed hard and beckoned Chloe closer. She stayed where she was. "What are we going to do with her?" she hissed.

"We cannot keep her here. I will relay a message to Congress

Hall for Araminta. I hope she can come here tonight. She'll know what to do. I wonder if the poor girl had any family. I will send for Lysander, too. He'll help us."

"Will the people at Congress Hall be suspicious of Araminta receiving a message from us?" Chloe asked.

"Don't worry about that. Araminta and I have long had a plan for urgent messages, and she must be made aware the poor girl passed away. We need to know what to do with her body."

"She won't stay with me, will she?" Emeline, her eyes widening, wiped her nose with her sleeve.

"For now, she must remain up here," I said. It was positively ghoulish to ask Emeline to stay with a body all day long. "We will keep the shutters closed so it is safe for you to be downstairs in the kitchen."

I walked slowly to the attic door and turned around before descending the stairs. "We didn't even know her name."

I poured a cup of tea and left the leaves to steep while I returned to the house and dressed in a day gown. I hastened with my toilette and returned to the summer kitchen to eat a hurried breakfast.

Emeline came downstairs just as I was about to leave to arrange messages for Araminta and Lysander. "I heard you did a fine job with scalding the wooden bowls," I told her. "Ask Chloe what tasks she would like you to do. And Emeline, I am truly sorry you had to experience the girl's death by yourself. We'll make sure her body is removed as quickly as possible."

When I arrived at my destination, Solomon's house, his wife Lydia answered the door swiftly after my knock. She took a deep breath when she saw me.

"Good morning, Mizz Holt. Thank the Lord it's you and not the sheriff." She stood aside to allow me to enter.

"I have thought of you often, Lydia. How are you and the children?"

Lydia sighed and beckoned me to be seated at the kitchen

table. The room closed in oppressively with heat and humidity from the laundry she was washing. "We're doin' the best we know how. Have you heard anything 'bout Solomon?"

"The sheriff told me the magistrate in Cape May Court House is ill, so all trials have been postponed until he can return to work. That is good news for Solomon. We need the court to delay his trial as long as possible."

"Thank the Lord." Lydia closed her eyes for a moment.

When she opened them, I spoke again. "In addition to checking on you and letting you know about the trial, I came here for another reason." I lowered my voice and leaned toward her. "I need someone to deliver two messages—one to a cook who works at Congress Hall and the other to Lysander Greaves. You know him?"

Lydia nodded.

"Can one of your girls run those errands for me?"

"I'll have one of 'em go right now if you want."

"Excellent. I will relay my messages to the child myself, if you don't mind."

"I don't mind. Lucy!" she called.

A girl, not much younger than the poor child whose body lay in my attic, came into the kitchen through the back door. Her hair was bound up in a kerchief and her forehead glistened with sweat. She curtsied briefly to me, then turned to her mother. "Yes, ma'am?"

"Mizz Holt has a message that you need to take over to the big hotel, then another to Mr. Greaves. You remember him?"

Lucy nodded, then turned to me with a question in her eyes. "Thank you for doing this, Lucy." I smiled to put her at ease. "The first message is for Araminta Ross, a woman who works at Congress Hall. Here is the message: 'please bring a basket of chard to The Chestnut Wig tonight.' Can you remember that?"

Lucy nodded and repeated the message and the recipient's name, looking at her mother out of the corner of her eye. She no doubt wondered why I was sending her to ask for chard rather than sending one of my employees to the market for it, but she was polite enough not to ask.

"The second message is for Mr. Greaves. Please tell him that tonight, I would like him to bring me a dozen cases of the brandies he brought me last Easter. Will you be able to remember that, too?"

"Yes'm." Lucy repeated the message, then departed immediately.

As my most trusted employee, Solomon was well aware of my activities on behalf of fugitive slaves. He had, with my and Daniel's blessing, shared that knowledge with his wife. Lydia squinted at me. "You wouldn't send my Lucy with a dangerous message. Right, Mizz Holt?"

"Absolutely not. If I thought I was putting her in danger, I would never have asked her to go."

"In that case, thank you for trusting her."

"It is I who should be thanking you for allowing her to run those errands. They're very important."

Lydia gave me a knowing look. I did not have to ask whether she knew the messages were in code—she knew.

"Now, is there anything I can do for you and your family?" I asked. "It cannot be easy for you with Solomon still sitting in that wretched jail cell."

"There's nothin' you need to do, Mizz Holt," Lydia replied. "With the extra work I'm gettin' from you and other good folks, I'm makin' enough money from the laundry. Maybe you can find out somethin' about Solomon."

"I will do my best, I promise." I paused and coughed lightly. "Lydia, I don't know how to say this, so I shall just come out with it." I lowered my voice. "It has come to my attention that Solomon may have done something wrongful—and gotten into trouble with the law because of it—prior to moving to Cape May."

Lydia's eyes turned wary. "Are you askin' me?"

"I suppose I am. What happened?"

She shook her head and made a noise of disgust. "It was only wrongful if you call it wrong to feed your family."

"I would say feeding one's family is never the wrong thing to do. Can you elaborate?"

She sighed, her eyes fixed on something only she could see. "Before we lived here we lived up Gloucester way. Solomon didn't have no steady job and I was mighty sick the year after Lucy was born, so I couldn't take in laundry." She picked nervously at a fingernail.

"It got so bad that we had nothin' to eat. We didn't have no neighbors, so there was no one around who could help us." She blinked and intertwined her fingers tightly.

"One night Lucy was cryin' and we couldn't get her to stop. Poor baby was starvin'. Solomon left. Said he'd be back soon." Her gaze shifted to meet mine.

"I asked where he was goin', but he didn't answer me. It didn't matter. I knew where he was headed. When he came back, he had a box of food. Some dried beef, some salt pork. Apples. We fed the baby and we ate a little ourselves."

Lydia shook her head. "The next day the sheriff came. It seems someone saw Solomon breakin' into the general store miles from our house. He took Solomon away and charged him with thievery. He was in jail for a year."

He was lucky to avoid the hangman's noose, I thought. "How did you feed yourself and Lucy while Solomon was in jail?"

"When the negroes in the town heard about Solomon, they came to help. I took Lucy and we lived with another family that whole year. I recovered from bein' sick and I was able to take in laundry to pay for our keep."

She gave me a sad smile. "Soon as Solomon got let out, we came here. I'll never forget them folks who helped us."

Solomon had been imprisoned for stealing food for his

starving family. That was the basis of the rumor floating around. Poor Solomon. When pushed to his limits, he chose to do the thing his family needed him to do. And he had paid a steep price for that.

"And that's the only time Solomon has ever been in trouble with the law?" I asked.

Lydia nodded and I stood to take my leave. At the door I placed my hand on her arm.

"Thank you for telling me everything. I am sorry you and Solomon and Lucy had to go through that."

"Thank you, Mizz Holt."

I was crossing the threshold when Lydia called me back. "Mizz Holt?"

I turned and gave her an inquisitive look.

"I know you won't tell no one about this. Solomon don't need for more people to know he went to jail. I'd rather have folks guessin' about him than knowin' for sure."

I had no intention of sharing the information with anyone, including Chloe. Her sense of rule-following concerned me at times. I loved Chloe as though she were my own sister, but following the law was not always the right choice. If Solomon had followed the rules, he and Lydia and their baby might have starved to death.

"I will not say a word."

CHAPTER 17

When I returned home, I found Chloe reading in our private parlor on the first floor. I sat on the sofa fanning myself while I waited for her to close her book.

When she did, she placed it slowly on the table beside her. A number of emotions crossed her face. She opened her mouth, then closed it again. I remained silent, as there was obviously something she wanted to say. Finally she took a deep breath and spoke in a low voice.

"I am growing increasingly concerned over the body in our attic." She wrung her hands. "Suppose it starts to emit an odor? What shall we say to the staff?"

"The staff will not be here until tomorrow. I have sent word to Araminta that we must see her urgently. If she doesn't come round after dark tonight, I shall be quite surprised. Besides that, there is absolutely nothing we can do while it's still daylight."

Chloe gazed into her lap. "Jeannine, do you think it wise to continue assisting Araminta? We are putting ourselves, not to mention our staff and The Chestnut Wig itself, in grave danger by doing so."

I momentarily closed my eyes in disappointment. I had

hoped her fear of being caught helping fugitive slaves would not get the better of her. She spoke again before I could formulate a response.

"Because if word gets around that we harbor—"

I cut her off with a cough. Her voice was rising as she became more agitated. I knew we were alone in the house, but one never discussed the subject of harboring runaways in a normal tone.

Chloe took a deep breath and lowered her voice. "If people believe we're engaging in certain, erm, prohibited activities in this house, they may decide they want nothing to do with The Chestnut Wig."

"I don't believe that will happen. Daniel and I have always kept our railroad activities in strictest confidence. Only people whom we trust implicitly know anything about it."

"But the body in the attic ..." Her voice trailed off.

"Will be taken care of this evening. And you cannot think the body will begin to spread an odor less than twenty-four hours after death."

"It's summer, Jeannine. Odors can be quite strong in weather like this."

"Chloe, I beg you to go about your business and let me handle this situation. I promise you, no one will be the wiser after the body has been removed."

She left the room and I heard her climbing the staircase. I hoped she would remain in her rooms for the rest of the day. I didn't care to discuss the issue with her further.

My nerves became more tightly wound as the afternoon and evening lengthened. I tried reading, needlework, and gardening, but I could not stop thinking about the dreadful secret that awaited Araminta when she arrived later that evening.

If *she arrived*, I thought.

If she couldn't leave Congress Hall and get to The Chestnut Wig without attracting any attention, it would be too risky to come. And if Araminta wasn't able to come to provide burial instructions, then Lysander would be coming for no reason. It would not do to have him making too many trips to The Chestnut Wig, especially late at night. Neighbors would become suspicious.

I took supper after dark in the summer kitchen. Left to her own devices all day, Emeline had not only cleaned the insides of all the cupboards, but she had also prepared a simple meal of cornbread, seasoned beans, and stewed greens. The food was delicious. When Chloe joined me, she agreed.

After supper I returned to the parlor and Chloe returned to her rooms. Emeline remained in the summer kitchen, as it was the safest place for her. Two hours passed during which I paced and fretted. When I heard Chloe coming down the stairs, I stepped out of the parlor.

"I'm going outside to wait," I said.

Chloe nodded. "I'll wait in the summer kitchen." She opened the back door and disappeared. After I made sure the front door was locked, I turned down the gas sconces and went outside to sit on the bench between the house and the summer kitchen. For several minutes I heard only the nighttime insects and the breeze. It sighed mournfully in the trees, echoing my own sentiments. The poor young girl who died deserved better than a secret burial under cover of darkness.

My macabre thoughts were interrupted by a rustling of leaves. I sat deathly still, hoping it was Araminta or Lysander, but keenly aware it could be Mr. Cowan looking for Emeline or the deceased young girl's owner seeking her whereabouts and, possibly, retribution.

A dark shadow slipped from behind the trees along the side of the property and I recognized Araminta's distinctive tiny silhouette in the shadows. I let out the breath I had been holding and stood up so she could see my outline.

"I got your message, Mizz Holt."

"I am alone. You can come out."

Araminta stepped slowly from her hiding place among the trees and into the scant moonlight. "She died, didn't she?"

"Yes." I moved toward the summer kitchen and Araminta followed. We said nothing more until we were inside with the door firmly closed behind us.

"I figured she wouldn't survive, but I had to try. Thank you for takin' her in." Araminta's eyes were deep pools of sorrow.

"I only wish we could have done more. Our main concern now is finding a place to give her a proper burial. I have asked Lysander Greaves to come here tonight to take the body away. I hope you know of a place where he can take the poor girl to rest in peace."

"I do," Araminta said.

CHAPTER 18

e were all climbing the attic stairs a few moments later when there were four familiar raps on the door: one loud, two soft, and another loud. I relaxed. It was Lysander, using our coded knock. Emeline's eyes widened in fear.

"Don't fret, Emeline. I have asked a friend to come. I have complete trust in him. Go upstairs with Chloe and Araminta and wait for us there." I hurried to the door and opened it just enough to allow Lysander inside. When he stepped into the kitchen, I locked the door behind him immediately.

"Thank you for coming," I said. "We've had an unfortunate event." I gestured toward the attic. "Araminta is upstairs. A girl whom she brought here yesterday has passed. I sent for you because we need your help to give the girl a proper burial."

Lysander closed his eyes and his lips moved in silent prayer. When he opened them, they were filled with pain. "We can put her in my wagon. I'll take her wherever Araminta tells me to go."

"Thank you. I knew we could count on your assistance and discretion." I gestured for him to follow me up the attic stairs.

We found Araminta kneeling on the floor next to the girl's

body while Chloe and Emeline looked on. A candle burned near the top of the attic steps, giving just enough light to see without alerting anyone outside that people might be in the attic. Araminta glanced up and nodded a greeting to Lysander. He moved to stand next to her, glancing at Emeline as he did so. Emeline looked at him warily.

"This is Lysander, my dear. He is a trusted friend," I told her.

She nodded and turned her attention back to the body.

"Does she have a family?" Lysander asked Araminta. "They'll wanna know where she's buried."

Araminta shook her head. "None that I've heard of. The other slaves in the big hotel said she's alone."

Lysander nodded solemnly. "You comin' when I take her?"

Araminta pushed herself into standing position. "No. I have to get back to work." In a low voice, she gave Lysander directions to the place where the girl was to be buried. "You take her and see that her body is buried proper. But don't tell Mizz Holt or Mizz Cooper where she is. It's safer if we're the only ones who know."

Lysander knelt and positioned his arms under the girl's thin frame, then slowly straightened up. Emitting a quiet grunt, he positioned her stiffened body so he could carry it as if it were a stack of firewood. Chloe bent to gather the linens that Emeline had used to cover the girl.

"She don't weigh more than a sack of potatoes." Lysander's voice was filled with sorrow.

We made a grim procession down the stairs and into the kitchen. I opened the door and peered out into the darkness, watching and listening for any sign that someone might be nearby. All the others stood close behind me. When I determined no one was out there, I eased the door open and stepped outside. Lysander followed, carefully turning so the girl's head would not hit the door frame.

"Where is your wagon?" I asked in a whisper.

"That way." He gestured with his head toward the stable. Chloe followed him. Araminta glided between the trees alongside the kitchen and slipped away. She would return to the hotel, hopefully without anyone realizing she had ever left.

I turned to Emeline. "You stay in the kitchen. It isn't safe for you to be outside. Lock the door, and I will knock four times, slowly, when we come back." She nodded, her eyes wide, and I hurried after Chloe and Lysander.

He had somehow managed to maneuver his wagon into the trees between the summer kitchen and the stable. His horse whinnied nervously and swished his tail when Chloe and I approached, and Lysander shushed him. I glanced around quickly to ensure no one was nearby. When Chloe gripped my hand, I could feel her trembling.

"We'll get back inside as quickly as we can," I assured her. In the faint moonlight coming through the treetops, I could see several items in the wagon. "Help me move these things."

She let go of my hand and followed close on my heels. Lysander had piled wooden boxes near the back of the wagon. They were empty save for a few bottles, so they were relatively light. We placed several boxes on the ground while Lysander stood nearby, still holding the girl.

"Now push those other boxes to the sides of the wagon," he instructed in a whisper. Chloe and I did as he told us. Beneath the boxes was a long, wide plank. "Slide the plank offa there," he said in a hushed voice.

We removed the plank, revealing a secret compartment in the bottom of the wagon. It was large enough to hold the girl's body. Chloe and I moved out of the way and Lysander set her down on the floor of the wagon. Then he hopped up beside her and moved her gently into the hidden compartment. With great efficiency and in much less time than it took Chloe and me to unload the boxes, he had replaced the plank over the girl's body and replaced the boxes to cover the plank. He hurried to untie his horse from the tree.

"I'll take care of her from here," he said. "You go back inside."

"How will you bury her by yourself?" Chloe asked.

"Don't you worry about that. One of Solomon's neighbors helps me with that in exchange for a bottle of brandy."

"Can we trust him?" Chloe asked.

I took her hand gently. "If Lysander trusts him, we can trust him. Besides, we have no choice right now. Come, we need to go so Lysander can get to work." I turned to him. "Lysander, thank you for all your help. You are a good man."

Lysander never asked for payment when he assisted us with tasks involving our secret visitors, but I always paid him as a token of our gratitude. I slipped him a small envelope as he lifted the rein in one hand. He tipped his hat and was gone.

CHAPTER 19

It seemed an offense to the girl's memory to go about our business the next morning as if nothing had happened, but there was nothing more we could do for her. We would each mourn her privately.

My first call was to the home of Benjamin Graham, the man Violet Curtis had recommended for our coachman position. I knocked on the door and his wife opened it to me. I introduced myself and explained I was there to see her husband about possible employment.

"Surely. He's in the back. I'll get him." She showed me to the parlor and gestured for me to be seated while she fetched Benjamin.

When he entered the parlor, I was a bit taken aback at his appearance. He sported a grizzled beard and graying blond hair that was far too long. He bowed to me.

"At your service, ma'am."

I introduced myself and handed him the letter of introduction Violet had composed. He appeared to be able to read, because he spent several seconds scanning the note before looking up.

"I would like to talk to you about working for me as my coachman."

We spent some time discussing the requirements of the position, and he seemed a good candidate.

"In addition to the duties of coachman, I shall require you to exercise the horses, feed them, and otherwise care for them," I said. "You will be expected to keep the stables clean at all times. You must be able to treat common equine ailments and have the horses reshod as necessary. We will require your services six days per week." I named the salary I was prepared to pay.

He nodded. "That sounds right perfect for me. I been driving horses since I was a lad."

I smiled. "Then shall we give it a try? You come highly recommended by Mrs. Violet Curtis."

Benjamin beamed. "When do I start?"

"You may begin tomorrow, first thing in the morning. I will show you the stables and the horses, which are now being tended to by a young boy in the neighborhood. I don't require you to wear a uniform, but I do require cleanliness and appropriate length of hair." I gave him a pointed look.

He laughed. "I just wear it this way to bother the missus. Drives her mad. I'll have her cut it today. She'll be happy, I reckon."

I left shortly thereafter, leaving Benjamin smiling broadly on the steps behind me. I hoped the arrangement would work out.

My next stop promised to be less cheerful. I ascended the steps of the Branson home and knocked on the door. A servant answered and I gave her my card, asking if I might speak with Bert Branson. She asked me to wait on the porch while she disappeared to ask him if he were accepting visitors.

She returned presently and admitted me into the foyer. The house did not look as if the Bransons were suffering financially, though appearances could be deceiving. I followed her through a sumptuous parlor and into a darkly paneled office filled with heavy furniture, including a great number of bookshelves, a lovely stone fireplace, and a huge desk, behind which sat Bert.

He stood awkwardly without the help of his cane when I entered the room but did not extend the courtesy of offering his hand. Instead, he gestured for me to be seated across from him on the other side of the desk before he resumed his seat. The servant left the room, closing the door softly behind her. I wondered briefly about the house girl they had recently let go. Apparently they had enough money to retain at least one servant.

"What brings you here this morning, Mrs. Holt?" Bert asked. He did not smile, and I attributed his stony countenance to the likelihood that he knew precisely the reason for my visit. I wondered if his wife knew of my presence.

I sat straighter. "I confess this is not a social call, Mr. Branson. I am here about the matter of money owing to The Chestnut Wig."

He frowned. "And how much are you alleging I owe, Mrs. Holt?"

I did not care for his tone, and I disliked his use of the word 'alleging,' as if I did not keep proper records. I took from my reticule a piece of paper detailing the dates of his visits to The Chestnut Wig and the amounts in which he was in arrears. I did not read each of the dates and amounts but instead gave him the total. Upon hearing the number, he gave me a look of cold indifference.

"Surely you cannot be serious."

"I am quite serious, Mr. Branson."

"You shall have your money, Mrs. Holt. I must say, I didn't realize your establishment was in such financial difficulty that you need to visit your patrons in this manner. It must be most embarrassing for you."

I fixed a thin smile on the man. "The Chestnut Wig is not a bank, Mr. Branson. Neither the general store, nor the cooper, nor the butcher, nor the blacksmith would allow a client to continue purchasing goods without paying his debts at some point. My business is no different."

"I thank you for calling on me, Mrs. Holt, but I do have work to do, as you can plainly see." To illustrate his point, Bert lifted a pen from his desk and glanced down at a stack of papers in front of him.

"I shall see myself out." I stood and left the office without looking backward. The man was infuriating. How dare he suggest I should be embarrassed when it was *he* who should be ashamed of his failure to honor his debts?

As I reached for the front door handle, I saw a figure out of the corner of my eye. Expecting the servant to say something, I glanced behind me. But the servant was nowhere to be seen—instead, Mrs. Branson stood imperiously in the hallway.

I would not be so rude as to ignore the mistress of the house, so I bowed my head slightly. "Good day, Mrs. Branson."

"What are you doing here?" she demanded.

"I had business to discuss with your husband."

"Hmph. Business, indeed. I can only assume you were discussing your refuge of vice."

Perhaps when one's husband is in a position of indebtedness, one may decide it best to blame the lender, I thought. "In fact, we *were* discussing my 'refuge of vice' as you refer to it. If I might be so impertinent as to make a suggestion, Mrs. Branson?"

She stared at me saying nothing, so I continued.

"If you desire civilized entertainment some evening, you might ask your husband to teach you to play faro. I believe he is well acquainted with the rules of the game."

Mrs. Branson inhaled sharply at my reference to the popular game of chance and her husband's fondness for it. She opened her mouth as if to blurt something but clamped her lips shut almost immediately. She nodded to me. "Good day, Mrs. Holt."

I smiled to myself as I left the house and closed the door

behind me. I should have been sorry for my behavior, but in truth I was delighted at vexing Mrs. Branson and causing what would very likely be a tense row between husband and wife.

I made my way home with a lightness of step I had not expected. When I arrived, I went directly to the summer kitchen to discuss the evening's menu with Chloe. She was in the storage cellar under the kitchen, so I chatted with Emeline while I waited.

Emeline was up to her elbows in hot water, scrubbing various kitchen implements. She smiled at me. "I been hard at work, Mizz Holt. Mizz Cooper told me to wash these things." She nodded toward the tub of soapy water.

"Thank you, Emeline. If you are going to work for us, though, we will have to provide you with remuneration."

She looked at me blankly.

"We'll pay you for your work," I explained.

The young woman's face broke into a smile as wide as the Delaware Bay. "You gonna pay me for this?"

"Of course. We would not expect you to work for nothing." I named an amount and her eyes became saucers. She started laughing, and once she began she could not stop. I had to laugh, too. I have rarely seen such joy on someone's face at the prospect of making a bit of money.

When I had assured her I was not teasing about her pay, she set to scrubbing even harder, promising to do all the work we could find for her.

Chloe returned from the cellar and I spoke to her about the evening's food and beverages, minding her advice to serve the Madeira first. The guests had already consumed the brandy Lysander provided us. While we waited for him to drop off our order for more pear and apple brandies, we had a good deal of wine to serve.

After the staff arrived for work that afternoon, the house

was ablur with dinner and gaming preparations until it was time to open the doors. I was not surprised that Bert Branson stayed away that night.

CHAPTER 20

Benjamin Graham presented himself at the back door of The Chestnut Wig early the next morning. He seemed as eager to start his job as I was to have a new coachman. He followed me through the yard, behind the summer kitchen, and down the shaded path to the stable. I left him there to become acquainted with the two horses, the carriage, and the other equipment he would be required to maintain.

It would not take Benjamin long to acquaint himself with the horses and the equipment, so as long as I was paying him for a day's work, I decided to make use of his services.

I had been thinking a great deal about Solomon. Other than Lydia and their daughters, I was sure no one in Cape May worried about Solomon as much as I did. I had not heard a word about his condition or whether the magistrate in Cape May Court House was again healthy enough to preside over a trial.

I had not forgotten the promise I made to Lydia—that I would do my best to unearth information about Solomon. I had also promised myself to try to learn the identity of Gideon

Welch's real killer. Since I could not visit Solomon in jail, there was no way for me to talk to him, to ask him questions about what he may have witnessed the night of Gideon's death. But I could visit the sheriff and try to obtain information about Solomon's well-being.

I asked Benjamin to prepare the carriage and pick me up in front of the house. When I climbed into the seat, I directed him to take me to the sheriff's office. I hoped this visit would prove more fruitful than my last.

A deputy sat at a desk outside the door to the sheriff's office. When I told him I was there to see the sheriff, he disappeared through the door behind him. Whispered voices issued from the office and a moment later the sheriff himself emerged and walked toward me.

"Mrs. Holt. My deputy tells me you wish to speak to me."

"That is correct. I have come to ask if there is any news of Solomon Sanders or of the magistrate's illness."

"The magistrate is still bed-ridden, but I hear he is improving. What sort of news are you hoping to learn about Solomon?"

"News of his condition, of the progress of his case, and of the evidence against him, for example."

He regarded me in silence for several long moments. There were a number of thoughts, all uncharitable, that I wished to shower upon him, but I kept them to myself and held his gaze. I would not be the one to cow first.

At last he spoke. "Surely you are aware of Mr. Sanders' iniquitous past."

So he knew about Solomon's imprisonment. I had told Lydia I would not discuss it, but as long as I was not revealing any more than the sheriff already knew, I would advocate for Solomon's good character. "I am aware of the events leading to up to his 'iniquitous past,' as you call it. I must say, I do not believe any man who is merely trying to feed his family some fruit and a bit of dried meat deserves to lose his liberty and possibly even his life for it."

The corner of his mouth lifted a bit. "But you don't make the laws, Mrs. Holt. Solomon Sanders got what was coming to him under the law. Just like he'll get what's coming to him now that he's gone so far as to kill another man."

I glared at him. "Surely you don't think that Solomon is a murderer simply because he stole food years ago. He hasn't been in trouble with the law since then."

"He's been convicted, Mrs. Holt. Once a criminal, always a criminal. You know how these negroes are. I'd say Solomon Sanders has pulled the wool over your eyes."

The nerve. I longed to say something smart, something that would get under his skin, but I also knew doing so would probably be a mistake.

I took a moment to gather my thoughts, then said in what I hoped was a strong and sure voice, "Solomon Sanders may have stolen food a long time ago, but he has not run afoul of the law since. His character is above reproach. If necessary, I will go to Cape May Court House and inform the magistrate myself of the extenuating circumstances around Solomon's encounter with the law. Good day, Sheriff."

My pace was sedate and dignified as I left his office, but my heart raced. The one piece of good news I had learned was that the magistrate was not yet well enough to return to his judicial duties. But there was no good news of Solomon. I knew him to be a good man with a strong sense of right and wrong—now I needed to get the sheriff to see that, too, and to continue his investigation into Gideon's death.

When I unlocked the front door at six o'clock that evening, Violet Curtis was one of the first to arrive.

She complemented me on my gown of robin's-egg blue, then asked, "Did you talk to Benjamin Graham?"

"I did, and he began working here today. Thank you for providing the introduction. He appears to be a hard worker and he cleaned himself up at my request."

Violet grinned. "He does present a woebegone figure, does he not, with that long hair and the dreadfully wrinkled clothing?"

"I was pleased to see the efforts he made to look presentable. I only hope he finds me an agreeable employer, because I have already grown accustomed to having a coachman again." I smiled broadly as Violet made her way to the dining room.

Isaac Campbell was in attendance that evening, too, and I asked him if I could speak to him after the close of business regarding his views about the proposed railroad between Camden and Absecon Island. He agreed, so after all the other guests departed, Isaac and I sat in rocking chairs on the front porch. We talked for thirty minutes or more as he expounded upon the extent of his own substantial investment in the proposed railroad, as well as the economic promise and benefits of a health spa on Absecon Island. I found his enthusiasm quite persuasive, especially as it agreed with my own feelings and predictions about the project.

My preference was to invest in the company that would be tasked with building the railroad connecting Camden to Absecon Island. In my opinion, it made more sense to invest in the railroad than the health spa directly because the railroad was a more immediate prospect. I was no stranger to making investment decisions, and I believed this was a project that was likely to garner considerable returns. There were no guarantees, of course, but I had a strong feeling that investing in the future of the New Jersey seashore was a wise choice.

By the time Isaac departed, I had decided to invest a not-insignificant sum of money in the railroad. According to him, the venture was still in need of investors. Having made the determination, I was eager to visit Mr. Shaw, the bank president, the next morning to direct him to facilitate the transaction.

CHAPTER 21

It was well before dawn the following day when I awoke to a terrific pounding. I must have been sleeping soundly, because I looked about my bedroom in startled confusion, wondering where the noise was coming from. I pulled on my robe and hurried down the stairs. Upon rounding the landing between the second and third floors, I could hear Chloe clattering down the steps behind me.

"What is that?" she cried.

I didn't answer, but as I reached the bottom step, I realized the din was coming from the back door. Under normal circumstances, it was unthinkable to open the door wearing only a robe and my nightgown, but the incessant knocking had startled me so that I was not quite in my right mind.

Chloe skidded to a halt behind me as I flung open the door, my heart in my throat.

"Lysander! What in heaven's name are you doing here so early, making such a hubbub?" I opened the door to allow him to enter, for the man's eyes were wild with—was that fear? Or confusion?

Once inside, Lysander slammed the door behind him. "Mizz Holt, there's trouble."

My insides froze. Chloe gripped my hand. "What sort of trouble?" I asked. He kept looking behind him through the glass panes in the door, so to help him focus I drew him further into the hall. "Tell us, Lysander. What is happening?"

"I heard it from one of my neighbors, who heard it from a waterman," he began. He referred to one of the many negro men who worked on the docks.

"Heard what?" I was trying not to sound impatient, but the man needed to get to the point of his visit. I did not personally know any watermen, but I knew they were instrumental in passing coded messages to local negroes about runaway slaves and the fiends who sought them. My stomach was clenched in fear.

"Is Mizz Emeline still staying here?"

"Yes." I spoke tersely, impatient for him to continue.

"The waterman, he said he heard Emeline's master hired someone to find her. Whoever it was has been here already. Came here late one night and got spooked somehow."

Chloe and I exchanged glances. My body responded viscerally with perspiration and a rapid heartbeat.

The face in the window.

Chloe's grip tightened, crushing my hand. I tried to ease it gently out of her grasp, but she was having none of that.

"Those people are mean, Mizz Holt. You know how awful they are." Lysander paused. He was right—I knew how mean they could be. I had heard too many stories from fugitives I sheltered. The slave catchers were ruthless mercenaries who let nothing stand in the way of getting the money they would earn by recapturing a runaway slave. Or even capturing a free negro and selling him into bondage in the South.

"And I hear they've already caught one runaway from the

Delaware side of the bay and brought him into town. I dunno where, though."

Unfortunately, we could not help the man the slave catcher had already snared, but it was not too late to help Emeline.

Lysander's mouth was set in a grim line. "Word's gettin' around. I heard the sheriff visited Congress Hall last night lookin' for hidden runaways."

"The sheriff? Why?"

Lysander shrugged. "He musta heard the rumors, too. He'd be embarrassed if the catcher could find the runaway but he couldn't."

Apparently I am not the only one trying to do the sheriff's job for him, I thought wryly. Aloud I said, "In that case, we have no time to lose." I turned to Chloe, who finally released my hand. "You go to the summer kitchen and fetch Emeline. Bring her into the house, along with food and water sufficient for several days."

Chloe was gone in an instant. I swept down the hall, my peignoir billowing behind me. "Lysander, please come with me."

I ushered him into the private parlor. He had never been in the room. I closed the door behind him and hurriedly pulled down the roller shade in each window. I turned on one gas sconce to dispel the darkness as he glanced around at the furnishings and decor.

"I need you to help me move this furniture and the carpet. We must hurry." I pointed to the two grandfather armchairs arranged across from the sofa. Between the chairs, the ottomans, the sofa, and the occasional tables with their curios, it was going to take several minutes to complete our task.

I stooped in front of one chair and pushed the heavy thing until it was off the carpet and against the nearest wall. Lysander did the same with the second chair. Then, while I took the trinkets and ornaments off the occasional table, he moved the ottomans and placed them near the chairs. After he moved the table out of the way, I beckoned him to my side. Together we bent down and began to roll up the carpet, revealing the shining wooden floor beneath it.

Lysander inhaled sharply.

Carefully constructed so its outline would match up with the wooden planks, a narrow trapdoor was built into the floor. Where a door handle would normally be, a small wooden bar sat flush with the planks, nearly invisible by design. When I plucked at it gently with my fingertips, it lifted to allow me to grasp it and open the door.

"Mizz Holt," Lysander breathed, "I never knew you had such a thing in here."

"We have seldom needed to use it, thank heaven."

He was quiet for a moment while I tested the door. Its hinges had not been oiled in a long time, so it opened and closed with a noisy creak.

"Would you hold the door for me, please, Lysander? I want to make sure the steps are safe."

"Lemme do that, Mizz Holt. I don't wanna see you gettin' hurt. Here, you hold the door." He held it until I swapped places with him, then he started down the narrow wooden steps gingerly. His head disappeared into the darkness below, but a moment later he spoke. "I can't see nothin' down here, but the steps are good 'n' sturdy. You want I should come up now?"

CHAPTER 22

*L*ysander clambered up the steps quickly, his pupils wide and black from the darkness below. At the top, he stepped into the parlor and took my place holding the door. "You puttin' Mizz Emeline down there?" He frowned. "You think it'll be safe for her?"

"That is exactly my plan. We will open The Chestnut Wig for business as usual tonight, but I cannot watch every patron all evening long. If anyone were to disappear in order to search for Emeline, I might not notice."

"But isn't she safe in the attic of the summer kitchen?" he asked.

"She is as long as people are around. My concern is for anyone who might leave the gambling salons and hide somewhere on the property until all the staff have left and Chloe and I have retired to our rooms. We lock the summer kitchen, but if someone were to get inside, we might not realize it until it is too late."

"But you weren't concerned about this before now?"

I chafed at the implication but knew Lysander was asking out of concern for Emeline, not condemnation of me. "Not until we saw a face in the window of the summer kitchen several nights ago."

"You think it was the slave catcher?"

I nodded. "It's very likely. I have worried about Emeline since then, but I didn't want to take the step of putting her in the hidden room until absolutely necessary. Now that you have heard news from the waterman, I fear she will no longer be safe in the attic of the summer kitchen. She will have to go into the secret cellar until we get word the slave catcher has left town."

"It's scary down there. S'awful dark."

"I will give her candles and matches. Don't worry about her, Lysander. She will be safe down there. Safer than she would in the summer kitchen."

He nodded, worrying his lips with his teeth. The parlor door opened. Lysander and I gave a start but heaved a sigh of relief when Chloe stepped into the room, leading a frightened Emeline. Each woman held a basket of provisions. Poor Emeline's eyes were wide with anxiety as they cast about the room and focused squarely on the open trapdoor. I crossed the room and put my hand on her shoulder.

"My dear, there is no need for alarm." I gestured toward the trapdoor. "We are moving you from the summer kitchen temporarily. There used to be a very large root cellar under our home's first floor, but years ago my husband and I decided to erect a solid stone wall that would create two rooms—one for the root cellar and one for a hiding place. There are two wide benches down there and a sleeping mat, as well as several warm blankets. There are candles, too, and I will give you plenty of matches to keep the candles lit. There is a chamber pot, but I hope you can come out at least once every day to use the privy."

"Someone's lookin' for me?" she asked.

I glanced at Chloe, who shook her head in response to my unspoken question. I was not sure whether she had told Emeline of the slave catcher's presence in town. It would be my job to tell her, and there was no sense in lying about it or pretending it was not a very serious matter.

"It has come to our attention that Mr. Cowan hired someone to look for you."

Emeline put one hand over her mouth.

I held her frightened gaze. "We will keep you hidden, but the summer kitchen is not safe enough for you right now. It is necessary for you to hide. Chloe and I, Araminta, our staff captain Solomon, you, and Lysander are the only living persons who know this hidden cellar is here. Will you go down there and stay until it is safe for you to come out?"

The girl swallowed, the muscles in her throat working, and clenched her teeth. It was a struggle, but I managed not to look at my watch or indicate that time was of the essence. I did not wish to scare her further.

"I'll go," she finally said.

"I am glad to hear it." I lit a candle I had taken from the mantel.

Lysander reached for the basket she was carrying, then held out his hand to me and I handed him the candle. He preceded her down the stairs, then came up again and took the basket of food from Chloe. After he delivered those to Emeline, he came up again.

Taking a tin of matches, I went downstairs next to reassure Emeline and make sure she had found the rest of the candles and the blankets. "I am sorry we have to do this, but it is for your safety. Once we hear from our sources that the slave catcher is gone, you can come out from hiding. It may be a few days. Can I trust you to stay resolute?"

"Yes'm. Can I have my handiwork?"

I hadn't even thought to have her bring her sewing from the summer kitchen attic. "Of course," I said. I climbed halfway up the steps and called quietly to Chloe. "Would you please run out to the attic and fetch Emeline's sewing? She needs something to pass the time while she's down here. And take Lysander with you. Show him where we keep the oil so he can grease the hinges on the trapdoor."

Their footsteps pattered overhead. We sat in nervous silence awaiting their return.

Presently Lysander descended the steps to deliver Emeline's sewing basket, then climbed up again into the parlor. I followed him up the steps. As he knelt to grease the hinges, he turned and spoke to me over his shoulder. "She'll be safe down there, right, Mizz Holt?"

"Yes. I hate to have to put her down there, but it is essential."

It was time to close the trapdoor and conceal it beneath the carpet again. I knelt on the floor and called down the stairs to Emeline. "My dear, take heart. We will try to get you out of there for a few minutes each day. And as soon as we know the slave catcher has left Cape May, you can go back to the summer kitchen. God be with you. Light the candle so you are not in complete darkness."

Pushing myself to a standing position, I motioned for Lysander to join me. Together we closed the trapdoor. After that Chloe helped us replace the carpet and furnishings. When everything was in order, we stood in the parlor doorway and gazed carefully at the room to make sure nothing appeared amiss.

I turned to Lysander. "You should leave now so no one will know you have been in the house this morning. It would be highly suspect. Be aware that we have a new coachman." I glanced toward the pane of glass in the front door. "But the sun isn't even up yet, so I'm sure he will not be in the stable."

He nodded, fixing me with a grave stare. "I know you can get in a heap o' trouble for this, Mizz Holt. I mean, for hidin' Emeline. You and Mizz Cooper are good people." He nodded at us, then took his leave.

Chloe and I still stood in the back hallway after he left. "Are you going back to sleep?" she asked.

"I couldn't possibly fall asleep after everything we've done this morning. Are you going back to bed?"

"No. My heart is still racing. I certainly couldn't sleep now."

By unspoken agreement, we made our way through the dewy grass to the summer kitchen, where Chloe put the kettle on to boil for tea and I went up to the attic to make sure there was no evidence that someone had been staying up there. I took Emeline's blanket and linens back to the house and placed them in a large basket I used for soiled laundry.

Chloe had set our tea things on the small table in the summer kitchen. It was too dark to eat outside in the garden. As our tea steeped, I spread a slice of bread with butter and honey. Chloe sat motionless, watching the steam rising from her cup.

"Would you care for bread and honey?" I asked.

She blinked, as if she had forgotten where she was. "Oh. No, thank you. I couldn't eat a bite right now."

"Because you're worried about Emeline?"

"I am concerned about Emeline's well-being, of course. But to tell you the honest truth, Jeannine, I'm worried about us."

I suspected as much. Poor Chloe, with her natural tendency to avoid anything not sanctioned by law, was finding it difficult to harbor a fugitive even though she knew the poor woman was safer with us than back with her master.

"What if we're caught?" She spoke in a whisper and looked around as if there were people in the kitchen who could over-hear us.

"We will not be caught."

"But you can't know that for sure." Her eyes were shiny, as if she were blinking back tears. "We could go to *jail*, Jeannine. I can't bear even thinking about it. Not to mention the fine that could be imposed on us both if we're caught harboring Emeline here."

"We are simply going to have to go about our business as if we have never heard of Emeline. The slave catcher is bound to look for her further north if he can't find her in Cape May. By the time he leaves, hopefully Araminta will have formulated a plan for the next step of Emeline's journey and she will be on her way. After she has left, no one will speak of her again. Daniel and I have done this many times, my dear, whereas you've only lived here for a few months."

I paused, leaning forward. "We have taken all the necessary precautions to keep Emeline safe and to keep our own participation in her shelter a secret."

She sighed. "I wish I shared your confidence."

I smiled gently. "If you do not share my confidence, then you will have to trust me."

THE SUN ROSE on another warm day as Chloe and I finished our breakfast. By the time we left the summer kitchen and returned to the house, the humidity already hung in the air like a wet cloak.

Chloe fanned herself with her hands as we entered the house. "Mourning frocks are so uncomfortable in this heat."

I smiled. "The discomfort doesn't last forever. Once autumn arrives, you'll be much happier. Be thankful you need not wear a wig."

Chloe giggled. "I suppose I am glad of that. Those wigs must be dreadfully hot."

We turned when a loud knock rattled the glass in the front door. I glanced at Chloe.

"I'll go upstairs. No one else needs to see me in my night-clothes," she said.

I debated whether to open the door to a second visitor

arriving inappropriately early that day, but the pounding persisted, so I set my doubts aside and opened the door.

The sheriff stood on the porch, his hands on his hips and a menacing look on his face. "May I come in?"

"Whatever for?" I asked. My legs turned to jelly, but I could not let him see I was nervous. There was only one reason he could be there.

He glowered at me. "There's talk you're hiding a fugitive."

CHAPTER 23

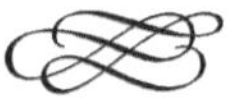

I recalled close brushes with danger on rare occasions when Daniel was alive. The few times he had been asked, he had stood firm in his insistence that there were no fugitive slaves to be found at The Chestnut Wig. Those memories gave me the strength I needed to draw myself taller. I did not flinch or blink when I returned the sheriff's glare. "That is absurd."

"If it's so absurd, you won't mind if I search your property," he said.

"Of course not. But surely you cannot expect me to stand here in my peignoir while you rifle through my home and belongings. Will you please wait here while I dress?"

He stared at me with undisguised suspicion but nodded toward the stairs. I hurried up to my dressing room to change into a day gown, then returned to the foyer.

"Chloe's rooms are on the fourth floor, but as you are aware, she is in mourning. We would be appreciative if you could allow her to go to the summer kitchen before you search her rooms."

"Very well." He put his hand on the doorknob to our private parlor and my insides froze. I hoped my face didn't betray my nerves. He pushed the door open and stepped into the room.

"Why are the shades pulled?" he demanded.

We had forgotten to lift the shades. I came up with an excuse quickly.

"The morning sun is so strong that we fear our furniture will fade. We open the shades later in the day." Once the words were out, I realized the sun beat against the other side of the house in the morning. I hoped he wouldn't notice my mistake.

He didn't seem to. He grunted as he checked under the horsehair sofa and the desk. He moved the drapes to check behind them. He even went so far as to run his hands along the walls to check for a hidden door. Perspiration slid down my back as I waited for him, watching from the doorway. If he thought to check under the carpet, we were all in a great deal of trouble, with the worst consequences falling upon Emeline.

It took all my strength not to slump in relief when he left the room, apparently having satisfied himself there was no one hiding in there. He continued his search in much the same way through every room of the house, including the gaming salons, my rooms, Chloe's rooms, our other private spaces, and even the privy. Afterward, he continued his quest in the summer kitchen. Chloe tensed when he mounted the steps to the attic, but I gently placed my hand on her arm and gave her an encouraging smile before following him. Since I had already taken away any evidence of Emeline's presence, the sheriff found nothing of note in his search up there.

He returned downstairs to the summer kitchen. His face was becoming red, whether from exertion or frustration I neither knew nor cared. Chloe and I followed him outside, where he took a slow walk around the perimeter of the property, gazing into the trees as if he expected to see Emeline hidden among the branches.

Finally he went back into the house and straight to the foyer, looking into each room as he passed. He turned to us upon reaching the front door. Sporting an icy glare, he shook his finger at us.

"I don't believe for a minute that you don't know where the missing negro woman is. Hear me, Mrs. Holt and Mrs. Cooper. I will find her and when I do, I will make her tell me what you did to aid her escape. And after I get that information out of her, I will be back here and you will face the consequences."

He opened the door and slammed it behind him. I locked it promptly. When I turned around to talk to Chloe, I let out a cry when I saw her crumpled on her knees behind me, her back against the wall. "Chloe!"

I helped her to her feet and guided her into the dining room. I pulled out the chair nearest the door and helped Chloe sit, then sat beside her.

Neither of us said anything for several long moments. Chloe's eyes were closed, but her lips were moving. I wondered if she was praying or simply trying to calm herself. Finally she looked up at me with dull eyes. "My nerves are shattered, Jeannine. I cannot live with the threat of a jail sentence hanging over me."

I took her hands in mine. She gently, but firmly, removed them and folded them in her lap.

"Chloe, my dear cousin, I know you're fearful. I am, too. But think for a moment of Emeline's terror right now—locked in a dank cellar in near darkness with no one to talk to and nothing but her sewing to keep her company. She knows only that a predator is stalking the streets of Cape May and she is the prey. We have a duty to help her."

"We do not have any such duty. Our duty is to the law, and the law says we can be prosecuted for helping her. Let Araminta find her a place to go, but let Emeline hide in someone else's house until then. I do not wish to be part of this scheme any longer."

I stared at Chloe, stunned. My face was growing warmer and my hands were clammy. "You cannot mean that," I whispered.

"I mean exactly that, Jeannine. You have to find a way to get Emeline out of this house or I will tell the sheriff where she is."

I leapt to my feet. "You would not dare do such a thing!"

She stood then, her eyes flashing with a look of defiance. "I intend to do exactly that if you do not find a way to get rid of Emeline."

"How can you be so cruel?"

Her expression became pained. She slumped, sighing deeply. "I don't mean to be cruel, Jeannine. But I can't sleep for fear that you and I are going to jail for harboring a fugitive. I feel terrible for Emeline, but I don't know if I can continue with my nerves in such a state all the time."

"Chloe, if you reveal Emeline's whereabouts to the sheriff, we are certain to face severe consequences. But if you say nothing, there's a chance no one will ever know about it."

"If I tell the sheriff, I believe he'll be lenient. He'll be so relieved to know where Emeline is that he may not prosecute us."

Chloe did not know the sheriff like I did. I knew better than to hope for leniency from him.

"Chloe, please give me a few days before you make any decision about going to the sheriff. I promise to tell Araminta we need to move Emeline along as quickly as possible. I will not tell her why, so the blame will fall on me. But I beg of you, do not go to the sheriff yet."

My cousin stared at me for what seemed an eternity, her face revealing nothing. At last, she nodded. "Very well. You have three days. After that I will have to tell the sheriff for the sake of my own nerves."

"Thank you. Now please, take some time to rest and relax. Go into the garden and read. Leave everything to me."

"I do not have time for leisure right now, as much as I wish I did. The cooks have been canning vegetables this week and I need to start taking the jars to the root cellar and organizing them." She frowned. "There is no end to the work of running a gaming house, is there?"

Her question did not require an answer, as we both knew it was the truth. Setting up jars of food for the fall and winter, not only for our own use but for our guests, was tiresome. Chloe disliked going down to the root cellar because not only was it dark and musty, but it was cramped since the other half of the cellar was Emeline's hiding place. There was hardly enough room to store all the jars of food the cooks made, and organizing them was a headache.

Chloe left the room and climbed the stairs slowly. I listened intently at the bottom of the staircase until I heard her bedroom door close three flights above me. I hurried out the back door and through the copse of trees to the stable, where I found our coachman filing one of the horse's hooves.

"Benjamin, I apologize for interrupting your work, but I have a message for you to deliver to Congress Hall."

He looked up and smiled. "I don't mind, Mrs. Holt. I can always come back to this." He set the file aside and patted the horse's flank. He glanced toward my hand. "Where's the message?"

"It is merely a verbal message."

He waited, an expectant look on his face.

"There is a cook at Congress Hall named Araminta Ross. She knows someone who grows a variety of tomatoes that are hard to find at the market. I would like to create a tomato tart using the rare variety, and I am hoping she can procure some for me. I need you to find Araminta Ross and ask her to bring me several pounds of those tomatoes as soon as possible."

"You need several pounds of rare tomatoes as soon as possible, right?"

"Yes."

"I'll go to the hotel this very minute."

"Thank you, Benjamin."

I disliked lying to him, but it was necessary. I needed to speak to Araminta urgently and if I went to Congress Hall to deliver the message myself, people might become suspicious of my motives. Within thirty minutes Benjamin came to the door to tell me he had completed the task.

I found it difficult to focus on my household duties that day, what with the goings-on so early in the morning. My tense exchange with Chloe weighed heavily on my mind, too. She seemed to avoid me as much as I tried to avoid her. I feared she might change her mind about giving me three days to send Emeline on her way if I did anything to pique her further.

A wicked thought arose as I pondered Chloe's ultimatum and our predicament. If she was so uncomfortable with my activities for the underground railroad, she need not continue living at The Chestnut Wig. I had invited her to live with me in sympathy of her plight as a new widow, and it was not her place to make demands on my actions. I could ask her to leave.

But even as that thought surfaced, I knew I could not and would not do that. She needed the routine and companionship that I offered, and I had discovered over the past several months that I needed the same from her. I knew from three years of widowhood that it could be a lonely existence, and with her under my roof, neither one of us had to face the experience alone.

When Chloe came in search of me an hour before it was time to open for the evening, I was surprised and alarmed, as she seemed flustered. I was in my sitting room at the desk. I set aside my paperwork immediately and gave her my full attention.

"Is anything wrong?" I asked.

"I'm sorry to bother you while you're working, but I've learned something I felt you ought to know."

My brows furrowed. "What is it?"

"Eliza told me this afternoon that she has spoken to the house girl who was let go from the Branson household recently."

I recalled my conversation with my friend Eunice, who thought the Bransons had let the girl go because of Bert Branson's debts. Debts which presumably included monies owed to The Chestnut Wig.

Chloe continued. "According to Eliza, the house girl told her that Bert Branson was heavily indebted to Gideon Welch."

My mind buzzed with questions. If Eliza's information was correct, and if the Bransons' maid did indeed have knowledge of Bert's financial situation, that gave Bert a powerful motive to kill Gideon Welch.

CHAPTER 24

I stood abruptly upon hearing the news. "I wonder if the sheriff knows this. I should tell him."

"I doubt the sheriff is likely to listen to anything you have to say right now. He was quite angry when he left this morning."

I could feel my face flame. She was right. I was probably the last person the sheriff wanted to see. Besides that, it was almost six o'clock and I needed to get ready. "You're correct, of course. Perhaps I will go to his office tomorrow. You and I seem to be doing his job for him," I scoffed.

"To be fair, though, he may have already looked into that possibility."

"Perhaps. But we do seem privy to much of the town gossip here, and if the sheriff questioned Bert in connection with Gideon's death after his initial interview the night of the murder, I assume we would have heard about it. One thing we do know—the sheriff spent far more time interviewing the negro witnesses than the white ones."

Chloe nodded and left without a word. I could hear her footsteps ascend the stairs to her own rooms. My head hurt and my stomach had been roiling all day over our conversation about

Emeline. I was torn between doing what I knew was right on Emeline's behalf and doing what I knew would please Chloe.

I understood her concern—recently widowed and still in first mourning, the last thing she needed was to worry about going to jail. My physical discomfort was a direct result of the guilt I felt for putting her in such a position.

And now she had to spend the evening doing one of her least favorite tasks—organizing the jars in the root cellar. Well, there was something I could do to help her with that. As soon as I was dressed and wigged, I hurried across the yard and through the trees to the stable. Benjamin was brushing down one of the horses and he looked up at me with a smile.

"What can I do for you, Mrs. Holt?"

"Benjamin, I would like to give Mrs. Cooper a small respite from her duties. The cooks have finished canning much of the summer produce, so I would like you to take the jars down to the root cellar. Mrs. Cooper detests the job and she has had quite a trying day. I think it would be a nice surprise if she does not have to transport all those heavy jars herself. She will organize them, of course, but it would be such a help if you can put them in place for her. There is a bulkhead leading to the root cellar along the side of the house."

"Of course I'll be happy to do that for you."

"Thank you, Benjamin. If you start now, you could probably have it done by the time she comes down from her rooms before our guests start arriving. Take the wheelbarrow and it will go much faster for you."

I pointed to the wheelbarrow leaning against the wall. He put the horse brush on a shelf, grabbed the handles of the wheelbarrow, and followed me to the summer kitchen. I explained to the cooks what Benjamin was doing and they offered to help him load the wheelbarrow between trips to the root cellar. Chloe would be so relieved.

When it was time to begin receiving guests, I checked my

wig in the looking glass one last time, tucking a long curl behind my ear. I unlocked the front door and stepped onto the porch, hoping my welcoming smile masked my private turmoil.

Isaac Campbell arrived shortly after we opened for business. At the sight of him, I recalled my earlier intention to visit the bank president that morning.

What with everything that had transpired beginning with the pre-dawn visit from Lysander and ending with the discovery that Bert Branson had motive to kill Gideon Welch, I had forgotten all about going to the bank. I made a mental note to go the following day.

Late that night after all our patrons had departed, the waiters and I had tidied the rooms, and my bookkeeping was complete, I went to the summer kitchen to boil the kettle for tea. The staff members had already left. I walked around the structure closing the shutters, then went inside. Chloe was waiting for me, wearing a frown.

"What is the matter?" I asked.

"Did you tell the coachman to take the jars of canned food into the root cellar?" Her voice was hard, accusing.

I blinked in surprise. "Yes. Did he do a poor job?"

"No. He did a fine job. My question is, why did you ask him to do it? Are you trying to show me how easily I can be replaced here?"

It was my turn to frown. "Absolutely not, and I am offended that you would think something so preposterous. I know you've had a long day, and that was in no small part because of me. I thought if I asked Benjamin to take the jars down to the root cellar, you would find it a welcome surprise. You dislike going down there, so I thought I was doing a good deed."

She stared at me for a moment, then her voice softened almost imperceptibly. "In that case, I apologize for misunderstanding your intent."

"I accept your apology." I no longer wanted tea. I removed the kettle from the stove and walked out.

The next morning I tried studiously to avoid Chloe, since my very presence seemed to irk her. I longed for a return to our easy companionship, but I could not betray my own heart or my late husband by abandoning Emeline to the evil that surely awaited her if she were discovered. If Araminta could not secure safe passage for her to get to Philadelphia in the next few days, I wondered if Chloe would really carry out her threat to go to the sheriff with Emeline's whereabouts. The thought of it made me shudder with apprehension.

After I breakfasted alone in the garden, I double-checked that the front door was locked, then went into the private parlor and closed the door behind me. I pushed one of the grandfather chairs in front of the door to slow down anyone trying to enter. I wished Lysander were there to help. Kneeling on the floor, I pushed the carpet away from the trapdoor as best I could.

I put my face close to the floor. "Emeline?" I called quietly. I strained to hear her voice in reply but heard nothing. I called her name again, a bit louder. Still, nothing.

I knocked on the floor four times slowly. I had done that for her once before, and I hoped she remembered the code.

Finally I heard her answering from the cellar and I heaved a sigh of relief. I leaned close to the floor again. "Emeline, it's Mrs. Holt. I am going to open the door now so you can use the privy."

I lifted the trapdoor and there stood Emeline, looking up and blinking from the sudden light.

"I didn't want to scare you by opening the trapdoor suddenly. Come on up."

Emeline did as I instructed.

"How are you coping down there?" I asked.

"I'm fine, Mizz Holt," she assured me. She emerged into the parlor and stood in the middle of the room while I closed the trapdoor.

"Are you warm enough?"

"Yes'm, the blankets are plenty warm."

"The sheriff was here looking for you yesterday, so we moved you down there just in time. He still thinks you're nearby, though, so I don't think it's safe for you to return to the summer kitchen yet. I am very sorry."

"That's all right, Mizz Holt. As long as I have plenty of candles, I'll be jes' fine."

"And do you think you have enough food and water, and candles and matches, to last for at least another day or two?"

"Yes'm, don't be worryin' about me."

"Good. I will show you where the privy is. After you've used it, you should go back down to the cellar quickly. Does the chamber pot need to be emptied?"

"Not yet, ma'am."

I opened the parlor door and peeked into the front hall. I did not see or hear Chloe, so she was probably still up in her rooms. I didn't want her to come down and demand to know why I was letting Emeline out of the cellar.

I beckoned for Emeline to follow me and we hurried to the privy. I waited in the hallway and when she was done, I ushered her back to the parlor. I opened the trapdoor and she descended into the dim cellar again. At the bottom, she looked up at me.

"Thank you, Mizz."

"Be well, Emeline. I'll do everything I can to get you out of there as quickly as possible."

The young woman moved away out of my sight. I closed the trapdoor, struggled to replace the carpet, and put the furniture back where it all belonged. Finally I brushed off my day gown and used a handkerchief to mop the perspiration from my face and neck.

Chloe was descending the staircase when I opened the parlor door and stepped into the foyer. We greeted one another politely, then I went up to my rooms immediately. My face must have been red, but if she wondered about it, she said nothing. In my room I donned a shawl, then took up my reticule and went back downstairs. Chloe was nowhere to be seen. I left the house and set off on foot in the direction of the bank.

When I arrived, I asked to see Mr. Shaw. I only waited a minute or two, then he came into the vestibule. "Good day, Mrs. Holt. It's lovely to see you. How may I be of service?"

"Might we talk in your office?"

"Of course." He smiled broadly and beckoned for me to precede him into his office. He closed the door behind him and offered me a chair opposite his own across a wide, gleaming desk. He folded his hands on the desktop. "How can I help you today?"

I related what I knew about the proposed railroad from Camden to Absecon Island. I concluded by saying, "I would like you to arrange an investment in the railroad for me. As I understand, there are still shares available for the financing of the project." I named the amount I wished to invest.

Mr. Shaw listened without interruption, then leaned back in his chair and laughed. "My dear Mrs. Holt, you are a wonder. Inside that head of yours is a brain that is keener than many around here."

I smiled and inclined my head in thanks at the compliment. "Will it be possible for you to assist me?"

"Certainly. I'll look into the particulars today. I'll deliver the stock certificate to your house as soon as I receive it."

"Thank you. Good day, Mr. Shaw."

"It's my pleasure to be of service. Good day, Mrs. Holt."

CHAPTER 25

When I returned home from the bank, I looked out the window and saw Chloe in the back garden. She sat on a wrought iron bench, staring at what looked like nothing in particular. I wondered if she were as unhappy as I with the state of our friendship. I thought about going outside to talk to her but decided against it—I didn't know what to say to her.

Then I thought of a topic we could discuss: my conversation with Mr. Shaw. The more I thought about it, the more enthusiastic I was becoming, and I wished to share that with her. In fact, it was my duty to discuss it with her since I considered it her money, too, that we were investing. Several minutes later I eased myself onto the bench beside her.

She looked up with a faint smile. "It's quite muggy today. I have no energy to do anything but sit. This black dress does not help matters."

"I believe we will both be glad to see the arrival of cooler weather." I paused. "Chloe, there's something I would like to discuss."

Chloe spoke at the same moment. "I've been thinking."

"About what?"

She fixed me with an earnest gaze. "I behaved monstrously after your thoughtful gesture of having Benjamin deliver all the glass jars of food to the root cellar. I recognize it was your way of trying to make me happy, and I am truly sorry I was so ungracious. It was kind of you and I had no cause to react the way I did."

I smiled as a bit of my spirit lifted. "Thank you. I know it's an unpleasant job."

Chloe stood and smoothed her skirt. "Well, I am all done with the organizing because of the work Benjamin did for me yesterday, and I have you to thank for it." She smiled. "I am going to lie down for a bit." She rose and walked into the house.

I could have stopped her to tell her about my trip to the bank, but as we had apparently reached a detente, I decided to wait.

Instead of gathering in our private parlor after the close of business that night as we normally would, Chloe came to my sitting room on the third floor. Lounging in the parlor felt like a mockery of the poor woman hidden beneath it. We each had a cup of tea as we sat comfortably on my settees across from each other. It was less formal than any of the rooms on the first two floors, and much cozier. It was a relief to be on friendlier terms with my cousin. Chloe leaned back into an armchair with a sigh. "It must have been crowded downstairs tonight. The cooks and I never stopped moving from their arrival until closing time."

"It was, indeed. After everyone left I looked through the ledger to approximate our earnings so far this month, and we are quite ahead of what we expected. To think people assume men can run businesses better than women ..." I shook my head. "And speaking of business, I wanted to tell you something. Something about the railroad."

Chloe leaned forward with an expectant look. "What is it?"

"I have directed Mr. Shaw, the bank president, to facilitate our investment in the railroad between Camden and Absecon Island."

Her face fell. She sat back with a sigh.

"Is something wrong?" I asked.

"When you said 'railroad,' I assumed you meant the underground railroad. I expected you to say Araminta had secured passage for Emeline," she said in a quiet voice.

My stomach fell. My desire to tell her about the railroad project evaporated. I tried brushing her concern away lightly. "Not just yet. Soon."

We sipped our tea in silence until she left to retire.

I was restless when I awoke the next morning. I needed something to keep my mind off the situation with Emeline, as there was nothing I could do about it until Araminta was ready to take her to the next station.

There was something I had been mulling over, and I decided to try it. It was mid-morning when I walked out to the stable. I was dressed in a traveling day gown. Benjamin was inside, examining a saddle. He turned and smiled when he heard my step in the doorway.

"Good morning, Mrs. Holt. What can I do for you?"

"I need to go to Cape May Court House this morning. Could you please prepare the carriage and bring it around to the front of the house? I shall be ready when you get there."

He raised his cap. "Certainly, ma'am. I'll do it immediately."

Before returning to the house, I stopped in the summer kitchen and prepared a basket of food to take with me. I included bread, butter, cheese, dried beef, and several plums. Then I went to my rooms, where I donned my favorite hat, adjusting the quail feather and tying the ribbons below my chin in front of the looking glass in my dressing room. I descended the stairs to wait for Benjamin in the foyer. He was true to his word and arrived quickly.

The carriage ride was long, bumpy, hot, and dusty. I was in a foul mood by the time we reached Cape May Court House, ninety minutes after departing from The Chestnut Wig. I directed Benjamin to let me out at the jail and to wait in the tavern down the street for me to finish my business.

Upon walking into the jail, I was greeted with stares from two men sitting across from one another at a table inside. "Good day. I am here to talk to Solomon Sanders. I am his employer."

The men exchanged glances. One of them, bulbous with a crumpled shirt and one brown front tooth, spoke up. "Can't let you do that, I'm afraid."

"Why not?"

"Against the rules."

"What rules?"

"The rules that say you can't see 'im."

The second man nodded in agreement. I had anticipated such a reception, and I had prepared a response. I rose to my full height, which was still quite a bit shorter than either of the two men appeared to be, and pursed my lips. "In that case, I need to speak to the person in charge here."

"That'll be me," said the second fellow. He grinned and I could feel my blood begin to boil.

"I have brought food for Solomon and I wish to give it to him personally."

"I told you, you can't see 'im."

"Very well, you can explain to the magistrate why you refused me entry. I have just been at his home and he told me I was permitted to see my employee."

I turned on my heel and had gotten as far as the door when the second fellow called out, "Wait a minute. You can see 'im. Just don't take too long."

I breathed a sigh of relief. I had been prepared to leave immediately if one of the men called my bluff and went to the magistrate to verify my story, but I was not the proprietress of a gambling salon for nothing. I was a fair gambler myself, and this gamble paid off.

I waited in silence until the first man stood and waddled over to a door on the opposite side of the room. He unlocked the door and only then did I step forward. I followed him down the hallway on the other side of the door. There was very little light and the place smelled of waste. I put my hand over my mouth to keep from gagging.

He stopped in front of another door and rapped on it with hands the size of small hams. "You in there. You got a visitor." He unlocked the door and stood aside for me to peer into the room beyond.

Solomon sat on a bed that was little more than a thin corn cob mattress on top of a slab of wood. He jumped up and exclaimed aloud upon seeing me.

"Mizz Holt! What are you doing here?"

I suppressed a gasp when I saw him. His face was bruised and one of his eyes was almost swollen shut. Blood encrusted one ear. He had lost weight and his eyes were dull, but his grin lit up the entire dismal place.

I turned to the jailer beside me. "Is there a place I can talk to Solomon besides this room?"

"No."

"Will you at least excuse us?"

He offered a sneer and clumped back the way he had come, leaving Solomon's door open. I handed Solomon the basket.

"I brought you some food."

"Thank you, Mizz Holt." He set the basket on the floor.

I tilted my head and gazed at his injuries with concern. "They have treated you dreadfully. I was afraid of that."

"Could be worse. I'm sorry you have to see me like this,

Mizz." He gestured to the bed. "You can sit right there. I wish I had a nicer place for you." There was no chair or stool, so he leaned against the wall while I sat.

"I'm sorry *you* have to live like this," I said. "How are you doing?"

"'Bout as well as can be expected, I 'spose. Have you seen Lydia? My girls?"

"I have, and they are doing fine. A lot of us in town have seen to it that Lydia is busy with laundry, but not too busy to care for the children and keep your house. They are eager for you to come home, as are the rest of us at The Chestnut Wig."

Solomon closed his mouth and his cheeks worked as if he were clenching his teeth. Tears shone in his good eye. "I don't think I'm comin' home, Mizz Holt."

I swallowed around the lump in my throat. "We have not lost hope. We are doing everything we can to get you home, and I am here to ask you some questions."

CHAPTER 26

"What sorts of questions?" he asked.

"First of all, I want you to know that Lydia told me about the incident in Gloucester. It is simply sinful that people are not paid enough to feed their families. You cannot be blamed for doing what you had to do. In fact, I would go so far as to say you acted heroically."

He hung his head. "Thank you, Mizz Holt, but I know what I did wasn't right."

"As I have recently had occasion to reflect, 'legal' and 'right' are not always the same. What you did may not have been legal, but it was right. Like any father, your first responsibility is to your family." I paused, taking a deep breath. "But now I need you to tell me if you know why the sheriff insists that you killed Gideon Welch."

"I don't know, Mizz. Once I got the job with your husband, God rest his soul, I never did nothin' that would put my freedom at risk. I never did nothin' that would make Lydia ashamed of me."

"In other words, the only reason the sheriff suspects you of killing Mr. Gideon Welch is that a long time ago you stole food to feed your family."

"That's 'zactly right."

"Now, I need you to remember as much as you can about the events leading up to Mr. Welch's murder. Leave nothing out, even if it seems insignificant. And take your time. I will stay until those two miscreants in the office force me to leave." That elicited a smile from Solomon.

He closed his eyes and was silent for at least two full minutes. Finally he opened them and spoke.

"I'm sure you remember there were a whole lot of people in the dining room that night," he began, and I nodded.

"I was busy, between servin' the guests and makin' sure the other waiters were takin' care of their own tables. Mr. Welch told me to bring him a glass of claret. You know I worked for him a while back."

I nodded again, refraining from blurting out my opinion of Mr. Welch. I did not wish to interrupt Solomon's recollection of that terrible evening.

"I know you like to pour the wine for the folks who come to your house, but when I turned around to ask if you wanted to serve Mr. Welch, you were busy talkin' to those two lady gamblers." He referred, of course, to Violet Curtis and Ada Miller.

"So I figured I'd do it my own self. I poured a glass of the claret and was almost to Mr. Welch's table when I tripped. It was on account of my own clumsiness and I'm sorry. The wine ended up all down Mr. Welch's shirt front and I ended up on the floor. I was scared to death, Mizz Holt. I thought he was gonna beat on me right then and there. I tried to apologize. I reached for a linen cloth to hand him, but he started yellin' at me and I knew better than to make an excuse for myself. I just stood there and listened to him, Mizz Holt. I felt bad for ruinin' his shirt. Matter of fact, I was already thinkin'

I'd have to tell Lydia we'd need to buy him a new one somehow."

He shook his head. "Everything happened so fast. Before I knew it, all the negroes were rushin' over to me, and all the fancy men were gatherin' around Mr. Welch, and them fists started to fly. I don't remember who started the fight. I remember bein' hit and tryin' to fend off the blows, but I don't remember who all was right there next to me."

Solomon reached down for a tin cup sitting on the floor. He took a sip of water from it. "And then you were there scoldin' everyone for fightin' and you looked down and saw Mr. Welch lyin' there, and he'd been stabbed." Solomon paused. "I didn't do it, Mizz Holt."

"I believe you, Solomon. I have never for one moment thought you were responsible for Mr. Welch's death. What do you remember about the other people in the room while the fight was going on? Anything in particular?"

"I remember seein' the lady gamblers and thinkin' they'd faint dead away, but they didn't. I remember food all over the floor. Before I knew Mr. Welch was dead, I remember thinkin' what a terrible waste of good food. Soup spilled, meat trampled on the floor. But when I saw all the blood and knew Mr. Welch was hurt real bad, I figured the food wasn't the most important thing."

"And was there anyone in particular you noticed acting strangely?"

Solomon closed his eyes again, then opened them several moments later. "To tell you the truth, Mizz Holt, the only one I saw behavin' strangely was Mr. Branson."

That was interesting, as I knew Bert Branson owed money to Gideon Welch. And, I recalled now, he was the one who offered to fetch the doctor as soon as we realized Gideon was hurt. Perhaps he wanted to leave to hide the bloody knife in the bushes?

"And what was he doing that struck you as strange?"

Solomon stared over my shoulder as if he would find the answer written on the wall of his little room. Finally he met my eyes again. "He seemed almost afraid, ma'am. He was jumpy-like. Every time someone raised their voice, Mr. Branson would flinch and look up quick. It looked to me like he was almost 'spectin' something to happen."

"That is helpful. Is there anything else you remember?"

Solomon shook his head. "I'm sorry I can't help more, Mizz Holt."

"There's no need to apologize. I will tell the sheriff about this so he can question Mr. Branson."

"I think about that night all the time. Almost as much as I think about Lydia and my girls." Solomon looked at the floor and clasped his hands in front of him.

"I do, too. But I am hopeful you will be out of this dreadful place soon. The more information I can provide the sheriff, the more likely he is to investigate other suspects."

I thought a change of topic might distract Solomon from his growing melancholy, so I told him about his friends at The Chestnut Wig. I dared not tell him about Emeline in case anyone was listening to our conversation. It was not long before the portly jailer appeared in the doorway.

"You've had 'nuff time in here," he said. "Let's go." He motioned for me to stand.

I took Solomon's hands in mine. "I wish you strong faith and clear thoughts. I shall be back to visit."

"Mizz Holt, please don't tell Lydia about my face. She'll worry."

I nodded. He gave me a faltering smile and thanked me. I followed the jailer to the doorway. He removed a ring of keys from his pocket and I stood beside him in the hallway while he swung the door closed, leaving Solomon alone again.

I MUSED about Bert Branson the entire ride back to Cape May.

He owed money to The Chestnut Wig and despite my attempt to discuss it with him, he had neglected to repay his debt. More importantly, Chloe had discovered through the network of kitchen staff gossip that he was heavily indebted to Gideon Welch.

I didn't doubt Solomon's recollections of the events from the evening Mr. Welch was murdered. Despite the melee going on around him, he had remained watchful. In fact, his memories of the events correlated with mine, and I had not been in the middle of the throng of fighters. I had not paid much attention to Bert, though. It was intriguing that Solomon felt Bert was afraid of something.

I wondered what questions the sheriff had asked Bert that horrible evening. I wondered if he knew about Bert's indebtedness to the victim.

It was essential that the sheriff receive this information if he didn't already have it. Even if he would not listen to me, I had to try. I leaned out the carriage window and called to Benjamin. "Could you please stop at the sheriff's office before we go home?"

"Certainly."

Settling in my seat, I watched the scenery flash past as we made our way back to Cape May. My mind remained in a constant state of turmoil throughout the drive. Solomon was top-of-mind, of course, followed quickly by Emeline, still in the cellar beneath our private parlor. It had already been over forty-eight hours and I felt sorry for the young woman.

As so often was the case, the ride to Cape May seemed to pass more quickly than the ride away from it. When Benjamin pulled the carriage up to the door of the sheriff's office, I alighted, asked him to wait for me, and went inside. The deputy was not at his post, so I went directly to the sheriff's open doorway and knocked on the jamb.

Bathed in bright light from tall windows on three sides, the sheriff sat behind a wooden desk. He looked up when I knocked.

"Good day, Mrs. Holt. To what do I owe the pleasure?" He barely hid the sarcasm in his voice, which I found offensive and disrespectful.

I nodded in greeting. "I have information I think you'll find interesting."

He looked at me blankly, as if he couldn't be more bored.

I dared not tell him I had lied to the jailers so I could see Solomon, so I didn't mention my visit to Cape May Court House. "Did you know Mr. Branson is in debt to Gideon Welch?" I paused to emphasize the gravity of my statement, "That is, he *was* in debt to Mr. Welch."

I watched closely as the sheriff squinted ever so slightly, but he quickly resumed his bored expression. *A-ha,* I thought. *This is information he is hearing for the first time.*

"Are you suggesting, Mrs. Holt, that Mr. Branson killed Gideon Welch because he wished to cancel a debt?" He scoffed. "That is ludicrous. Mr. Branson is an upstanding member of the community and, I am sure, pays his debts in a timely manner."

"He is indebted to my gaming house and has thus far failed to make good on his account. I am sure you were unaware of this."

He shrugged. "The way you pursue your debtors, Mrs. Holt, is of no concern to me. That is, as long as you do so legally." He glared at me.

"You mistake my point, Sheriff. The fact is, Mr. Branson does not pay his debts in a timely manner, contrary to what you believe. If he owed money to Gideon Welch and was unable to raise the necessary sum, which I understand is significant, he might be tempted to commit an act of violence to avoid having to reimburse Mr. Welch."

The sheriff folded his hands over his thick belly and sat back. His face was stony. "Mrs. Holt, I understand why you're trying to deflect suspicion from your employee, but the facts of the case are simple. Gideon Welch was Solomon's former employer and it is commonly known that Mr. Welch did not treat Solomon in a way that Solomon felt was fair. Frankly, Solomon was lucky to get any job after the, uh, incident in Gloucester County when he was found guilty of theft. Anyway, on the night of his murder Mr. Welch said things—perfectly legal things, mind you—that angered and embarrassed Solomon. And Solomon, with his history of criminal behavior, saw his opportunity to make Mr. Welch pay for what he saw as disrespect."

I did not reply immediately, making an extraordinary effort to control my anger. I took a deep breath. "I will not presume to tell you how to do your job, Sheriff, but you are making a mistake in failing to consider the motives of other people in that room. Mr. Branson had a strong motive to kill Mr. Welch. I hope you will take my information into consideration and, at the very least, make inquiries of him."

CHAPTER 27

Benjamin took me straight home after my interview with the sheriff, and I went up to my rooms to sulk. I had intended to visit Lydia and tell her about my visit with Solomon, but I decided that should wait until my mood improved.

I did not wish to see or speak to anyone until I had calmed myself and could manage a civil conversation. I sat at my desk and spent the next few hours answering correspondence from friends and relations living far from Cape May. Doing so eventually proved a balm to my spirit, and I was ready to get dressed, don my chestnut wig, and greet my clients by six o'clock.

I spoke with Chloe for a few short minutes before I unlocked the front door. Any longer than that and I might have found my mood souring again. I did not wish to entertain conversation about Emeline, Araminta, the hiding place under the parlor, or any other unpleasant topic before the evening's business began, but Chloe and I did need to discuss the food and wine that I would serve that night. Lysander had brought more brandy while I was out on one of my errands, and it was proving popular with our patrons, as always.

"I believe we are going to have to place another order with Lysander," Chloe said.

"I will send Benjamin to him tomorrow with a message to bring more," I said. "Perhaps I should serve something else tonight—too many of Lysander's brandies and we shall have to increase our fees to play."

Chloe smiled. "If you think they would pay more to come here and taste the best brandy available while they play at the tables, we should take advantage of their appetite for both drink and spending."

I grinned. It was the sort of reasoning that made The Chestnut Wig such a profitable endeavor.

The evening passed quickly, and to my relief Bert Branson was not in attendance. I did not wish to lay eyes upon him again until he paid his debt to The Chestnut Wig.

Very late that night, after Chloe had retired to bed, I sat in my rooms upstairs, wondering whether I should check on Emeline. I feared that I would startle her if I woke her up at such a late hour. If she could sleep down there, I had better let her sleep. She would need all the rest she could get if she were to continue her journey northward in the coming days. Besides that, she had a chamber pot if she needed it.

I decided to leave her alone for the night and check on her first thing in the morning. I was an unusually early riser for someone who kept late hours, so I planned to see her before Chloe was awake. It would be easier for all of us. And as long as it was before sunrise, I could assume the sheriff would not come knocking to search my home again.

I did not think for one minute that he had eased his relentless pursuit of Emeline. I could only place my faith in Araminta's ability to spirit her away before he returned to look for her again. I did not expect to be so lucky, but I harbored hope.

Worry about Emeline caused me to toss and turn during the night. I finally arose long before dawn and went downstairs to the parlor. I moved the furniture to the edges of the room, then knelt and pushed and coaxed the carpet away from the trap-door. I found myself perspiring most unpleasantly by the time I lifted my hand to knock slowly four times. There was no response. My heartbeat quickened, though I knew it was likely the young woman was still asleep.

I fetched a candle from the desk, lit it, and pulled the wooden bar set into the door. The door opened slowly, noise-lessly, allowing me to peer into the gloom below. I could see nothing, so I started down the steps.

When I reached the bottom, I lifted the candle aloft to peer into the dim recesses of the cellar. I expected to see Emeline asleep on the wide bench, but she was not there.

My breath caught in my throat. Turning around in a circle, I squinted into each corner of the room. Emeline was nowhere to be seen.

That could mean only one thing: she had discovered my secret, the one I had kept from her for her own safety.

Hidden in the wall, so cleverly concealed that even I had trouble finding it, was a door. That door, when pushed with sufficient strength, opened into a passageway leading from the hiding place below the parlor to the cellar underneath the summer kitchen. Emeline must have been desperate for a way out of her dungeon and discovered the door.

My teeth clenched in frustration. Had the woman no idea the danger she was in? What could have possessed her to leave the safety of her hiding place? Then I had another thought: if she had gone down the passageway as far as the summer kitchen cellar, would I find her there?

I needed to bring her back immediately. I started for the steps to go back up to the parlor and run out to the summer kitchen, then changed my mind. I should check to make sure she was not hurt somewhere in the hidden corridor.

The door to the passageway was disguised so cunningly that

it took me several minutes to find it. But find it I did, by sliding my fingers up, down, around, and across the walls until I felt the outline of the door cut into the stone. The only way to open it was to push very hard on that portion of the wall, since it opened inward onto the passageway. I left the door ajar as I started down the tunnel.

If I had not held a candle, I would certainly have had to return to the parlor for one. The passageway was dark as night. I was no little bit frightened as I moved forward, the cold, damp stone walls pressing in on me.

As I drew closer to the cellar below the summer kitchen, the air around me became fresher and even a bit cooler, thanks to the iceboxes there. When icemen delivered the ice, Chloe or one of the cooks would direct them to the cellar, where they would place the sawdust-packed ice in the iceboxes. What a miracle it was when we started using ice!

In the cellar of the summer kitchen, the door leading to the passageway was camouflaged in a way similar to that under the parlor, so anyone going down to the cellar would not know there was a door there. But from inside the passageway, there was an iron handle to open the door. It was closed, and I found it quite stubborn to open. I did not wish to scare Emeline, so I purposely made a bit of noise and called her name as I pulled on it.

"Emeline, it is Mrs. Holt."

The door suddenly swung open and I practically stumbled against the tunnel wall behind me. I stepped into the summer kitchen cellar.

Emeline was nowhere to be seen.

CHAPTER 28

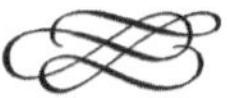

My mouth agape, I turned in a slow circle, searching for the young woman. I knew I had not passed her in the tunnel—it was too narrow for anyone to hide. And the only exits were at each end, so there was no other place for her to disappear.

Confound it, she must have gone up into the summer kitchen. I shook my head in disbelief that one could be so dismissive of one's own safety.

But then I softened. Perhaps she could no longer bear the silence and relentless dimness of the cellar. Perhaps she longed to return to her attic sanctuary.

I climbed the stairs and opened the door into the summer kitchen. It was empty.

I hurried to the attic stairway and peered up, listening for any movement. There was nothing. I ran up the steps lightly.

The entire story was shrouded in darkness. "Emeline," I called in a soft voice. There was no answer. "Emeline?" I was still holding my candle, so I moved around the attic, peering into the far corners and along all the walls. The young woman was not there, nor was there any evidence that she had been.

My heart thudded against my ribcage. I could not think where she might have gone.

I stood for a full minute in the attic, trying to calm my breathing. It would not do to panic. I descended the stairs and was closing the door when Chloe stepped into the summer kitchen from the yard.

"Oh!" Her hand flew to her chest. "Jeannine, you startled me. What are you doing out here?" She paused. "You're as pale as a sheet. What happened? Are you all right?"

She reached for my hand and led me to the small table. She placed her hands on my shoulders and pushed me gently into a chair, then sat across from me. "Tell me what's happening."

"Emeline is gone." I croaked the words, still aghast at her disappearance.

Chloe's eyes widened and she inhaled sharply. "Are you sure? You've checked her hiding place?"

I nodded. "I checked there first."

"Where else have you looked?"

"I walked the passageway leading to the cellar below the kitchen. I didn't see a single sign of her. I also checked the attic."

Chloe frowned. "Have you checked the house? Or the yard?"

"No."

Chloe was rising as I spoke. "You look around outside. I'll look in the house. Don't worry, Jeannine. We will find her."

Even through my confusion and distress, her words soothed me. A glimmer of hope flickered in my heart, both for Emeline and for Chloe herself. Perhaps my cousin was warming to the idea of helping our runaway.

She strode purposefully toward the house. "I shall meet you back here shortly," she called over her shoulder.

I hurried toward the side of the yard where the trees grew in a thick grove. Stepping into the shade, I cast my eyes in every direction—even above me. She was not there. I continued moving around the back and the other side of the property, searching through the trees. When I didn't see any sign of her, I retraced my steps to the path leading through the thicket between the summer kitchen and the stable. I walked the entire length of the path, scanning my surroundings as I went.

Upon emerging from the trees, I walked straight to the stable. Benjamin was arriving for work at the same time. He looked at me in surprise, then smiled. "Good morning, Mrs. Holt. You're out early."

"Yes. Good morning, Benjamin." Since he was not aware of Emeline's existence, I could not discuss the matter with him. But I had to try to determine if he had seen her that morning.

And that was when an alarming thought struck me—I had not communicated with Emeline for over twenty-four hours. She could have disappeared last night, and might be even farther away by now. I chided myself for not trying to contact her before going to bed. I might have been able to find her quickly if I had realized then that she was missing. Not only that, but I had told her I would try to get her out of the cellar for a few minutes each day. I had failed her.

I tried pushing that thought from my mind lest I be paralyzed with fear, but my heart continued to race and I could feel droplets of perspiration running down my back. I swallowed hard and addressed Benjamin. "Did you see anything out of the ordinary last night or on your way to work this morning?"

He cocked his head and gave me a questioning look. "I don't believe so. Nothing that I can think of. Are you all right, Mrs. Holt?"

I ignored the question. "Have you seen anyone around here who shouldn't be here?"

"No, ma'am. But I'll keep my eyes open and come for you if I see anyone." He looked at me with concern.

"Thank you."

"If you think someone is lurking around, make sure you keep the house locked," he warned.

"I will, Benjamin."

I made my way back through the wood, searching again in every direction, and stepped into the summer kitchen. Chloe was at the stove, adjusting the heat under the tea kettle. She turned to me with a look of anguish. "She isn't in the house. I looked everywhere, even in your rooms and mine."

"She is nowhere to be found. I don't know what to do." I wrung my hands.

"Do you suppose Araminta came for her?"

"Araminta doesn't know about the underground passageway between the hiding place and the summer kitchen cellar, so she would have had to fetch Emeline by going through our parlor. She would have had to break into our house, take the young woman, perfectly rearrange all the furniture and the carpet in the parlor, and disappear without saying a word to me. It would have been impossible. Besides, that's not her way."

"But suppose someone told her about the passageway? She could have come into the summer kitchen during the night, found the door to the passageway, and spirited Emeline away."

"You and I and Solomon are the only ones who know about it. I didn't tell Araminta, and I assume you didn't, either. Solomon wouldn't have said a word to Araminta or anyone else." I shook my head in despair. "Besides that, getting into the passageway from the summer kitchen would have been impossible because the door was locked until you came in a short while ago, just as the house door was. If anyone had broken into the summer kitchen, I would have noticed when I emerged from the cellar at this end of the passageway."

Chloe stared at me. "When I came into the summer kitchen this morning, the door was not locked. I assumed you had unlocked it."

I inhaled sharply when I realized what she was saying. "Someone has been in here."

Chloe nodded slowly, covering her mouth with her hands.

Finally she let them fall to her sides. "Let's not be too hasty. Could it be that one of us forgot to lock the summer kitchen door last night? And that Araminta happened to have found the passageway and come to fetch Emeline while we slept?"

"I suppose that is possible, but it seems highly unlikely. It would simply require too many coincidences."

Chloe's frown deepened as she walked to the door. She bent to examine the locking mechanism. "I do not understand ..." She felt the side of the door and looked up at me. "Jeannine, this lock is broken. I think Emeline is in danger."

CHAPTER 29

My knees felt weak. I staggered to the table and sat heavily. I could not bear the thought of Emeline being taken from our house. I had promised her she would be safe.

"Emeline may yet be safe—we cannot know." Chloe came to sit by me. "But we need to start making inquiries to determine what, exactly, has happened."

I shook my head. "I hope that's the case, but my heart tells me she's been taken." I thought for several moments. "I will send a message to Araminta. I must also ask Lysander if he's heard anything about Emeline."

"But if Lysander knew something, wouldn't he come to us immediately?" Chloe asked.

I had to admit that was true, but I was desperate for a ray of hope. "It can't hurt to ask him." I paused. "I'll ask Benjamin to take me. I can't waste a single moment."

"Will people find it suspicious if you go to Lysander's house?"

I shrugged. "I hope anyone who sees me will simply assume I need to discuss a business arrangement with him."

Chloe looked doubtful, but I could think of nothing else.

After managing to stomach a slice of dry toast and a cup of tea, I asked Benjamin to prepare the carriage. We set off for Lysander's house, arriving in mere minutes. I called for Benjamin to wait for me, then hopped from the carriage without waiting for his help. I strode to Lysander's front door.

Lysander greeted me with a look of surprise. "What's wrong, Mizz Holt? You look like you seen a ghost."

"May I come in?" I glanced over my shoulder to see if anyone was nearby, but none of Lysander's neighbors lived within shouting distance and Benjamin was murmuring to the horse. We were alone.

He opened the door and stood back to allow me to enter. He offered me a chair, but I remained standing.

"Have you seen Emeline?" I blurted.

His eyes widened. "No, ma'am. She ain't under your parlor?"

I shook my head. "Chloe and I have looked everywhere for her. She is not at the house or anywhere on my property. And one of the locks on our doors was broken. If you have not seen her or had word of her, my next stop will be Solomon's house to ask Lydia or their daughter Lucy to take a message to Araminta at Congress Hall."

"I haven't heard a thing. Do you want me to go asking? There's some folks I trust."

If Lysander trusted them, I probably could, too. But my nerves were as taut as wires and I dared not bring someone new into my confidence at the moment.

"Not yet, Lysander. If that time comes, I'll tell you. Right now I just need you to keep your eyes and ears open for any information you might glean."

"Course I'll do that, Mizz Holt." He paused. "Do you think she's hurt?"

"I hope not, but there's no way to know. We must keep faith that we can find her and bring her to safety. If you see or hear anything, please come to my house and notify me at once."

"I will, Mizz Holt."

I departed quickly, with a feeling of dread settling in my stomach and preventing me from thinking about anything other than what could have happened to Emeline. I had urged Lysander to remain hopeful, and I still had faith that we could find her safe and sound, but my faith was dwindling with every minute that passed without word of her whereabouts.

From Lysander's house I went straight to see Lydia Sanders. She opened the door to my loud knock in much the same way Lysander had, with a look of surprise.

"Have you got news of Solomon?" She covered her mouth with one hand, her eyes wide with fear.

"Yes, and I will tell you all about it in a moment. But first I need someone to take a message to Congress Hall as quickly as possible. Lucy delivered a message for me last time I needed Araminta, and I need someone to take Araminta that same message again."

My face must have looked ghastly with alarm, even panic, for Lydia did not waste any time asking questions. She yelled for Lucy out the back door. It was not long before the young girl hurried into the house, wiping her hands on her apron, her face ruddy and covered with a sheen of perspiration.

"What is it?" she asked.

"Mizz Holt needs you to go to Congress Hall and ask for that same woman again. Do you remember the last message?"

"That Mizz Holt needs a basket of chard? From the tiny lady?"

Lydia looked to me and I nodded. "That is exactly the message, Lucy. Her name is Araminta Ross." I managed a smile. "You're a smart girl."

The girl curtsied and ran out the back door.

"She'll be fine, Lydia, so have no fear."

Lydia gave me a nervous smile.

"I don't have long to talk because there is something that requires my urgent attention at home, but I wanted to let you know I have been to see Solomon in Cape May Court House."

"You have? Is he all right?"

"He's in good spirits. He remembered some information about the night of Gideon Welch's murder that we didn't have previously. I have already spoken to the sheriff about it." I did not mention what the sheriff thought of the information because I simply could not bring myself to dash Lydia's hopes that Solomon would be exonerated.

CHLOE WAS WAITING for me at the front door when I returned home. She closed the door behind me as soon as I went inside. "Has Lysander heard anything?"

"No. He offered to ask other people, but I told him to wait. Solomon and Lydia's daughter Lucy took a message to Araminta at Congress Hall. I expect we'll see her late tonight." I exhaled shakily.

"Poor Emeline," Chloe murmured.

"I must tell you, I am encouraged by your concern for her," I said. "I feared you might be relieved at her disappearance."

Chloe frowned. "I'm not a monster, Jeannine. Of course I feel terrible that she's missing."

"I apologize. I didn't mean to imply you are a monster."

"I think we should probably change the subject before we both get angry again." Chloe offered me a smile. She was right. It was best for us to focus all our energy on locating Emeline, not arguing with each other. I had a strong feeling this subject would come up again between us, though.

Chloe pulled a piece of paper from her apron and read me the menu she had planned for the evening. As usual, it sounded divine. I was grateful for her attempt to focus my attention on our work instead of our differences.

I spent the rest of the day doing chores around the house to keep my hands busy, but all the while I thought about Emeline. I couldn't think where she might be, and I couldn't ask anyone else about her without risking her life. The longer she was gone, the more likely it seemed that she was in danger. The arrival of guests that evening only created more disquiet in my mind.

The evening seemed to fly by with the activity of overseeing the gaming tables and making sure the guests had plenty of food and drink to keep them sated. As the time inched closer to closing, though, I found myself becoming increasingly anxious about what Araminta would have to say when I saw her later. By the time the last guests departed, my hands were shaking. I clasped them in front of me so no one would notice my agitation.

Chloe brought tea to our private parlor when her work in the summer kitchen was done. She handed me a steaming cup, but I couldn't drink it for the uneasiness roiling my stomach. My ears were highly attuned to any sound that might indicate Araminta was outside.

"Would you like to meet with Araminta by yourself?" Chloe asked. "I can go to my rooms."

"No, I think I would like you to stay with me." I wrung my hands. "Where can she be?"

"She will be here, Jeannine. Try to be calm."

Chloe's suggestion that I be calm had the effect of agitating me further and I wished I had told her to go upstairs. We sat in silence for many long minutes before there was an almost imperceptible tap on the glass window. I leapt to my feet.

"Wait," Chloe whispered loudly. "Let's make sure it's Araminta before we go dashing outside." She stood and turned the gas jets off so the room was completely dark. We crept to the window and I pulled the curtain aside to peer out.

It was definitely Araminta standing out there in the grass below the window. In the faint light of the crescent moon she looked this way and that, as if prepared to run at the slightest sign of danger. As usual, her hair was wrapped in a long scarf. It looked huge atop her tiny figure. I tapped on the glass in return to alert her that I was coming outside. Her head jerked toward the window at the sound, then she melted into the shadows.

Chloe and I went out the back door. Araminta was waiting for us beneath a large spreading oak tree. "Why did you send for me?" she asked without preamble.

"Do you know where Emeline is?" I asked. I heard the small woman's sharp inhale.

"She's gone?"

"Yes. We've looked everywhere and earlier today I went to Lysander's house to ask him. He knows nothing of her whereabouts."

"This is bad, Mizz Holt. This is bad."

CHAPTER 30

My heart turned to ice.

"What should we do next?" I asked.

Araminta was silent for several moments.

"I will do anything to find her," I said.

Finally she spoke. "I'll talk to some other people and see if I can figure out where she's got to. That slave catcher's been layin' low. I haven't heard a thing about him."

Until now Chloe had been silent, but now she spoke up. "Should we search for her somewhere?"

Araminta's eyes narrowed as she turned toward Chloe. "And where do you think you gonna search? No, there's nothin' for you to do until I done some lookin' around myself. I'll let you know if I learn anything."

"Thank you, Araminta. I am terribly sorry this has happened. We have taken the utmost care in keeping Emeline's hiding place a secret," I said.

"Well, someone knows about it," she said. "And the worst part is, I arranged the next leg of her journey. I was gonna come for her tomorrow night."

The cold fear gripping my chest tightened. My stomach was

in knots. How terrible to have lost Emeline when her escape was so close.

Araminta had every right to be angry with us, but she did not seem to be. Her voice belied only concern and dismay. Without another word she turned away and departed, slipping into the trees behind the house. I could not even hear her footsteps, so stealthy was she.

Chloe and I went back indoors, locking the door behind us. "Would you drink some tea now?" she asked.

I shook my head. "I cannot drink even a sip. I'm going to bed, though I know I shan't sleep a wink."

Chloe followed me upstairs, then continued up to her own rooms. I performed my nighttime toilette automatically, barely aware of what I was doing. I climbed into bed, pulled the sheet over me, and closed my eyes. But as I had predicted, sleep eluded me. Instead, my thoughts were filled with images of disastrous and horrifying scenarios, all involving Emeline and what she might currently be experiencing.

I tried to think sensibly and logically about what could have happened. There were only three living people who had known about the underground passageway.

I could eliminate myself from suspicion, obviously. And I could eliminate Solomon, since he was in jail.

That left Chloe. The thought that she could be responsible for this dreadful situation was paralyzing, and I did not wish to think about it.

There had to be an explanation. Was it possible Solomon had shared the information with Lydia? It was plausible, of course, though I was absolutely convinced Lydia would do nothing to endanger anyone's safety. I trusted Solomon to be judicious about the information he shared, and if he trusted Lydia, then I did, too. I did not actually think he had told her of the existence of the hiding place or the passageway, though—

such knowledge could potentially put Lydia's safety at risk, and Solomon would never do that.

My thoughts turned to the cooks and waiters in my employ. Most of them had been with Daniel and me for years. I knew all of them well. I knew their families. Occasionally one of them would have to stop working because of old age or illness, and when that happened they were almost always replaced by a trusted family member. That insured a ready supply of people I could depend upon.

But one could not know everything about everyone, which is why Daniel and I had always avoided discussing our underground railroad activities with any of the staff save for Solomon. I suspect, of course, that many of them knew or had guessed the work Daniel and I were engaged in. But no one ever brought up the subject or questioned me about it, despite those occasional rumors that The Chestnut Wig was a station along the railroad.

I had to admit, though, that the cooks and waiters were frequently in the cellar below the summer kitchen. In fact, one or more of them was in that cellar six days a week to put something into or take something from the iceboxes. It was certainly possible that one of them had unwittingly discovered the door leading to the passageway. Perhaps curiosity got the better of them and they explored the length of the passage to find the hiding place at the other end of it. I wondered what they might do with such information. Would they gossip about it or keep it a secret? I could not very well ask them—if they did *not* know of the hiding place, questioning them was tantamount to divulging the secret.

My musings about the cooks and waiters were leading to nothing but more questions. What of Lysander? He did not know about the underground corridor, but could he have told someone about the hidden room, then that person searched for a way to reach it?

Absolutely not. I shook my head to rid it of the thought. Lysander had never been anything but helpful to me and Daniel, and he had proved worthy of our trust on many occasions.

Then I wondered if it were possible one of his neighbors noticed or suspected that he was helping us. None of them lived close enough to overhear my conversation with him at his house, but perhaps someone followed him to The Chestnut Wig out of curiosity the night he buried the girl who died in my attic. Maybe that person let slip the information about our activities, leading to suspicion that we harbored more runaway slaves.

But even if that had happened, and I fervently hoped it had not, no one would know of the existence of the hiding place beneath the parlor.

I was left with Chloe. She knew as much as I about Emeline, she knew about the hiding place, and she knew about the passageway.

And she had expressed a clear desire to be rid of the young woman.

But Chloe could not be behind Emeline's disappearance. The very idea was unthinkable.

CHAPTER 31

I never did sleep that night. I tried reading a book by the light of a candle on my bedside table, then I tried writing a letter, also by candlelight on my desk, and I tried sleeping, but I tossed and turned about until the first rays of the sun appeared in the eastern sky.

My head, heart, and stomach churned with nerves over Emeline's fate and the identity of the person or persons behind her disappearance. Every few moments I looked out the windows, hoping to see Araminta coming toward the house with news that Emeline was safe. But I knew better, of course— Araminta would never visit the house during the light of day.

No, I would have to accept that Emeline was beyond my help, at least for the moment. I prayed she was safe. I would have given anything to know what had happened to her, even if it was horrible. It was the uncertainty that was hardest to bear, as it is so often.

I was sitting in the garden, lost in my dark thoughts, when Chloe joined me earlier than usual. The first thing I noticed that morning was her complexion: two spots of high color stood out on her cheeks. She must not have had much sleep.

"Jeannine, dear, I hope you don't mind my saying you look dreadful," she said uncharitably. When I frowned she hastened to add, "I say that out of concern, of course. Did you not sleep last night? I'm quite worried about you. I'm going to prepare a pot of tea right now and I expect you to drink a cup." Without waiting for a word from me, she walked quickly to the summer kitchen and disappeared inside.

She returned many minutes later carrying a tray laden with a teapot, cups, a small pitcher of cream, the sugar bowl, and a plate of buttered toast. She set it on the table near the bench where I still sat.

"Come and join me," she directed. I did as she bade me, since my thoughts were too jumbled to refuse. I wished she had slumbered late that morning. I didn't wish to talk to her, for as much as I hated to think she was behind Emeline's disappearance, I could not avoid it. She briskly poured a cup of tea for me, then when she saw I had no intention of touching it, she added a lump of sugar and a dribble of cream. She even stirred it for me.

"I can do nothing more, short of drinking it for you," she said. She sat down opposite me. "Jeannine, I insist that you eat and drink something. I do not want to have to send for the doctor. Refusing to take food will not help Emeline."

With a sigh, I reached for the teacup and drank from it. It did taste good, and I had to admit I was thirsty. Chloe watched me with satisfaction, as if I were a baby bird and she the doting mother. She slid the plate of toast toward me. "Now eat this."

I shook my head. "I appreciate your efforts, Chloe, but I can't bear the thought of food passing my lips right now. Just thinking about it makes me ill."

"Very well. At least you have had something to drink. I am content with that for now."

"Thank you."

We attended Sunday services that morning. The pastor's message was about hope, and concentrating on his words helped buoy my spirits a bit. I refused to give up hope that Emeline would return to The Chestnut Wig and that I would find the evidence necessary to prove that Solomon was not Gideon Welch's killer. Where there was hope, there could be justice. My mood had lightened by the time the service ended and we left for home. Though we tried not to work on Sundays, Chloe and I did chores all afternoon so I would be able to spend more time during the week trying to help Emeline and Solomon.

THE NEXT MORNING I was in the front garden trimming some of the flower beds when Mr. Shaw, the bank president, came up the front walk. I rose from my knees to greet him.

"Good day, Mrs. Holt," he said with a smile. He pulled an envelope from a pocket in his coat. "I have brought you the stock certificate from the Camden Railroad Company."

"Wonderful, Mr. Shaw. I appreciate you doing this for me." I accepted the envelope. "Would you care for tea?"

"No, but thank you for the offer. I must be getting back to the bank."

He waved jauntily as he walked away. I went indoors and up to my sitting room on the third floor to put the stock certificate away for safekeeping. I opened the envelope first and checked it to ensure it was accurate.

Holding a stock certificate in one's hand was a small thrill. It was beautifully printed on thick, cream-colored paper. Just its weight and appearance lent a sense of substance and security.

That afternoon I spent several hours preparing monthly bills to send to my clients. That task finally finished, I had ample time before six o'clock to go for a walk to clear my head of accounts and take some fresh air. I donned a walking dress and took a parasol to protect my skin from the bright sunshine.

My footsteps took me on a winding stroll down Hughes Street, a wide avenue with colorful homes and lovely gardens. I could feel my shoulders begin to relax as I ambled slowly, breathing in the salty ocean air. Many men and women were out walking, some bustling, some taking their time.

I recognized Gideon Welch's eldest son, Caleb, coming toward me. He wore a black arm band and black attire, but men did not suffer the same constraints as women during the period of mourning following a family member's death. It was presumed that men still had to go out into the world to make their living and provide for their families, so their mourning protocols were substantially more relaxed.

I slowed as we neared each other. He nodded graciously toward me.

"Good day, Mrs. Holt."

"Good day. How is your mother coping?"

"She is doing as well as can be expected under the circumstances. I will tell her you were asking after her."

"Thank you." I took a step forward to continue on my way, but the young man stopped me.

"Excuse me, Mrs. Holt, but I've been wondering ... did you happen to notice anything peculiar about my father the night he died?"

I thought back to that awful night, speaking my recollections aloud. "Your father arrived with Isaac Campbell. He was talking about some sort of mistake the bank had made regarding an investment in the Camdem Atlantic Railroad. I moved away from the table. The next thing I knew, he was, erm, angry over something one of my staff members had done. He said something to the staff member and all of a sudden men came from every direction and joined in the fracas that erupted. Only when it was over did I find your father on the floor, already deceased. I am so sorry."

The young man rubbed his beard. "He mentioned something

earlier in the day about a problem with the stock certificate. He was quite angry. But he didn't wish to discuss the matter right then, so I'm not privy to the details."

My brow furrowed.

"As I understand it, your staff member is awaiting trial for my father's murder. Is that correct?" Caleb asked.

I nodded. "It is, but with due respect to your father's memory, I have asked the sheriff to investigate other suspects."

He frowned. "Why is that?"

"Because I think it is unlikely my waiter killed your father. He is a quiet, reserved man without a violent bone in his body. Forgive me for repeating gossip, but I have heard your father held debts from people in town. It is my opinion one of his debtors might have killed him."

The man's eyebrows rose. "Which one? There were plenty of people in debt to my father."

"I dare not say the person's name in case I'm wrong. But I have provided the sheriff with the information and trust that he will act appropriately."

"Perhaps I should call on the sheriff. I don't want to see the wrong man in jail for my father's murder simply because arresting him was the most expedient outcome."

I was taken aback by his words but in a rather heartening way. It seemed Caleb might not share his father's feelings of superiority and disdain for negroes.

"I would encourage you to talk to the sheriff," I said with a smile. "Perhaps he'll be more receptive to you than he is to me."

"I will do that." The young man doffed his hat and wished me a good day.

I turned around at the end of the street and walked home deep in thought. I was curious now about the problem with Gideon's stock certificate. When I arrived at home, I went up to my sitting room to examine the certificate Mr. Shaw had delivered.

Everything appeared to be correct. My name and address, the company's name and address, and the number of shares were all printed on the certificate underneath an artist's charming rendering of a train chugging through a cleared field.

I wondered how I could learn more about the issue with Gideon's shares.

CHAPTER 32

That night a well-dressed man arrived alone about an hour after opening. I led him to the dining room and told him to help himself to the buffet while I fetched the wine. He seated himself at a table away from other clients and opened a conversation as I poured his beverage.

"How long has The Chestnut Wig been here?" he asked.

"Sixteen years," I replied with a smile.

"This is my first visit to Cape May. What a charming town."

"I agree. Where are you visiting from?"

"Richmond, Virginia," he said.

I had noticed his drawl, though it was not as pronounced as I would have expected. "That is quite a long trip," I said.

"I am thinking about buying two steamships that travel between here and various southern ports and I wanted to ride on one for myself to see if it was as grand as I've been told."

"And is it?"

He nodded. "Indeed it is. The trip was smooth and I was able to spend much of the time enjoying the view on the water."

"How lovely. There is a man here in town who owns

steamships that also run between here and points south. You might wish to talk to him while you are visiting."

"Isaac Campbell?" he asked.

"So you have heard of him." I smiled. "He comes here to The Chestnut Wig on occasion."

"Mr. Campbell is the one selling the steamships. I have corresponded with him, but we have never met in person. He doesn't know I'm in town. I didn't want him to know I planned to travel on one of his boats. I wanted to experience the trip as anyone else would, without special accommodation."

"I didn't know Mr. Campbell had put his boats up for sale."

"Those boats are worth a pretty penny. Now that I've ridden one in person, I'm eager to close the sale. I will contact Mr. Campbell while I'm in town and hopefully we can work out the details before I go back to Richmond."

"I wish you luck and speed, sir."

He smiled and turned to his meal.

That evening I grew more tired as each minute passed, so I was glad to lock the door at the close of business. As soon as the staff went home, I went straight to my bedroom.

But to my frustration, sleep would not come. Staring into the darkness from my bed, I could think only about Emeline and Solomon. I thought some reading might help calm my mind. I got out of bed and turned on the gas sconce above my settee, then settled down with *Uncle Tom's Cabin* by Harriet Beecher Stowe. I had heard the title discussed by a number of people and it seemed to be generating a wide mix of opinions, so I wanted to read it for myself. It was hardly the calming balm I needed, but I was riveted by the end of the first page.

I had just finished Chapter One when a shout from outside the house distracted me. I held my place with my finger and listened intently, but heard nothing more. I went back to the book, falling quickly into the story again, and was startled many minutes later when there was a loud pounding at the front door.

I thrust the book aside and reached for my wrapper, hastily tying it around my waist as I hurried down the stairs. Chloe was already yanking the front door open as I reached the foyer and grabbed a candle from a table. I struck a match with shaking fingers.

To my surprise, Lydia Sanders stood on the front porch. A large basket sat on the floor behind her.

"Whatever is the trouble?" I looked from her to Chloe and back again, then gestured behind me. "Come in, Lydia."

She shook her head. "Just around the corner." She was panting from exertion. "There's a body on the ground. You have to send for the sheriff. And the doctor."

My blood ran cold. In the flickering light of the candle, the color drained from Chloe's face.

"Is the person moving?" I asked.

"No." Lydia's voice quavered.

"Is it a man or a woman?" My voice faltered as I felt my heart shrink into a hard knot of nerves. *Please, do not let it be Emeline*, I thought. I willed it to be someone else.

"I think it's a man."

I breathed a sigh of relief. "I'm going out there. Maybe I can help."

"No, Jeannine!" Chloe cried. "How do we know it's safe for you to be out there?"

"If the person is still alive, we have to do everything we can to save him," I said.

"Please, Jeannine, please think of your own safety," Chloe pleaded. "Do not go out there."

I sighed. "Very well. I'll saddle one of the horses and fetch the sheriff."

Chloe exhaled and closed her eyes, allowing her body to slump slightly in relief.

"You stay here with Lydia while I run out to the stable. I shan't be long." I didn't wait for her to object to me running through the thicket of trees in the middle of the night, but ran up the stairs to my rooms as quickly as I could. I couldn't very well present myself at the sheriff's house in my nightclothes.

I had barely plunged my arms through the sleeves of my simplest gown before hurrying down the stairs and out the back door. I flew through the copse of trees to the stable, where I startled the horses by bursting in upon them. I spoke to them soothingly and pet their muzzles quickly before saddling the smaller one. Once that was done, I was off.

The filly ran like the wind, likely more from fright than from my ability as a horsewoman. I brought her to a stop in front of the sheriff's house, tied her to a post in the yard, and raced up the front steps. I pounded on the door, much like Lydia had done at my own house, and stood back to wait for someone to answer.

The sheriff flung the door open and held up a lantern, peering into the darkness. "Mrs. Holt! What are you doing here?"

"Sheriff, there's a body on the ground near my house. I came as quickly as I could."

"Wait for me." He slammed the door and I hugged my arms around myself while I counted the seconds before he returned. Pushing his arms into a jacket, he commanded, "I'll saddle my horse and meet you out here." His wife stood in the doorway, looking bewildered as she watched her husband run around the side of their house. It wasn't long before he returned on horseback. "Follow me," he called. He turned his mount toward The Chestnut Wig.

I followed and in only a few minutes we were back at my house. A small but growing crowd had gathered. News of the wounded man had spread quickly. I recognized Benjamin among the group, as well as Bert Branson, Isaac Campbell, and a number of my neighbors and guests from Congress Hall.

The sheriff dismounted and walked toward the crowd. They

parted to allow him through to the man lying on the ground. I tied my own horse to a post by the street then joined Chloe and Lydia, watching events unfold from the front garden. I gripped Chloe's arm.

"Send for the negro doctor," the sheriff called over his shoulder. "This man is still alive."

I recalled that the negro doctor had been in Philadelphia when the unnamed girl passed away in the attic, and I had no idea if he had returned to Cape May, so I called out, "Bring Doc Parsons, too."

One of the men in the assembled crowd ran off in the direction of the negro neighborhood, but no one ran for Doc Parsons. I would have to go myself. I turned to leave, but Chloe gripped my arm.

"I am not letting you go away again. If the negro doctor isn't available, someone else can go for Doc Parsons."

I had every intention of wresting myself from Chloe's grasp, but one look at her steely gaze made me reconsider. "But—" I said.

"Shush. I am not willing to let you put yourself in harm's way when it is quite likely the negro doctor will be here any minute." Her eyes shone and she lowered her voice. "Nothing can happen to you, Jeannine. You are all I have."

I nodded and turned my attention to Lydia. "What were you doing out here so late?" I asked. I fear my tone sounded more accusing than I intended, for Lydia gave me a sharp look before answering.

"I got no time to rest with Solomon in jail." She paused as I winced at her acidic tone. "I can't be sittin' on my hands. Mrs. Davis sent me a message that she got three sick children. They've soiled ev'ry one o' their linens. She needs 'em cleaned as soon as possible so her babies got fresh bedclothes by tomorrow. I was on my way home with the load."

"I apologize for my tone, Lydia. I meant nothing by it. You understand, I am simply beside myself."

She nodded, keeping her gaze focused on the group of men surrounding the person on the ground. The sheriff left the rest of the men and stalked toward me and Chloe and Lydia.

"Who found him?" he asked.

"Who is he?" I asked. He glared at me. He probably didn't appreciate me answering his question with one of my own.

"I asked, who found him?" He frowned.

"I did." Lydia stepped forward and straightened her shoulders.

The sheriff looked her up and down in the light of his lantern. "And how did that happen? What were you doing out here in the dark?"

"I had just picked up a load of dirty wash from the Davises, around the corner. I was on my way home."

"Where do you live?" He looked away toward the men surrounding the body, but jerked his head back toward Lydia when she answered him. "You're Solomon Sanders' woman."

"I am his wife, yes," she answered in a dignified tone.

"Go sit over there." He pointed to the porch steps.

I spoke up. "May I ask why?"

He stared at me for a moment, a challenge in his small eyes. "Because I want to ask her more questions. This is my investigation, not yours, Mrs. Holt."

Chloe took my arm gently. "Come, Jeannine. We should let him do his job."

I clenched my teeth, but followed Chloe without protest as we walked with Lydia toward the porch. I looked over my shoulder and saw the sheriff talking to another man, nodding toward Lydia. The other man joined us a moment later. He said nothing, but stationed himself, arms folded in front of his chest, beside Lydia. Chloe and I stood on her other side.

The man who had left for the negro neighborhood came

back several minutes later, apparently in no hurry. "Negro doc ain't home."

"Someone *must* go for Doc Parsons," I called loudly. This time another man walked off toward the doctor's house. Thankfully, it was only a few moments before everyone turned at the sound of a carriage rattling toward us. It jerked to a stop in front of The Chestnut Wig and Doc Parsons clambered down from the rumble seat. In the light from the lanterns carried by all the men, I watched his eyes search the crowd. When they settled on the sheriff, the doctor moved toward him. The two men spoke together in low tones.

I couldn't hear what was being said, but the crowd parted as the doctor made his way toward the person on the ground. Silence fell as he conducted a brief examination of the person by lanternlight, then he said something to the people closest to him. One of them came walking toward me.

"Doc needs a blanket."

Without a word, I hurried into the house and returned only a moment later with a woolen blanket, which I thrust into the man's arms. He turned on his heel and returned to the doctor.

A few minutes later, I realized what the blanket was for—a litter to carry the injured person. Four men wrestled the body onto the blanket, then each picked up one corner of it. They marched with the body slowly toward my house. Chloe and Lydia and I stood aside, giving the men as much space as possible to get up the steps and onto the porch, but they placed the man on the ground. I still could not see who it was.

"Take him inside," I ordered.

"But he's a negro," one of the men said.

"You heard me." I stood with my hands on my hips. Slowly, the men lifted the litter again, grumbling.

"The doctor won't have to strain his eyes to see the patient indoors," I said by way of explanation. That seemed to ease their bigoted minds.

Chloe opened the front door and the men proceeded into the foyer. Their bodies prevented me from seeing the man in the litter. Chloe and I followed them and I directed them into the parlor. Lydia tried to join us, but was stopped by the man appointed by the sheriff to guard her.

Chloe hurried to turn on the gas lamps while I made my way to the side of the injured person being placed on the sofa.

It was Lysander.

CHAPTER 33

I gasped when I saw the gash of red across Lysander's forehead.

The doctor peered closely at the wound and reached into the black leather bag he had placed on the floor next to him. He pulled out a roll of bandages. "I need strong spirits," he said over his shoulder.

Everyone turned to look at me. I hurried from the room. I should have realized immediately that the doctor would need spirits to cleanse the wound, and I berated myself for not fetching it sooner. It only took a moment for me to grab a bottle and return to the parlor, but I worried that I had wasted precious seconds—seconds that mattered, since I appeared to be the only one in a hurry. As I thrust it toward the doctor, I realized with wry irony that the spirit I had grabbed was Lysander's brandy. The doctor poured a liberal amount over the wound, causing the amber liquid to mix with the blood and dribble onto the sofa.

I stood back, watching the doctor unroll bandages of cloth and place them over the wound and around Lysander's head. In only a minute or two, the bandages were soaked through with blood, or perhaps it was a mixture of blood and brandy. The doctor grunted, removed the bandages, and replaced them with fresh ones from the supply in his bag.

"I'll need more linen strips," he said, casting his eyes over his shoulder and toward me and Chloe. "As long as the wound continues to bleed, he'll need fresh bandages."

I left the room again, this time to fetch linens from a closet on the third floor. While I did that, Chloe hastened to the summer kitchen and returned with shears. Together we cut the linens into strips and handed them to the doctor. The other men who had helped bring Lysander into the parlor stood at a distance around the perimeter of the room, watching us and the doctor work. Every now and then I looked up and saw them exchange glances. I knew what they were thinking—it was highly improper for me to insist on bringing an injured negro into my parlor.

But their prejudices didn't matter to me at the moment. The most important consideration was Lysander's health.

Presently the flow of blood began to slow and the doctor requested fewer new bandages. Lysander's eyes, which had been closed from the time he was brought indoors, finally fluttered open. They widened when he gazed around the room and took note of all the people staring at him. He opened his mouth, but no sound came out.

The doctor stood and addressed me. "I have laudanum in my bag. I'll give him some to dull the pain. Does he have family who can come get him?" I shook my head. He did not appear terribly concerned about Lysander's wound, but I didn't know whether that was because he expected Lysander to make a full recovery or because his patient was a negro.

I stepped forward. "Lysander, how are you feeling?" The poor young man looked at me in confusion. "It is I, Mrs. Holt.

You've been in an accident," I said in a soft voice. "You are in my house and the doctor has bandaged your head."

He began to inhale and exhale more slowly, then closed his eyes. He did not wince or cry out, though he must have been in a great deal of pain. The doctor appeared at my elbow and touched Lysander's shoulder. Lysander opened his eyes again. "Take this," Doc Parsons said. He held out a dropper full of reddish-brown liquid. Lysander opened his mouth and the doctor gave him several drops of laudanum. Lysander made a face upon tasting the bitter medicine.

When the doctor had returned the dropper to his bag, he closed it and called me to his side. We moved toward the door. "He appears to have suffered a sanguine apoplexy brought on by a fall."

"What is a sanguine apoplexy?"

"An injury to his brain. He may have trouble walking or talking for an undetermined amount of time. He may not even understand what people are saying to him. Someone should stay with him for a day or two. If his condition worsens, they can send for me until the negro doctor returns to Cape May. At that time I will transfer the patient's care to him." He gestured toward the men still idling against the wall. "One of these men might be willing to take him home for a small fee."

"That will not be necessary," I stated. "He can stay here while he recovers."

"That is highly unusual, Mrs. Holt. I should think you would be better off if he were with his own kind."

I clenched my jaw and took a breath before answering him as courteously as I could. "Lysander is one of my vendors. Thank you for coming to take care of him. You may send me the bill for your services, and I would appreciate it if you would come back in the morning to check on him."

The doctor raised an eyebrow, but did not reply. He merely

nodded and left. The men who had carried the litter into the parlor filed out after him. Chloe and I were left alone in the room with Lysander, who opened his eyes and turned his head slightly toward us. I knelt on the floor next to the sofa. "Can you tell me what happened?"

His mouth twisted as if he were attempting to speak, but only garbled sound came out. His eyes widened. He must have been frightened.

"There is a deep gash on your forehead. It's covered with bandages," I hastened to explain. "The doctor cleaned it with spirits, but said you might have trouble walking and talking for a while. Don't try to talk any more. Perhaps you can rest and feel better tomorrow. I'll check on you during the night."

Lysander lifted his hand slowly and touched the bandages on his head.

"Can I get you anything to make you more comfortable?"

He gave me a bewildered look, but I didn't know what else to say. Perhaps he didn't understand my question. Chloe and I sat in the grandfather armchairs beside each other. We watched him as his eyes closed and his breathing slowed and became more regular. Thankfully, the laudanum appeared to be having its effect.

"Perhaps I should stay in here with him," I whispered.

"A woman sitting up all night in her parlor with a man who is not a relation is exceedingly improper," she said.

Dear Chloe, always following the rules.

"Suppose he should need help suddenly?" I asked.

"Jeannine, it's only because this is an emergency that I am not insisting he leave tonight. He is not likely to need help suddenly. The laudanum will keep him still."

I nodded, trying to remind myself that Chloe was nervous and upset, and those feelings prompted her to talk that way. Nevertheless, there would be no silencing her if I stayed awake all night by Lysander's side. The doctor had not seemed unduly concerned about his condition, so it was probably acceptable for me to go to my rooms. I could check on Lysander occasionally. I followed Chloe up the stairs and readied myself for bed.

My last thought before I fell into a fitful sleep was that I should not have left Lydia on the porch earlier to face the sheriff's questions by herself.

I awoke with a start several times during the night. Each time, I crept downstairs and into the parlor to make sure Lysander was not in distress. He was asleep each time I checked, though he murmured unintelligible sounds now and then.

By morning I had a wretched headache. I left my bedroom just after sunrise to find Chloe going downstairs.

"Were you able to sleep?" she asked quietly.

"Not as much as I would have liked," I answered ruefully. I followed her down the stairs and into the parlor. Lysander was still sleeping. I sat in the chair I had occupied the night before while Chloe left to prepare tea and toast. As I massaged my temples, Lysander opened his eyes.

"Good morning, Lysander. Do you remember where you are?" I spoke quietly as I rose to stand next to the sofa.

He stared at me, his expression worried.

"You are at my house, at The Chestnut Wig. Can you remember what happened last night?"

His eyes widened, but he remained still.

"You were found on the ground nearby. You were badly hurt."

He squinted at me. I swallowed, a burgeoning sense of alarm encircling my chest, squeezing. If Lysander had indeed lost the ability to speak and comprehend, would it ever return?

"Are you able to speak?" I asked.

He moved his lips, but the effort was in vain. Only muddled utterances came out of his mouth. He struggled to lift himself onto his elbows but fell back.

I frowned. "Your body is still exhausted from your injury. Don't try to move—the doctor should return this morning."

Lysander's eyes bulged. I could see how frightened he was of the entire situation. I put my hand on his arm. "Everything will be all right, do not fear."

Chloe opened the parlor door a few minutes later carrying a tray of tea things and a stack of buttered toast.

"How is he?" She spoke quietly as she set the tray on a small table.

"Unfortunately, he's still unable to speak," I whispered.

Her brow furrowed. "I wonder what exactly happened."

I shook my head and shrugged in response.

Lysander's eyelids fluttered open. I offered him a plate of toast and set a cup of tea in front of him.

He ate slowly, but his color improved with every bite. It appeared he was only able to use his right hand. Chloe and I chatted softly while we ate. I hoped Lysander would join in our conversation, but he did not. We took turns staying with him in the parlor until there was a knock at the door around noontime. While Chloe stayed with Lysander, I opened the door to find Doc Parsons standing on the porch. I had begun to wonder if he would ever visit.

"Good day, Doctor. Thank you for coming. Please come in."

"How is he?"

"He can't speak. I am quite concerned." I closed the door behind him.

"As I said, he may not speak for some time, if ever. Is he able to walk?"

"I have not seen him walk."

He followed me in silence to the parlor. Chloe and I left the room while he examined Lysander. When he emerged several minutes later, his face was grave.

"Will he regain his power of speech?" I asked.

The doctor was silent for a moment. "I believe he will. But he must remain quiet and without undue excitement."

"We can have our coachman take him home today," Chloe said. "Will the carriage ride be too jarring?"

"Probably not, but it would be best if someone could stay with him. I heard this morning that the negro doctor will be back by evening, so he will look after the patient from now on. Contact him if you have any questions." Doc Parsons bade us a good day and was gone.

I turned to Chloe. I was about to speak when she anticipated my remarks and spoke first. "He has to go home, Jeannine. You must agree that he'll be more comfortable there."

"I do agree. But I think he should stay here one more night."

"He can stay here long enough for us to find someone to stay at his house with him. How could he get any rest with patrons coming and going for hours this evening?" Chloe asked. "I am going out to the summer kitchen to prepare a basket of food for him to take when he leaves. You go back into the parlor and stay with him until I can take your place, then you can find someone to stay with him."

I knew from the set of her mouth that she would brook no argument. Again, I was caught between my own tendency to ignore certain rules and Chloe's rigid adherence to them. The Chestnut Wig was *my* house. I should have control over what happened. The dreadful thought of asking her to leave flitted through my mind again.

But as irksome as Chloe could be at times, I had grown accustomed to her company. She was my cousin and I loved her. Besides that, she had nowhere to go if I asked her to leave. And her words made sense.

I returned to the parlor and sat in a chair across from where Lysander lay on the sofa. His eyes were closed. I kept watch over him until Chloe joined me. She set the large basket of food on the floor next to the parlor door.

"I'll stay with him now. You can go find someone to accompany him home."

I nodded and left the room. I went to my rooms on the third floor and donned a hat and gloves, then returned to the parlor to tell Chloe where I planned to go first.

But as soon as I walked into the room and saw her sitting on the sofa beside Lysander, I knew something was wrong.

CHAPTER 34

Chloe looked up with a grave expression. Lysander's left hand fluttered as his body moved slowly from side to side.

"Whatever is the matter?" I asked.

"I have no idea," she said. "He suddenly began to rock sideways and twitch."

"Perhaps he saw the basket of food and doesn't want to leave," I suggested. Chloe's eyes narrowed, but she said nothing.

I sat on the other side of him, no longer caring what Chloe's opinion was. "You are welcome to stay in this house for another night, but I fear I cannot offer you accommodations other than this uncomfortable sofa." He stilled, with no indication that he understood what I was saying. "Would you prefer that?" I asked. Again, no response. I wondered if he understood anything I had said.

My gaze met the grim expression in Chloe's eyes. Her mouth was set in a thin line. I did not need to ask her how she felt about such an arrangement.

But having blurted out the invitation, I wondered how we could possibly keep Lysander in our house. I knew Chloe did not want him there because of how it would look to the neigh-bors and others in Cape May, but there was a much more pressing reason to send him home: keeping him any longer might prompt people to start asking questions about our rela-tionship with negroes—and how far we would go to protect them. If rumors and suspicion began to bloom all over town, we might be forced to discontinue our assistance along the under-ground railroad, and that was a step I was not willing to take. I rambled along, despite the possibility that he could not under-stand what I was saying.

"Lysander, if it were up to me, you could stay here as long as it takes you to recover. But we have other considerations, such as ..." I nodded toward the floor, wondering if he remembered there was a hiding place beneath our feet. "And besides that, I am sure you'll find it much more agreeable to stay in your home, in your own bed and your own night-clothes."

He sat motionless, his brow creased with worry. His glance slid toward Chloe out of the corner of his eye. He might not understand my words, but I realized he understood something: he sensed Chloe wanted to send him away.

There would come a time, I was sure, when she would not place a great amount of importance on outward appearances. But until then, I wanted to keep the peace between us. Our friendship had faltered, becoming awkward and strained following her threat to expose Emeline (and thereby, our role in protecting her) to the sheriff. I had no desire to go through that again.

I wondered briefly if Lysander could stay in the attic over the summer kitchen or even the hiding place beneath the parlor, but discarded those ideas almost immediately. Lysander was a free man, and there was no reason to conceal him like a runaway slave.

It was time to talk to Lydia. She might know of someone

who could stay with the injured man. I stood and smoothed my skirt. "Chloe, would you mind—"

I stopped short when Lysander yelped and his hands tightened into fists. It was a most alarming display. I took a step backward, startled.

Slowly, he raised his hands and clumsily clasped them together. With a jerky motion, he gestured violently toward his head several times.

"What is he doing?" Chloe's tone was suspicious, frightened.

I swallowed. "I wish I knew." I paused. "There must be some reason he's behaving this way. Do you suppose he's trying to tell us something?"

"I assume so. But what?"

I shook my head, my eyes still focused on Lysander. As I watched him continue the strange movements, though, a slow realization began to dawn on me. "Chloe, do you suppose he's trying to tell us he was hit in the head?" My heartbeat quickened.

She turned to stare at me. "Are you saying he was attacked? I thought he tripped on something in the street."

"I did, too. But look at the motion. He is mimicking the act of hitting his head."

Chloe's mouth fell open. "I believe you're right."

I sat next to Lysander and took his hands in mine. I spoke in a gentle voice so he might know we understood him. "You are safe here, my friend." I looked up at Chloe. "How vicious! I wonder if he saw who hit him."

She shook her head and lifted her hands, then let them fall to her sides in a gesture of helplessness. "We have no way of knowing. Can he write? Perhaps he can write a name if he saw the person."

I grimaced. "I believe he can read. I don't know if he can write. Will you fetch a pen and a piece of paper from the desk? Maybe he can provide us with a name."

Chloe hurried to the desk in the corner, then set the items on the low table in front of Lysander. She pointed to him and to the table. He followed her motions with his eyes, but didn't move.

"He may have seen the person," I said to Chloe. "But it doesn't appear he's going to write the name." I stood again. "It's no wonder he seems so afraid. He probably doesn't wish to go home by himself. I am going to see the sheriff right away. He needs to know about this. Then I am going to Lydia's house."

"For what?"

"She may know someone who can stay with him. I hope to be back quickly."

She nodded and I left the room.

I walked to the sheriff's office rather than waiting for Benjamin to hitch up the carriage. It wasn't long before I was standing before the sheriff. I wasn't sure he would even listen to me since I was talking about an injury to a negro man, but I had to try.

"Do you realize Lysander Greaves' fall was not an accident?" I asked.

"What are you talking about, Mrs. Holt?" He fixed me with a look of utter annoyance.

"Lysander told me someone hit him in the head."

"The doctor told me the man is incapable of speech. So how did he manage to tell you anything?"

"He made a chopping motion toward his head with his hands."

The sheriff scoffed. "Are you sure you aren't overly analyzing his actions, Mrs. Holt?"

I bristled. "I am positive, Sheriff. A chopping motion does not require analysis."

"Very well. I will take this under advisement and see what truth there may be to it. I must tell you, though, I am sure it will amount to nothing and you are putting yourself at risk for a fine."

"A fine? For what?"

"For wasting the law's time."

"I know Lysander to be an honest man, Sheriff. He would not lie about this, let alone anything else."

"We'll see about that, Mrs. Holt. Now if you'll excuse me, I have pressing matters to look after."

With that abrupt dismissal, I left his office. I was quite sure he had no other pressing matters—unless one counted cleaning his fingernails or examining his navel.

And a fine! The very notion was ludicrous. The next time I made the trip to Cape May Court House, I might have to speak to the magistrate about the sheriff's high-handedness and blatant disregard for legitimate public concerns.

Next I went to Lydia's house. I had not spoken to her after Lysander was carried into my parlor, and I had a hunch the sheriff had questioned her harshly about finding him on the ground. Besides that, I needed her help.

As usual, she was working when I arrived. She wiped her brow with her apron as she opened the door to me. Her eyes widened.

I held up my hand. "Before you ask, Lydia, I don't have news about Solomon."

Her shoulders softened. "It happens ev'ry time, Mizz Holt. I open the door thinkin' someone's here to tell me Solomon's dead."

I couldn't imagine the strain she must be under. Before I could say anything, though, she continued. "The sheriff said it was Lysander Greaves I found lyin' on the ground last night. How is he?"

"He is conscious and alert, though he cannot speak and seems not to understand what we say to him. I'm grateful to you for finding him and bringing the situation to my and Chloe's attention."

She gestured indoors. "Come on in."

Once seated at her table, I folded my hands in front of me. "I did want you to know about Lysander, of course, but there are two other reasons I'm here. First, I want to apologize for leaving you to the mercies of the sheriff while I went inside."

She bowed her head and looked at the ground. "Mizz Holt, he is not kind to folks who look like me. He blamed me for Lysander's accident and said I'm no better'n my husband." Her fists clenched. "You know me and Solomon haven't done anything wrong."

"I know, Lydia. If I had stayed outside last night, perhaps the sheriff might have questioned you with more delicacy. Though since I'm not his favorite person, I can't be sure of that. And I am most certainly aware that you and Solomon are innocent of any wrongdoing."

Lydia sighed heavily. "Thank you. Will Lysander recover? Is there anything I can do to help?"

"The doctor thinks he will recover, given some time. He stayed at my house last night, but I believe he will recover more quickly at his own house, in his own bed. He is … nervous about going home." I had been wondering how much to reveal to Lydia, and there was no sense in keeping any of the truth from her.

She gave me a quizzical look. "What's he got to be nervous about?"

I lowered my voice in case any of the Sanders children were nearby, listening. "He did not fall last night—he was attacked."

Lydia's hand flew to her mouth. "That poor man," she said in a muffled voice. "Does he know who did it?"

I shook my head. "If he does, he's not able to tell us. And that brings me to the second purpose for my visit today. Do you know of anyone who would be willing to see him home and stay with him while he recovers? I think it would help put him at ease if he knew someone was looking after him. I would pay the person, of course."

Lydia thought for a moment, then disappeared into the other room of her house. When she came back, Lucy was following her. "Lucy's gonna take a message to my brother, Oscar. He makes furniture, so he can do that at Lysander's house. He can maybe stay with Lysander," Lydia said.

I smiled at Lucy—every time the dear girl saw me it seemed she was sent away with some message or another. She ran off while Lydia and I discussed who could have done such a thing to Lysander. Lydia was of the opinion that he was well-liked by everyone in the negro community and insisted the culprit did not come from their ranks.

That narrowed down the suspect list.

CHAPTER 35

By the time I left Lydia's house with confirmation that Oscar would stay with Lysander while he recovered, I had to hurry to prepare for the evening's guests at The Chestnut Wig. Chloe was rushing about, too, having been with Lysander while I was out. I consulted her regarding the food and beverages, then told her that Oscar was coming to fetch Lysander after The Chestnut Wig closed later that evening. I did not wish to leave Lysander alone in the parlor, but it was time for a dose of laudanum and by the time the first guests arrived he was sleeping soundly.

I was dismayed to see Bert Branson arrive an hour after opening. I gave him an arch look when he came into the foyer, but he evaded my gaze skillfully as he greeted another guest and was immediately swept up into conversation. I wondered at his audacity. It was the height of rudeness to ignore the proprietress of any establishment, particularly if she were standing directly in front of him, and particularly if he owed her money.

Not only that, but he could very well be Gideon Welch's murderer.

I made a special point of keeping my eye on him that

evening and was pleased to see him accumulating several handsome wins at different games. If I garnered some of his winnings, it finally looked like he might be able to pay at least a small portion of the amount due to me.

Once the evening was over and the guests had left, Chloe and I went to the parlor to keep watch over Lysander. He was still sleeping. I made notes and sums in the ledger while Chloe read a book in one of the armchairs. I turned to Bert's account and saw that he had won enough money to pay nearly a quarter of what he owed me.

I wondered if Gideon's sons would attempt to collect the money Bert owed their father. A shiver ran down my spine when I remembered Gideon lying on my dining room floor, covered in his own blood.

I recalled a conversation with Daniel long ago, shortly after we were married. We had opened our gambling house to the public and I was learning the ways of business. There was an incident one night when two men were arguing heatedly over a bet, each threatening violence to the other, and it had frightened me. Daniel said, "As useful as money is for a comfortable existence, it is also the root of evil. Too much makes men callous. Too little makes them desperate."

Daniel's words told a cautionary tale. It set me to wondering whether money—and in particular, too little of it—had played a role in Gideon's death. I had a strong hunch it did.

If I were ever to help Solomon clear his name and get him back to his family and his workplace, I needed to figure out if money was, in this instance, the root of the evil that had befallen Gideon. I wondered if the sheriff had questioned Bert yet about his debts.

It would be easy to become desperate, I thought, *if one owed money and could not repay it. Desperate enough to kill?* My thoughts returned again and again to Bert. How was I to find out the particulars of his debt to Gideon?

The most effective way to get information, I figured, was to ask our cook Eliza to do it. She was so good at gathering information without people realizing that was her goal. I wondered if she would be able to talk again to the house girl the Bransons had to let go, and whether the girl would know any details about Bert's debt to Gideon and possibly other people, too. If there was one thing I had learned from Eliza, it was that the servants knew everything that went on in their employers' homes.

A knock at the back door interrupted my musings. While Chloe stayed with Lysander, I hurried to answer the door and found a man who looked exactly like Lydia smiling at me.

"You must be Oscar. I would know you as Lydia's brother anywhere. I am Mrs. Holt."

"Pleased to meet you, Mizz Holt." Oscar was tall and stocky. He seemed friendly, but looked like he would not let anyone intimidate him. That was exactly what Lysander needed.

I invited him inside and he followed me to the parlor. Lysander was stirring. Chloe had set her book aside and moved to sit closer to him.

I explained to Oscar what the doctor had said about Lysander's condition. While we talked, Lysander woke up and pushed himself to a seated position. I introduced him to Oscar and Oscar took Lysander's hands in his and held them warmly.

Oscar had a wagon waiting outside by the stable, so I asked him to drive it around front. When he came back into the house, we tried getting Lysander to walk. He was unable to do it by himself. So Oscar half-dragged, half-carried him to the wagon and lifted him up into the back, where he had spread out a sleeping pallet. Once the injured man was lying as comfortably as possible, Chloe and I bid him goodbye and thanked Oscar. I promised to visit Lysander whenever possible. They drove away slowly into the darkness toward Lysander's house and I had a feeling my friend was in capable hands.

The next day when Eliza arrived at work I pulled her aside, out of the summer kitchen and the earshot of the other employees. When I saw the surprise and apprehension on her face, I was quick to allay any fear that she was being reprimanded.

"Eliza, I have a special job for you."

Her shoulders and face relaxed and a sigh of relief escaped her lips. "I'm happy to do it, Mizz."

"When you're at the market tomorrow fetching whatever Chloe asks you to get, I would like you to find the girl who recently worked for the Bransons. I need to know everything she can tell me about the money Mr. Branson owed to Mr. Welch—how much precisely, what it was for, whether he had paid any of it back, and whether Mr. Welch was demanding repayment. I would also like to know if Mr. Branson owes money to anyone else. Can you do that for me?"

"Yes'm. But what if she ain't there?"

"Then you can simply wait until the next time you see her. I thought perhaps she visited the market frequently."

"If she's there, I'll talk to her and get right back here quick."

"Thank you, Eliza. You may return to your work now."

I smiled as she hurried back inside the summer kitchen. She loved nothing more than to gossip, and I felt sure she would root out the information I sought.

DESPITE HAVING COME TOGETHER for the sake of caring for Lysander while he was at our home, Chloe and I were still treading lightly around each other. After bidding Lysander and Oscar a safe trip home the previous evening, we had gone back into the house, each to her own rooms. Now, during daylight hours, we studiously avoided each other. I missed our banter throughout the day, but did not wish to talk to her about Lysander, Emeline, or anyone else.

But that didn't stop me from thinking about them. Whoever attacked Lysander needed to be caught and brought to justice. It was a shame he had not seen his attacker's face.

I frowned. I wondered if the sheriff would take the time to investigate a crime against a negro. I doubted whether he would give it the attention it deserved unless and until a white man was attacked in a similar manner. Given how little investigating he was doing on the murder of Gideon Welch now that he had Solomon in custody, I was certain he would all but ignore the attack on Lysander.

As for Emeline, it seemed Chloe was getting her wish. Emeline was gone. In an ironic twist, I almost wished I could go to the sheriff and ask for help locating the young woman, but I knew in my heart that was the most unwise thing I could do. Besides, even if it were not illegal to harbor fugitive slaves, he would give short shrift to her plight. I refused to stop hoping she would be found, though.

CHAPTER 36

I had time the next morning to visit Lysander. Benjamin drove me to his house and waited while I went indoors.

Oscar greeted me pleasantly and offered me tea, which I declined. Lysander was sleeping soundly, he said, and he welcomed me to wait for him to awaken. We talked about Lysander's condition while we waited. Oscar had noticed no improvement in Lysander's ability to speak, but he had spent most of his time resting since arriving back at his own house. He did not seem to be in great discomfort, according to Oscar, and his wound seemed to be healing. Oscar had helped him walk the length of his porch, and he reported that Lysander was becoming a bit steadier on his feet.

I eventually left before Lysander woke up. I told Oscar I would be back the next day.

I spent the evening in the company of some of my most reliable clients. Violet Curtis was there, as well as Ada Miller, along with many of the same gentlemen and ladies from Congress Hall who had become habitués over the course of the summer.

The evening was rollicking fun for them, as evidenced by their laughter, good-natured teasing, and mirth.

Isaac Campbell was there, too, in a fine mood. That is, his mood was fine at first.

After eating his supper, he caught my eye and lifted his finger to call me to his table. He smiled and asked for a brandy, saying it always fortified his courage before a game of faro. As I poured it for him, I told him I had been surprised to learn that he was selling his steamships.

His smile vanished and he gave me a sharp look. "Who told you that?"

Oh, dear, I thought. *I wonder if I wasn't supposed to know about it.* Well, I had no choice but to tell him the story.

"A gentleman from Richmond was here several nights ago. He was visiting because he was interested in purchasing two steamboats. I suggested that he talk to you about it, and he said you were the seller."

Isaac nodded. "That is correct. I considered selling the boats."

I raised my eyebrows in surprise. "Did you not sell them? The man seemed quite keen to complete the transaction."

Isaac gulped his brandy all at once and sat the glass on the table. He set his napkin next to the glass. "My dear Mrs. Holt, I regret I cannot stay for faro this evening. I have just recalled something I need to do." I watched in bewilderment as he strode from the dining room.

Obviously I had vexed him, but I had no idea how I had done so. A steamship is a big thing to sell—surely he was not angry that I knew about that. Everyone on the docks must have known about it.

I sighed, dismissing Isaac and his temperamental behavior from my mind and replacing him with questions and worries about Emeline and Lysander. We had received no word of or from Emeline, and it had been almost a week now since she disappeared from the hiding place beneath the parlor. I had also heard nothing from Araminta.

To make matters worse, as Violet was leaving she lamented to me about "that poor, poor negro" who had been found on the ground around the corner two nights before. Her remarks were not what I needed just then, with my nerves as taut as a bowstring, but I tried to be polite.

"What on earth happened to him?" she asked.

"If only we knew. He's still incoherent."

Her eyes became saucers. "Oh, dear. He must have hit his head."

"There is no doubt of it. I hope the sheriff is able to figure out who attacked him."

Violet gasped, her hand to her breast. "Attacked? Surely you're mistaken."

"He did manage to communicate to us that he was attacked. But nothing else."

"Who would do such a thing in a town as peaceful as this?" She leaned closer. "Do you suppose it was a spat among negroes? The sheriff has enough to do without policing their disagreements." She pronounced "their" with an ugly curl of her lip.

I frowned at her distasteful remark. "I have no idea who it was," I said tersely.

She cocked one eyebrow, then responded by wishing me a good evening. She left with Ada, who had been waiting for her on the porch. No doubt Violet was wondering why I did not engage in her bigoted talk. She had spoken in less-than-flattering terms about negroes before, and my estimation of her dropped a bit more that night. That very moment she was probably gossiping with Ada about my sympathetic leanings toward negroes.

No matter, for what did I care of gossips? I closed the door and locked it, then retired to my desk to tally the evening's accounts. Chloe came into the house from the summer kitchen some time later.

"Would you care for a cup of tea before bedtime?" she asked.

"That would be lovely. Thank you." I smiled as I watched her leave the room. I heard the back door open and close. She probably yearned for a return to our routine as much as I did. Being at odds lately was taxing on me. It had to be troubling her, too.

We met several minutes later in our private parlor, where we enjoyed our tea in silence for a short while before engaging in conversation that had nothing to do with Lysander, Emeline, Bert, or the sheriff. It was refreshing and soothing. Though the ghosts of those topics hung in the air between us, we managed to take delight in one another's company as we used to do, and I slept well that night.

In the morning I breakfasted early and told Chloe I was walking to Lysander's house, as it was a beautiful day. She asked me to give him her regards, which I did promptly upon seeing him. He was awake and improved—I could tell immediately from his smile and healthy color. He had left our house with a sickly pallor and I was happy to see that being in his own home was helping him recover.

Oscar was an excellent companion. A checkerboard was set up on the table when I arrived, and a banjo stood upright in the corner of the sitting room. Clearly, the men had been enjoying their idle time.

Best of all, Lysander had regained a some of his ability to speak and understand spoken conversation. Haltingly, he told me how he was faring.

"I'm ... gettin' back ... to normal, Mizz." He smiled.

"I am so grateful to hear it, Lysander. We were all afraid for your life."

He nodded, his eyes glistening. "I'm ... gonna be ... just fine. Prob'ly soon."

"Well, my friend, it cannot be soon enough." I hesitated

before asking him the question I hoped he would be able to answer. "Do you remember what happened when you were attacked?"

He stared beyond my shoulder at something only he could see. When he spoke, it was in a soft voice. "I remember ... walkin' across the street ... It was late. I had ... been calling on ... a friend. Took a ... shortcut home." He paused, his eyes narrowing. "But crossing the street ... is the last thing I ... remember. Except ... I recall thinkin' ... there was someone else ... right close." He stopped speaking and looked as if the effort had exhausted him.

I dared not push him too hard, but the identity of the person close to him was of utmost importance to the sheriff's investigation. "Was it just one person?"

He nodded.

"Do you recall anything about the person?"

"It was ...prob'ly a man, because the footsteps sounded heavy ... like a man's."

"Do you remember if the man was white or negro?"

He shook his head. "It's just ... out of reach. I wish ... I had paid him ... more attention. I'm sorry, Mizz."

"Oh, Lysander. There's no cause to be sorry. Every bit of information will be useful in the sheriff's investigation of the attack." *If there's going to be an investigation,* I thought. Lysander and Oscar exchanged looks and I knew they wondered the same thing.

Not wishing to tire him further, I stood to leave. Oscar promised to keep me, as well as the doctor, apprised of any changes to Lysander's condition. "You're doing a fine job," I told him as I shook his hand. "Thank you. Lysander is a dear friend and I can't bear to think of him trying to recover by himself."

"Mizz?" I turned at Lysander's voice. "Any word ... about Emeline?"

I pressed my lips together and shook my head quickly, knitting my brows as I looked at him. I hoped he would not say anything else about her. I did not wish Oscar to know of Emeline's existence. As much as I liked and trusted him, the more people who knew about her, the less likely she was to return safely. "Nothing yet. If I hear, I will certainly let you know."

I stopped at the sheriff's office after leaving Lysander's house. The sheriff was not in, so I left a detailed message with his deputy repeating what Lysander had told me.

I walked the rest of the way home deep in thought. I wished I had been able to give Lysander good news about Emeline. I had a feeling we were running out of time to find the young woman and bring her back to The Chestnut Wig unharmed.

CHAPTER 37

The next morning found me at the sheriff's office again. The deputy wasn't there, and the sheriff was sitting at his desk when I knocked on the door jamb. He looked up at me with a slight frown, then quickly adjusted the set of his mouth into something between a grimace and a smirk.

"Good day, Mrs. Holt."

"Good day, Sheriff. I hope you're well. I trust your deputy relayed the message I left yesterday about the things Lysander Greaves said."

"He did."

I paused before speaking. He had confirmed receipt of the message I left for him, so there was little else I could do for Lysander. But it could not hurt to try to convince him of Solomon's innocence one more time. "I am here to inquire about the status of your investigations into Gideon Welch's murder and the attack on Lysander Greaves."

The sheriff sat back and folded his hands over his ample belly. He seemed to be contemplating how much to reveal. I adopted a conciliatory tone.

"Of course, I am not asking you to divulge anything confidential," I said. "But I hope you are able to share some information with me."

He nodded slowly. "Of course, Mrs. Holt. There are certain things I can tell you. Please, have a seat." He gestured to the chair opposite him on the other side of his desk.

I sat on the edge of the seat, my back straight and my hands in my lap. "I appreciate that, Sheriff." I gave him an expectant look.

"With regard to the person who attacked the negro near your house, we have learned that there was an unknown person seen in the vicinity just before the attack."

I suddenly recalled the voice I had heard that night, the one that interrupted my reading. I inhaled sharply as I realized that was probably either Lysander or his attacker. If only I had gone outside to find out who it was.

"I heard a shout several minutes before the attack. I believe it was a man's voice, but I can't be sure. Do you know any details about the person? I assume it was a man? Do you know his race?" I asked.

"All the information we have points to it being a man. A white man, though it was dark and witnesses can be unreliable in such circumstances."

I hid my distaste. It did not surprise me to hear the man hedging about the likely race of the perpetrator.

"We are still trying to determine the man's identity," the sheriff added unhelpfully. He paused. "As to the murder of Gideon Welch, there is no new information. I remain convinced we have the correct offender in custody."

"Have you looked into the relationship between Bert Branson and the murdered man yet? You will recall Mr. Branson owed him money."

The sheriff sighed, barely concealing his annoyance. "Mrs. Holt, if every debtor in Cape May were to become a suspect in

Mr. Welch's murder, there would be no end to my investigations."

I pressed my lips together in a thin line. "But you *are* continuing to investigate, correct? As you know, it is my strong belief that Solomon Sanders did not kill Gideon Welch. I know you cannot base your investigation on my opinions, but I am not the only one who knows Solomon is innocent."

"The moment you have any proof that Solomon did not kill Mr. Welch, please bring it to my attention."

"But surely you realize it is nearly impossible to prove someone's innocence. It is proof of guilt that is required in a court of law."

He frowned. "And as I have told you, I have sufficient proof of Solomon Sanders' guilt."

"What you have, Sheriff, cannot even amount to circumstantial evidence. That is certainly not adequate."

"Mrs. Holt, if you had any idea how many cases have nothing but circumstantial evidence to recommend them, you would realize it is common and, I daresay, necessary to allow prosecutions to proceed on such evidence."

This was nonsense, and I had to bite the inside of my cheek to prevent myself from telling him so. Very well, I would simply continue to look for clues as to the real murderer's identity.

I was in a disagreeable mood when I arrived at home. Chloe was in the summer kitchen working on menus for the fall. She invited me to eat luncheon with her in the garden, but I declined, not wishing to infect her with my irritability. I took a tray with some food up to my room and ate alone. There had to be *something* I could do to help either Solomon or Lysander.

After luncheon I sat down to make a list of the information I needed in order to continue my surreptitious investigations into Gideon Welch's murder and the attack on Lysander.

First, I needed to speak to Solomon again. This would serve two purposes: a visit would remind him that I had not forgotten about him and would also enable me to find out whether he had remembered anything else about the night Gideon was killed.

Second, I needed to speak to Eliza. I hoped she would have some news for me about Bert Branson's debts.

Third, I needed to speak to Lysander to make sure he was continuing to recover from his ordeal and to see if he recalled any more about the night he was attacked.

It was already early afternoon, and I certainly didn't have time to travel up to Cape May Court House to see Solomon before The Chestnut Wig opened at six o'clock. Eliza would arrive for work by three, so that meant there was time to visit Lysander before I spoke to her.

Taking the path through the trees behind the house to the stable, I found Benjamin eating his luncheon.

"I apologize for interrupting your meal, Benjamin, but I would like you to drive me to Lysander Greaves' house. I can wait until you have eaten your meal."

"No need, Mrs. Holt. I was just finishing up. I can take you now." He put the remains of his meal into his pail and set it aside. Several minutes later we were on the way to Lysander's house in my carriage.

I knew something was wrong as soon as we arrived. Oscar met me at the door with a worried look in his eyes.

"What has happened? Is Lysander ill?" I asked in alarm. I called over my shoulder, "Benjamin, please wait for me right there." Benjamin moved the horse and carriage to the side of the dusty road while I listened to Oscar.

"He's not well, ma'am. He's been cryin' and carryin' on, and he won't say what's botherin' him. He's not talkin' near as good as he was yesterday. I can't get him to eat or rest."

"May I see him?"

He stood aside so I could enter the main room of the house. It was dark inside, with curtains still pulled across the windows and no lamps or lighted candles in sight. Lysander sat at the table.

"Lysander?" I moved toward him slowly. "Is there something I can do to help you?" I waited for him to respond, but he said nothing. He sniffled, though, and dragged a hand across his face. Despite the dimness, I could see tears glistening on his cheeks.

I sat in the chair next to his and he turned his head toward me. He sniffled again.

"Can you tell me what the trouble is?" I spoke as gently as I could. "Do you feel unwell?"

He nodded and squeezed his eyes shut.

"Does your head hurt?"

He nodded again.

"Would you like me to fetch the doctor?"

When he did not respond, I asked the question again. This time he nodded slightly.

I stood immediately. "I'll send my coachman for him straightaway." I went to the front door and gestured for Benjamin to come closer. When he was at the foot of the porch steps, I instructed him to take a message to the negro doctor requesting that he attend Lysander as quickly as possible. Benjamin tipped his hat toward me and left, driving away at a quick clip. I returned to Lysander's side.

"The doctor should be here soon," I assured him. "In the meantime, tell me what I can do to make you more comfortable."

He shook his head, but it seemed to cause him pain. "There's nothin', ma'am," he said.

I chafed at my inability to help him, but as we sat together in silence, he seemed to calm. The sniffling stopped and the tears on his cheeks dried. Oscar stayed on the front porch while I was indoors. It was not long before we heard the sound of horse hooves on the road, and Oscar opened the front door. "Your coachman is back, ma'am. Looks like the doc is right behind him."

"Thank you." I rose and patted Lysander's arm. "I'll go talk to the doctor and be back in just a moment."

I met the doctor coming up the front walk and explained what I had witnessed since arriving. He nodded, listening intently. He told me he knew of Lysander's case from Doc Parsons. I accompanied him into the house while Oscar stayed on the porch.

I didn't wish to seem obtrusive, so I went to a window and raised the shade enough to look outside while the doctor examined Lysander. Presently he cleared his throat. "Mrs. Holt?" He gestured toward the door and I followed him outside.

Oscar joined us. "Will he continue to recover?" I asked.

To my immense relief, the doctor nodded. "What I see here is quite common when someone has had a grave head injury. Often the patient is overly emotional. Speech comes in fits and starts. But I believe he will eventually return to normal. His speech will improve. We just need to be patient and give him time to recover. Lysander is a strong young man."

"Thank you for coming to see him so quickly. Please send me your bill."

"I will. Good day to you, Mrs. Holt," he said.

"And to you." As soon as he climbed into his carriage, I went back inside. Lysander still sat at the table, but this time he was eating a fresh peach. I told him what the doctor had said. He exhaled and finally a smile crossed his features. No doubt he had been afraid that he might never return to the way he was before he was attacked.

"What a relief it is to know that your symptoms are normal and to be expected," I said. "You shall be back to yourself in no time."

I took up my reticule and went to the front door, pleased to see him stand and join me. He even opened the door for me.

"I shall return to check on you in a day or two," I said. He nodded, smiling. Oscar joined him and they stood together on the porch, watching as I walked to the carriage.

Benjamin had walked a short distance from the carriage. When he saw me emerge from the house, he called out to me, saying he would fetch the box to help me up into the carriage. I had no sooner set one foot on the box when Lysander screamed.

CHAPTER 38

 dropped my reticule onto the carriage floor and turned around. "Lysander! Whatever is the matter?"

Lysander's eyes rolled back into his head and he began to slump as I looked on in horror. Oscar immediately braced himself to catch Lysander under his arms. I picked up my skirts and ran back to the house. By the time I reached them Oscar was supporting Lysander awkwardly with his arms and legs so Lysander would not collapse onto the porch floor.

"Benjamin!" I called out. My coachman saw what was happening and ran up behind me. He helped Oscar shift Lysander's weight and together they carried him into the house and laid him on the bed. Benjamin left immediately so Oscar and I could minister to Lysander.

He woke after just a few moments, but his hands trembled and he blinked rapidly as if to hold back tears. His speech was unintelligible.

"Get the laudanum," I directed Oscar. He hurried to a cabinet across the room and was back just a moment later. I held Lysander's shaking hands as he gulped the laudanum, grimacing at the taste.

It was quite a large dose, so it did not take long for his breathing to slow and his eyes to close. Soon he was asleep. It was no wonder he fainted. The stress of everything that had happened must have been a terrible weight on his mind.

There was nothing else I could do, and I had a feeling Lysander would sleep for a long while. I departed again. "Please keep a very close watch on him," I said to Oscar. "If he awakens and is no better, please send for the doctor immediately."

"I will," he promised.

Though it was for a very good reason, I had spent longer than I intended at Lysander's house. When I arrived home, the cooks were already busy in the summer kitchen preparing the evening meal. I took Chloe aside to tell her what had happened. As she stared at me, dumbfounded, I told her of the measures Oscar and I took to calm Lysander and that he was asleep when I left for home. Finally she found her voice. "I hope the poor man is going to recover. He's been through so much in the past several days. What do you suppose caused him to faint?"

I shook my head. "The stress of everything he has experienced. He was ruthlessly attacked and is still barely capable of speech. And no doubt he wonders if he'll be able to get back to the work of making brandies. He must fear for his livelihood."

"Surely he'll be able to return to it," Chloe said. "Even if he can't speak, he can still listen to orders. And making the spirits doesn't require the power of speech, so he should be able to achieve it."

I knew Chloe was trying to comfort me, to maintain an optimistic view of Lysander's future, but I found myself feeling cross, as if she were dismissing the severity of his condition. I changed the subject before I could say anything I might later regret.

"Is Eliza here?" I cast my gaze around the kitchen, but did not see her.

"Yes. I sent her to the cellar. She should be back shortly."

Chloe returned to her work and I waited for Eliza. She emerged from the cellar a few moments later and smiled when she saw me.

"Eliza, I think Miss Jeannine would like to speak to you," Chloe said.

"Yes'm."

She approached me and I gestured to the door. I waited to ask her anything until I had closed the door behind us and we were out of earshot of the other cooks.

"Were you able to talk to the Bransons' former house girl?"

She nodded. "Yes'm. I talked to her. She told me Mr. Branson and his wife fight all the time, they do, and always about money. She's glad she don't work there any longer. She's got a better job now. She said she don't know how much Mr. Branson owes Mr. Welch, but it's a lot." Eliza took a deep breath and continued. "Mr. Welch even came to his house to demand the money, and told Mr. Branson if he didn't pay he'd tell everyone the Bransons couldn't be trusted." *It's no wonder Bert Branson looked fearful the night of the murder—he thought Gideon was going to embarrass him publicly.*

Eliza continued. "She said Mrs. Branson yelled at him somethin' fierce."

I suppressed a smile. I could only imagine what it must be like to live with Mrs. Branson, debt or no debt.

"I'm sorry she didn't know how much money he owes," Eliza said.

"You did a fine job, Eliza. I appreciate you talking to her for me. You may get back to work now."

She beamed. "You're surely welcome, Mizz."

All that evening as I worked at The Chestnut Wig, I fretted about Lysander. I hoped he was improving. His nerves must have been horribly strained to collapse like that.

I was so consumed by my distress over Lysander that I fear I was not a very attentive hostess that night. Several of my regular clients and friends were in attendance, but I was only capable of exchanging perfunctory greetings with them.

Even the sight of Bert Branson at the gaming tables did not faze me. But I hoped he was winning enough to repay me.

IT WAS ALMOST two o'clock in the morning when I awoke suddenly. I lay in my bed, listening intently. Had I been startled awake by a dream that was now slipping quickly out of grasp, or did something wake me?

When I heard nothing but the sighing of the wind through my open windows, I turned over and closed my eyes.

Then I heard it. A soft scraping sound coming from the back of the house. I crept from my bed and tiptoed to the window. Looking down, I could see nothing. The scant silvery light from the moon illuminated the tops of the trees behind the house, but the light was not strong enough to reach the ground. Then I heard it again: a faint scratch that only lasted a moment. Then one knock.

A cold fear slithered down my spine. What I heard was not an animal sound—it was human. Who could be out there, and why? Perhaps Araminta had finally returned with news about Emeline, though she usually sent word that she would be coming. I heard the scratch again, a bit louder and more insistent. I grabbed my wrapper and slipped into the hallway, where I promptly walked into a small table, knocking it into the wall. I steadied it, then descended the stairs as quickly as I dared, trying not to make more noise. At the bottom of the steps I paused, listening, and heard the sound again. Now that it was closer, it seemed more insistent.

With hushed steps I made my way toward the back door, picking up a silver candlestick on the way. I was now mere feet from the door. I sidled close to it, trying to peer through the window without being seen by the person outside. I could see no one. My entire body trembled with fear. What if the person meant us harm? What if it were Lysander's attacker? Or, I thought with chilling awareness, Gideon's murderer?

I had a choice: open the door and attack the person before he could break into the house, or wait until he broke in and surprise him before he could go any further. And if it was Araminta, I would have to pray I would recognize her before bringing the candlestick down.

I made my decision. Raising the heavy candlestick above my head with one hand, I gripped the doorknob with the other. I turned it swiftly and yanked the door open, ready to bring the candlestick down upon the head of the trespasser.

When I saw a huddled form lying on the ground in front of me, I gasped aloud, letting the candlestick fall to the floor in the doorway. It wasn't someone who meant us harm—it was someone in need of help.

I knelt next to the person, who rolled over and gazed into my face.

It was Emeline.

"Mizz Holt?" she asked in a choked voice.

I gasped. "Emeline, are you hurt? Let me get you inside immediately." I reached around her to grip one of her arms, but she whimpered and let out a low moan.

"You are hurt. I'll wake Chloe to run for the doctor." I leaned forward and placed one hand on the ground to raise myself into a standing position.

"No!" Emeline let out a feeble cry. Too late, I saw her eyes widen at something behind me.

Someone gave my back a rough shove. My neck snapped backward and I fell onto the stone steps. I saw stars as a pain in my head exploded.

I opened my eyes, feeling slow and sluggish as I tried to figure out what was happening. My shoulder felt as if it were on fire. My vision was blurry, but I could see someone pulling Emeline's arms. She protested weakly, but her hissing made it clear she had no intention of being taken without a fight. She thrashed her arms about, trying to shake her attacker's grasp.

I rolled over and heaved myself onto my hands and knees. I tried to think, but the darkness and confusion, combined with my injuries, addled my brain. I reflexively grabbed for Emeline's legs and started to pull, trying to ignore the pain.

I tried to get a glimpse of the attacker, but whoever it was wore a mask. I cried out with exertion and frustration. This tugging on each of Emeline's limbs was not getting us anywhere, and it could be causing her further harm.

Movement in the corner of my eye broke my concentration long enough to see Chloe framed in the doorway. She appeared as an angel, surrounded by light. It took me a moment to realize she had lit one of the gas jets in the hallway. I could have wept with relief. "Chloe! Help!" I shouted.

Even with the aid of the gas lamp, I could not identify our attacker. His mask was one of the most frightening things I had ever beheld. It had to be a man, I thought. His body was much larger than mine or Emeline's, and his strength was more than either Emeline or I could muster.

Chloe looked around for a moment, as if attempting to assess the situation in front of her, then bent down. A moment later she straightened up, brandishing the candlestick I had dropped.

She ran forward and swung it violently, but missed the attacker. The effort spun her around. Her steps faltered, but she recovered quickly. The man had continued to yank Emeline's arms, but now he turned his attention to Chloe. With a roar of anger, he charged toward her at lightning speed, his fist closed and deadly. She backed toward the doorway and ducked away from his fist, lashing out with the candlestick again. He howled in pain, gripping his head as he lurched backward and fell to the ground, but surprised me a few seconds later by dragging himself forward using his knees and elbows.

My wits were returning slowly. I limped over to Emeline and managed to move her a few feet away from the tumult. Chloe had dropped the candlestick and stood bent over with her hands on her knees, her chest heaving from the struggle. She did not seem to notice the attacker inching forward.

Leaving Emeline on the ground, I shouted a warning to Chloe when I saw the attacker stagger to his feet and lunge toward her. Her head snapped up as I flung myself forward. I landed on the ground just as the man reeled by me. I flailed out, catching his trouser leg in my fist.

His head made a terrific *smack* when it hit the stone step leading to the back door, then he lay still. For a moment no one moved.

"Chloe," I finally gasped, "are you hurt?"

"No. Are you?"

"Yes, but I think Emeline's injuries are worse than mine." I struggled to my feet and reached for the candlestick. It was sticky and wet.

Chloe straightened and moved toward Emeline, who was crying softly. "I'm sorry, Mizz Holt, Mizz Cooper. I didn't know he followed me here."

"Hush, now. We need to hide you somewhere," Chloe said.

"Take her into the summer kitchen, up to the attic," I directed.

"But—"

"No arguments, Chloe. Get her inside now. And then bring me some rope, please."

While Chloe supported Emeline as she limped away to safety inside the summer kitchen, I gripped the candlestick in both hands. I stepped toward our attacker, who still lay motionless. I reached out with my slippered foot and nudged him, but he neither moved nor made a sound.

Chloe turned and looked over her shoulder. "Jeannine," she hissed, "come with us, for heaven's sake. We will send for the sheriff. That man could wake up at any moment."

"I will come inside in just a moment. You take Emeline up to the attic."

The man still did not move, so as Chloe and Emeline disappeared into the darkness on the way to the summer kitchen, I reached toward his head. I still had the candlestick to hit him in case he awoke suddenly or was feigning injury, but I had a feeling his fall had knocked him unconscious.

Pulling the mask off his face, I moved slightly so the light from the doorway spilled over him.

It was our coachman, Benjamin.

CHAPTER 39

Chloe reappeared a few minutes later holding a length of rope. "Hurry, Jeannine. Whoever that is may—"

She stopped short, mouth agape, when she saw the face of the man who had attacked us.

"What is he doing here, at night and wearing that horrid mask?" she demanded, as if she expected him to answer for himself.

"I do not know, but I think I killed him. We will not need that rope."

She stood stock-still, staring at me. "He's dead?"

I put my fingers on Benjamin's bloody neck to feel for a pulse. I kept them there a full minute, but felt nothing.

"We need to send for the sheriff," Chloe said.

"No!" I shouted, then I lowered my voice immediately. "Not yet. Not until we know what is going on and we can tell the sheriff without saying anything about Emeline."

"Not this again, Jeannine."

I left Benjamin's body on the ground and walked to the summer kitchen, still holding the candlestick. I put the kettle on for tea, almost as if this were a regular evening. I lit a candle, and by its light I could see the sticky, wet substance on the candlestick was blood. Benjamin's blood. Chloe followed me up the steps to the attic, where Emeline lay on the wooden floor, curled into a ball.

I sat on the floor next to her while Chloe stood watching us. I took up the young woman's hand. "My dear, tell me where you're hurt."

The young woman looked up at me, her eyes large and dark in her sunken face. "Everywhere."

"I'll send for the doctor." I glanced up at Chloe and opened my mouth to ask her to fetch him, but Emeline interrupted.

"I don't want … no doctor. I'll be all right … if I can just get some food … and water. I ain't eaten … in a while."

I looked up at Chloe again.

"I'll fetch her something," she said. She hurried away.

I looked Emeline up and down to see for myself. Her arms and face were bruised, but in time they would heal. Her weakened state was of more concern. It did indeed look like she had neither eaten nor drunk in days. Her lips were dry and cracked, her skin pale and papery. No wonder she had been unable to knock on the door earlier—it had probably taken every last ounce of her strength to lift her hand to scratch for someone's attention.

Even now she could not lift her head from the floor. She was clearly struggling to stay awake: her eyes kept closing and she remained slack-jawed.

It wasn't long before Chloe appeared with a tray of food and water. She set it down on the floor beside Emeline.

"I didn't have time to warm the soup," she said in apology.

"I should think Emeline will be so glad to have food that she won't care about its temperature," I said. I looked at Chloe and she returned my smile.

In addition to a bowl of celery soup, Chloe had brought a thick slice of bread, a small plate of butter, a biscuit, and a cup of water. I picked up the spoon and dipped it into the soup. Chloe knelt behind Emeline and held the back of the young woman's head, lifting it enough to allow her to take a sip of the soup. We continued this way until we had fed Emeline several tablespoons. She shook her head slightly from side to side when I offered her a bit of bread, but instead asked for a drink of water.

When we had helped her take two gulps of water, she fell back against Chloe's hands and Chloe lowered her head gently to the floor.

"I'm feeling ... better already," Emeline took a ragged breath.

I knew it was probably best to allow her stomach to accustom itself slowly to the presence of food again. She seemed to know it, too, for she asked if she could have more food later.

I turned to Chloe. She would be dismayed by what I was about to say.

"Chloe, I hate to ask you to leave the house," I began. Chloe gave me a sharp look. "We need to tell Araminta immediately that Emeline has returned. She has arranged for the next step of Emeline's escape, and it must be done tonight despite her physical condition. We can't wait much longer before we summon the sheriff for Benjamin's body and Emeline should leave by the time he arrives."

"But I can't leave the house," she protested.

"Chloe, I think this is an appropriate excuse to deviate from the rules of mourning."

Even though she was loath to leave the house, especially in the middle of the night, she knew that if she did as I asked, Emeline would leave soon. Then she wouldn't have to worry about her personal involvement in a runaway's escape any longer.

I could see her weighing the positive and negative consequences in her mind. Finally she took a deep breath. "Very well.

I will go fetch Araminta. But surely you don't expect her to be at Congress Hall in the middle of the night."

"Ah, but I happen to know where she stays while she spends the summer working in Cape May." I directed Chloe where to find Araminta's boarding house and sent her off with instructions to bring Araminta to The Chestnut Wig with great haste. Chloe left immediately.

I turned to Emeline. "I have many questions for you before Araminta gets here. I hope you'll be able to answer at least some of them."

"I'll do my best, ma'am."

I gave her another sip of water and was pleased when she lifted her head unaided. Her strength was returning already.

"Did you escape from the hiding place beneath our parlor, or were you taken?"

"I was taken."

"By whom?"

"Benjamin Graham."

I had suspected as much when I realized he was the one under the hideous mask. "Did you find the entrance to the passageway under the house, or did Benjamin use the passageway to find you?"

"He found me, ma'am, when I was asleep. I didn't hear him. He sneaked up and put his hand over my mouth. I couldn't even scream for help. I didn't know nothin' about the passageway."

"Did he say how he discovered the passage?"

Emeline squeezed her eyes shut, as if she were trying to remember. When she opened them, they shone with tears. "He laughed at you, Mizz Holt. He said anyone who was ever in your root cellar knows that's not the only room under the house." She took a shuddering breath.

I wanted to ask her to hurry, but I remained silent. Presently she continued. "He said the root cellar is much smaller than it should be. It should take up a lot more space under your house.

There had to be another room under there, he said, and since there was no door, he knew the other room had to be a secret."

I groaned inwardly when I remembered sending Benjamin down to the root cellar with the foodstuffs the cooks had canned for the winter. I had been hoping to make Chloe's life a bit easier and instead, I had allowed a dangerous man with mischief on his mind to discover the existence of the concealed hideaway.

"But even if he knew there was another room under our house, did he say what made him go looking for the entrance? There are plenty of homes with secret rooms."

Emeline winced as she nodded. "He said none of those other houses are rumored to hide runaway slaves."

I inhaled steadily to calm my nerves. Benjamin must have heard rumors of my home being a waystation along the underground railroad and put two and two together when he realized there was a secret room beneath The Chestnut Wig.

Emeline continued. "He said he asked hisself, what would he do if he had a room hidden under his house? He said a smart man would have connected the house to the summer kitchen so it would be easier if someone had to escape. He said he broke into the summer kitchen and found the passageway without hardly any work."

"Did he tell you all this, or did you overhear him telling someone else?"

"I overheard him."

"Who was he talking to?"

"I dunno. But he said Master Cowan hired him." She choked back a sob. "I hope I never hear that man's name again."

So Benjamin must have been the one looking in the window of our summer kitchen. And to think he had done that before I hired him. The audacity.

I patted her hand. "And where did Benjamin take you?" I asked gently. I did not wish to upset the poor woman further, but after tonight I might never see her again to ask her all my questions.

He took me to a cellar. There was other negroes in there."

"Where was the cellar?"

"I dunno exactly."

"Was it far away?"

"No. I found my way to your house after I escaped from there. It was pretty close. I remembered the route to the place where Benjamin took me. It only took but a few minutes."

I smiled at her resourcefulness. She had the presence of mind to note where he was taking her over a week earlier, and she recalled the information after escaping from captivity. On both occasions, she must have been terribly frightened.

"And whose house were you in?"

She managed a shrug. "I dunno. It was a big house."

A big house, and one that was close by. Given that my neighborhood was filled with large, elegant homes, that meant it was very likely she was being held captive at the home of one of Cape May's wealthier citizens.

Perhaps even one who enjoyed the thrill of the gaming tables.

CHAPTER 40

I had to make haste if Emeline were to answer all my questions before Araminta arrived.

"Do you recall hearing any voices when you were being held captive? Voices from upstairs?"

Emeline thought for a moment. "I heard a woman's voice. And a man's voice."

That observation was not much help. Many of the wealthy men in town were married; Emeline could have been hearing anyone's voice. I wondered briefly if Benjamin had taken her to his own house, but then remembered visiting his house—it was quite small. Emeline would not have mistaken it for a large house.

"Do you think you could remember how to get back there?" I asked.

"Yes'm."

Unfortunately, she would not have time to show me. I dared not put more physical strain on her before Araminta arrived. Once Araminta took charge, she would whisk Emeline to the next stop along the railroad and not wait for her to show us where her captor's house was.

"I think I can guess the answer, but do you know why you were taken from my house?"

Her bottom lip trembled as she nodded. "They were gonna give me back to my master and get the reward. I had to get out of that house."

I put my hand on her arm and squeezed gently. "You are safe now. As soon as Araminta gets here, you'll be on your way."

One tear fell from Emeline's eye and made a track along her face to the floor. "Thank you for all you done for me. I'll never forget it."

"It is an honor to help you. I am only sorry that horrid man learned you were here and took you away."

She swallowed, nodding. "Is Lysander gonna be all right?"

I tilted my head and looked at her. "How did you know about Lysander?"

"Benjamin was the one that beat him. He was gonna kill him, but he heard someone coming and he took off. He told us about it. Told us the same thing would happen to us if we tried to leave."

I was too stunned to speak.

"Why would Benjamin attack Lysander?"

"Bejamin said Lysander was too big for his britches. Said Lysander shouldn'ta been walkin' through the white part of town. He used a brick to hit him."

What a disgusting, vile man. And I had foolishly had him drive me to Lysander's house. It was no wonder Lysander nearly fell apart when he saw Benjamin. Somewhere in his injured brain, he must have known Benjamin was the man who attacked him.

I stiffened when I heard the summer kitchen door opening. I flew to the stairway and peeked downstairs, then slumped with relief when I saw Chloe and Araminta.

"Araminta, thank goodness you've come," I called. "We must

get Emeline out of here. You will be shocked to hear all she has told me."

Chloe raised her eyebrows, but Araminta ignored me, a fierce look on her face. "No time for stories, Mizz Holt. We gotta hurry if we gonna get her away from here."

"Where are you sending her?" I asked.

"Best if you don't know that," Araminta said.

"How will you get her there?" Chloe glanced at Araminta, then Emeline.

"I'll take her where she's goin' next, but I'll need your carriage," said Araminta.

"It is at your disposal," I said. "But what if someone sees you?" I nodded toward the window. "It's almost dawn. My yellow carriage is rather distinctive. People are bound to know it belongs to me."

Araminta stood for a long moment, her hands on her hips. "Then we'll have to make people think it's you driving."

"And how are we going to do that?"

Another lengthy pause, then Araminta smiled. "You got any extra wigs? And a hat with a veil?"

It was my turn to smile. "I certainly do."

"If you don't mind me borrowin' 'em, I'll wear the wig and the hat with the veil and we'll get out of town as fast as we can. If anyone sees me, they'll think you're in a hurry to get some-where. You got gloves I can wear, too?"

"Of course."

"I don't want no one to see my hands."

Chloe and I exchanged glances. It just might work.

"I'll hide the carriage during daylight and bring it back tonight," Araminta said. "You'd best get those things now. We gotta go as fast as we can."

I hurried to the house and up the stairs to my rooms. Rummaging through my armoire, I found a plum-colored hat, one with a thick veil, and one of my more elaborate chestnut wigs. I plucked a pair of white gloves from the top shelf. I snatched up my reticule and practically ran back down the stairs and out to the summer kitchen. Chloe and Araminta had managed to bring Emeline down from the attic. She looked a bit peaked, but she was gamely trying to move about the room, testing her muscles.

While Emeline looked on, Araminta unwound the scarf she usually wore on her head and I helped her don the chestnut wig. With its curls and ringlets in the front and its long tresses piled high on her head, the wig completely covered her own hair. It took several precious minutes to firmly secure the wig on her head, but that was necessary considering the bumping and jostling she would endure driving the carriage.

Chloe busied herself in the kitchen while I assisted Araminta. By the time the wig was affixed, Chloe appeared behind me with a basket. Lifting the cloth that covered its contents, she revealed a pile of biscuits, a loaf of bread, a large hunk of cheese, several pieces of ripe fruit, and a tin cup. I took something from my reticule and tucked it among the foodstuffs.

Chloe spoke to Emeline. "This should hold your appetite until you get to your destination. Just remember not to eat too much too fast. Your body is still unused to very much food."

Emeline gave her a solemn nod and another tear fell from her eye. "Thank you, Mizz."

Chloe swallowed hard. "And Araminta, there's plenty for you, too," she said.

I confess to a lump in my throat as I looked on. I was sorry I had ever doubted Chloe's goodness. But I could not dwell long on sentiment, so I turned toward Araminta. "Let me help you with the hat and veil. Chloe, you take Emeline out to the stable and get her situated in the carriage. Araminta and I will be along as soon as we have completed her disguise."

Emeline grasped my hand and held it a moment. "I'll never be able to thank you enough, Mizz."

"You do not need to thank me. I'm only sorry I couldn't keep you safe the entire time you were here. I've placed the money you earned while you worked for us in the basket. Now go with Chloe. You will be safe now. Godspeed."

With that, Chloe and Emeline departed. That was the last I heard of Emeline.

And that was as it should be. Of all the people Daniel and I had helped over the years, we had never heard from any of them again. They knew they risked our safety if they sent a letter and it fell into the hands of the wrong person.

Araminta was trying to fit my hat onto the intricate wig, and I almost laughed aloud. "It'll require two people to get the hat on top of the wig correctly," I said. I was taller than she, so it was easy for me to adjust the hat and the wig until both were securely on her head. I handed her the gloves and she pulled them on quickly. I ushered her out the back door and was alarmed to see the sky turning a lighter gray with the coming dawn.

"Hurry up," she urged. We ran through the trees until we reached the stable, where Chloe had not only hitched the horse to the carriage, but settled Emeline as comfortably as possible on the floor of the carriage and placed a blanket over her. Emeline was perfectly silent as she waited for Araminta to drive away. Chloe held the horse's reins.

Araminta climbed into the driver's seat and Chloe handed the reins up to her. "It's gettin' light. We gotta go."

With that, she and Emeline disappeared down the street.

CHAPTER 41

$\mathcal{A}$s soon as Araminta and Emeline left, I went to my room and slipped into a day dress. It was time to let the sheriff know what had happened. Before I left, Chloe and I discussed what to say. We agreed to tell him we had attacked an intruder and say nothing of Emeline.

I saddled our other horse and rode quickly to the sheriff's house. It was too early for him to be in his office, and it was a Sunday morning at that.

It was surprisingly simple to tell the sheriff our story while leaving out any mention of a runaway slave. He had no trouble believing that Benjamin had intended to rob us, especially when he accompanied me back to The Chestnut Wig and saw the mask lying on the ground beside the body.

When he asked why it appeared Benjamin's blood had been coagulating for several hours, I showed him my injuries and explained that I was in shock. Chloe supported my statement, saying she had been afraid to leave me alone with my injuries.

When the sheriff left, he told us he was not going to arrest us … yet. "A man's dead," he said, "and someone's got to answer for that. But from what I can see here, it's a clear case of self-defense. I'll have Doc Parsons come and take a look at Graham's body. Then I'll make a decision about charges." He nodded and was gone.

Chloe locked the front door behind him. "We did what we had to do to survive," she said. "I would do it again if I had to."

"So would I. And Chloe, if the sheriff does end up charging us with something, rest assured I will get us the best lawyers in the country."

"I know you will."

After Doc Parsons left with Benjamin's body, Chloe and I ate a late breakfast together in the garden. We ate in silence, not daring to speak of the events that had transpired overnight, in case we should be overheard. When we went indoors, though, I gestured toward our parlor. "I must tell you everything Emeline revealed while you were fetching Araminta."

Chloe followed me into the room and I closed the door. We sat down on opposite ends of the sofa and she looked at me expectantly.

"Benjamin was behind all of it," I began, then related everything Emeline had told me: that Benjamin had realized there must be a hidden room under the parlor, that he had broken in and captured Emeline, that he had taken her to someone's house, that she was held prisoner there with a number of other negroes, that he intended to take her south and claim the reward for her, and that Emeline had escaped, finding The Chestnut Wig by recalling the route Benjamin had taken to the other house. I ended by telling her that Benjamin had attacked Lysander because he believed Lysander did not deserve to be walking in our neighborhood.

"I can't believe it." Chloe sat back, shaking her head.

I nodded. "It's all my fault, Chloe. If I hadn't hired him, he never would have figured out there was a room under the parlor. He never would have known of Emeline's existence."

Chloe reached out and took my hands in hers. "None of this

was your fault, Jeannine. Why, the risks you are willing to take to help fugitive slaves put me to shame. I am truly sorry I threatened to go to the sheriff with information about Emeline."

I didn't know what to say, so I remained silent. She continued. "I hope you can find it in your heart to forgive me. I was afraid. Afraid for my own safety. I have lived my entire life obeying rules and laws, without giving them any thought. Telling the sheriff about Emeline seemed the right thing to do, but I was wrong and I am sorry I threatened to put you and Emeline in danger. Having seen the pain and horror a runaway faces, and knowing I tried to make it worse, fills me with remorse."

I smiled. "If Araminta is able to trust me enough to bring another fugitive here, I hope you will help me."

"You have my word."

Chloe insisted that I lie down for the rest of the day. I did exactly that, and though I was sore and lame Monday morning, I felt rested and refreshed.

At mid-morning I donned a day gown and set out for a brisk walk. There were quite a few people outdoors enjoying the beautiful day. I walked with no particular purpose or destination in mind, but simply to clear my head.

As I passed the sheriff's office, the door opened and I was surprised to see Caleb Welch, Gideon's eldest son, come down the steps. His head was down and he appeared to be in a hurry.

"Good morning," I greeted him.

He looked up, startled. "Good morning, Mrs. Holt. What brings you here?"

"I am taking the air, as they say."

"If you're looking for the sheriff, he's not in there," Caleb said. He reached into a pocket and pulled out an envelope. "I brought this to show him." He waved the envelope. I could see the seal was broken.

"I'm sure you could leave it with the deputy," I said.

"I'd rather not. I want to speak directly to the sheriff about it." He lowered his voice. "I think it might shed some light on my father's murder."

My eyes widened. "How so?"

Caleb nodded toward a carriage parked nearby. "Let's sit in my carriage and I'll tell you."

I followed him to the carriage and he helped me inside. He sat opposite me and spoke in a low voice. "I found this letter last night among my father's effects. He wrote it the day before he was murdered." He pointed to the date at the top of the letter.

"What does it say?"

"It is addressed to the banking authorities in Trenton. It is an account of conversations my father had regarding shares he bought in the Camden Atlantic Railroad."

My heart thudded a bit faster. "I heard him talking about a mistake with regard to his stock certificate."

Gideon's son nodded. "My father had occasion to go to Absecon Island to look at property for a new hotel the week before he died. While he was there, according to this letter, he met the president of the Camden Atlantic Railroad. That man was visiting the island to oversee the very early stages of the railroad's development."

My eyes narrowed. I did not understand why this was important.

"Father told the railroad president that he had recently purchased a large amount of stock to help finance the railroad. The president appeared confused, telling my father he was mistaken, that there had not been shares available for funding the railroad in over a year, as the company met its funding goal."

My frown mirrored that of the young man.

"There had been no stock available for over a year?" I repeated.

"That's correct. In other words, my father paid for stock that did not exist."

My mind was spinning with questions. "But I invested in that same funding project, as did Isaac Campbell," I said. "Mr. Shaw delivered my certificate personally."

Gideon's son stared at me. "Something is not right about this entire situation, Mrs. Holt."

"Your father clearly didn't post the letter, since you found it in his effects," I said. "I wonder why he didn't mail it."

"Because he returned home from Absecon Island Friday night, the night before he died. He must have written it immediately upon getting back. I am sure he would have posted the letter on Monday morning."

"Since the next day was Saturday, he could not have gone to the bank to speak to Mr. Shaw about it until Monday," I mused. "What do you propose we do?"

"If I were you, I would go home, get my stock certificate, take it to the bank, and demand an explanation from Mr. Shaw. I will come back here later this afternoon and show the sheriff this letter."

"Thank you for bringing this to my attention," I said. "I will go see Mr. Shaw immediately."

"I'll drive you home," Caleb said.

He dropped me off in front of The Chestnut Wig with a promise to be in touch if he learned anything else. I pledged to do the same. I hurried upstairs and burst into my sitting room. I grabbed the envelope Mr. Shaw had delivered and slipped the certificate out.

I examined it as I had the day I received it, but again, I could find nothing amiss. I slid the certificate back into the envelope, tucked it under my arm, and went back downstairs. Chloe was coming in the back door.

"Where are you off to? And why are you so flustered?" she asked.

"I have to go to the bank. I am in a great hurry, but I will explain everything tonight." I paused, briefly wondering if I should hitch the horse to the carriage. I decided to do that, since it would probably save time in the end. I could get back to The Chestnut Wig quickly if my discussion with Mr. Shaw ran long.

It took a long time for me to prepare the horse and carriage, and I was perspiring and in a dreadful mood when I finished. I left immediately with the stock certificate under the driver's seat.

To my great disappointment, Mr. Shaw was not at the bank when I arrived. According to the teller, he might not return for some time. He offered me a chair to wait, but I found I could not sit still. I fidgeted and fumed and shuffled about until I couldn't stand being in the bank another minute.

I climbed into the carriage and pointed the horse toward home, but as I drew closer to The Chestnut Wig, I checked my wristwatch. As long as there was time before I had to ready myself for the evening, I thought Isaac would probably appreciate knowing there might be a problem with his stock certificate. It could not hurt to share the information with him. I knew him to be friendly with Mr. Shaw, so perhaps he could speak with the bank president and get the issue resolved quickly and satisfactorily. I wondered how many others in Cape May had done the same thing and might be facing the same situation.

I changed direction, heading toward the docks where Isaac Campbell kept his office. At this time of day, men milled about, hauling ropes, guiding boats to the piers, and swabbing decks. The entire place smelled of fish. I wrinkled my nose.

I tied the horse and carriage to a hitching post and walked up to the first man I saw.

"Can you tell me where Isaac Campbell's steamship office is?"

The man pointed toward a low, white clapboard building. Clutching my stock certificate, I hurried toward it.

Crossing the threshold from the bright sunshine reflecting off the water and beating onto the pier, I blinked several times for my eyes to adjust to Isaac's dark office. When I could see more clearly, I found I was in a huge open room. The boarded-up windows allowed only slivers of light to penetrate the darkness. Two large objects stood on either side of the room, both covered with sheets. I stepped forward, looking for a hallway or a staircase that might lead to Isaac's offices. *What a grim place to work*, I thought.

I saw a hallway leading to the side of the building along the waterfront. Quietly, I walked toward it. It felt silly to be quiet, but the place lent itself to a feeling of concealment.

There were several closed doors along the hallway, then I noticed that the last door had a shaft of light beneath it. That was probably Isaac's office. I approached the door and lifted my hand to knock, but lowered it when I heard two raised voices in a heated argument. I leaned close to the door to hear what was being said.

"I tell you, Shaw, we need to get out of here. Gideon figured it out. It's only a matter of time before other people start getting wise to us." It was Isaac.

"But you took care of Gideon. He's not going to tell anyone." The voice belonged to Mr. Shaw. He let out a chilling chuckle.

"True, but the woman who owns the gambling house found out I wanted to sell the boats. She's too smart by half. She'll figure it out before long."

Under ordinary circumstances I would have grinned upon hearing his estimation of me, but there was nothing ordinary about what I was hearing.

"Isaac, the more you panic, the more likely we are to make mistakes. I say we stick with our original plan and leave next week."

"Is all the money still hidden at the bank?"

"Of course."

There was a pause. "You wouldn't try to swindle me out of my share, would you?" Isaac asked.

"Don't be an oaf, man. You know how much money is there. Divide it in two and that's your share. I couldn't steal it from you if I tried."

I was in danger.

I needed to get out of the building. I turned quickly, but dropped my stock certificate on the floor. It landed with a whisper, but suddenly the voices behind the door stilled.

CHAPTER 42

"Who's there?" Mr. Shaw called out.

I grabbed the certificate and did not bother to soften my footsteps as I ran toward the building entrance. I had only gone a few steps, though, before I heard someone yank open Isaac's office door.

Boots pounded on the wooden floor of the hallway. The sound echoed off the walls like shotgun blasts. I ran as I had never run before, fear coursing through my body.

"You there!" yelled Isaac.

I was almost to the door when someone grabbed my arm and whipped me around. There were a couple seconds of silence, during which the blood thrummed in my ears, before both men erupted in laughter.

"Just look who it is, will you, Shaw?" Isaac held my arm in a grip that could have been an iron vise.

"The woman who's too smart by half!" Mr. Shaw let out a braying laugh.

"Well now, maybe she's not as smart as we thought," Isaac said. "If she was smart, if she knew what's good for her, she'd have stayed away."

"That is true, my friend." Mr. Shaw nodded back toward Isaac's office. "Do you have rope in there?"

"I surely do."

"Come along, Mrs. Holt," Mr. Shaw said with mock politeness. "We have been most inhospitable, Isaac."

"I could not agree more, Shaw." Isaac pushed me forward, none too gently.

"You cannot possibly think you'll succeed at whatever you're trying to accomplish," I said. My voice was an octave higher than usual, and I was furious with myself for letting them hear my fear.

"That is where you are mistaken, Mrs. Holt," Isaac said. He pushed open his office door and shoved me inside.

"Where's the rope?" Mr. Shaw asked.

"In my desk, bottom drawer on the right."

Mr. Shaw wrenched the drawer open and pulled out a length of rope with a triumphant smile. Isaac shoved me roughly into a chair and Mr. Shaw deftly tied my legs to it. He tied my hands behind me.

Isaac stood before me, watching Mr. Shaw work. "By the time people realize what happened, Shaw and I will be long gone. Shaw, you'll have to agree that we need to leave now, not next week. People will realize Mrs. Holt is missing by six o'clock tonight when she's not home to open the doors."

Mr. Shaw nodded, frowning. "We have a lot to do before we can get out of Cape May."

"The sheriff will find you both before you can get far," I growled.

Isaac laughed. "I'll be headed to the land of opportunity out West before the sheriff knows I'm gone. How about you, Shaw?"

It worried me that he would so freely announce where he was going. It did not bode well for me.

"I'll be headed in a different direction, you can be sure. But I'm not dumb enough to tell anyone where I'm going."

Isaac shot him a look. "Shaw's headed south, I'll tell you that much."

"Keep quiet, Isaac."

"Oh, Mrs. Holt isn't going to repeat anything to anyone. By the time they find her body, we'll have melted away with all the money we need to start fresh. It's a shame you don't have two steamships to sell, Shaw. I daresay my life promises to be more comfortable than yours."

My mind went blank. I couldn't think, couldn't plan, couldn't reason. All I could do was listen to the men talking and pray I could figure a way out of this.

"Isaac, I need you to print four more stock certificates," Mr. Shaw said. "Those'll be the last ones before we clear out."

"I told you not to accept any more orders." Isaac frowned.

"I don't take instructions from you, Isaac. This whole thing was my idea. I make the decisions." Mr. Shaw shot Isaac a dark look.

"Very well. Give me the names and amounts and I'll get them printed."

Mr. Shaw scrawled something on a piece of paper and handed it to Isaac. "Be quick. I need to get back to the bank this afternoon."

Isaac left the room. I glared at Mr. Shaw. "I know what you're doing. You and Isaac are forging stock certificates. You take the money, give the counterfeit certificates to innocent people, and then leave town, never to be heard from again."

Mr. Shaw laughed. "You *are* too clever by half, Mrs. Holt. It's a pity you'll not live long enough to share your revelations with anyone else."

Isaac had left his office door open when he walked out, and now I could hear metal clunking and sputtering. The echoes told me the noises were coming from the large, almost empty room at the end of the hallway. The noises explained the objects covered with sheets—counterfeiting equipment.

I scowled at Mr. Shaw, but he didn't seem to notice or care. He rifled through the papers on Isaac's desk and opened and closed desk drawers. Presently Isaac returned.

"The certificates are drying. You can take them when you leave."

Mr. Shaw grunted in return.

"How can you behave this way?" I asked suddenly. "You've stolen from your friends, your business associates. You cannot possibly think you're going to succeed."

Isaac and Mr. Shaw exchanged glances. "She wasn't listening." Isaac shook his head, making a *tsk tsk* sound while my blood boiled. "Mrs. Holt, my dear woman, we *are* going to succeed. Once we leave Cape May, there will be no trace of either of us. We'll go our separate ways, never to be reunited, and no one will be the wiser."

Mr. Shaw caught Isaac's eye. He nodded toward the hallway.

"Whatever you have to say, Shaw, you can say it in front of Mrs. Holt," Isaac said. "Sadly, she will not be able to share whatever she hears." His grin was positively reptilian. My stomach lurched.

"What are you going to do with her?" Mr. Shaw asked.

Isaac made a show of rubbing his beard. "I haven't decided. She is clearly a liability. What do you think I should do with her?"

Mr. Shaw was all efficiency. "You know my position. Leave no witnesses behind. She should receive the same treatment as Gideon Welch."

"Shaw, it hardly seems necessary to plunge a knife into Mrs. Holt's back. There are cleaner ways of addressing the problem she presents."

"I'm leaving it to you, Isaac. I am taking the stock certificates back to the bank now, so whatever you do, I can claim complete ignorance."

Isaac frowned. "Then go, so I can finish up here and follow."

Mr. Shaw walked to the office door and turned around. "Mrs. Holt, please understand this is not an attack on you *per se*. If you had not insisted upon treading where you don't belong, this would not be happening."

He went through the door and was gone. I listened as his footsteps echoed down the hallway. There was a brief silence while he must have been gathering the counterfeit stock certificates, then the footsteps continued. I heard the front door open and close, then silence descended.

I clenched my teeth. I needed to figure a way out of this situation. Isaac rifled through documents at his desk as if nothing of concern was happening.

"What are you going to do to me?" I asked when the silence grew too long.

He glared at me. "I haven't decided. But the more you talk, the more likely I am to end it here and now."

I closed my mouth.

"You know something, Mrs. Holt? If Gideon Welch had stayed home just a few minutes longer that terrible Saturday he died, he might still be alive today. It gives one pause to think of how a mere coincidence can change the course of someone's life."

"What do you mean?" I asked crossly.

"I mean, if Gideon had not gone to Absecon Island in the days before he died, he would never have met the president of the Camden Atlantic Railroad. And if he had not left his house when he did on the morning of his death, he would not have met me in the street and shared his suspicion that Mr. Shaw was involved in a scheme to issue counterfeit stock certificates. And if he had not shared his suspicions with me, I would not have known he presented a danger to my plans."

Isaac laughed. "And that brawl at The Chestnut Wig—if that fight had not taken place, I would not have had such an easy opportunity to prevent Gideon from going to the banking authorities, as he had promised to do when we met in the street." Here Isaac shook his head. "You see how coincidences can change everything? Gideon would have met a violent end, certainly, because he knew too much, but it was merely coincidence that it happened at your salon. I intended to follow him that night and take care of the matter without any witnesses, but the altercation in your dining room provided an opportunity too good to pass up."

I maintained a stony silence.

"May I ask what brought you to this building?" he asked.

"I mistakenly thought you'd appreciate knowing there was a problem with the stock certificate."

Isaac chuckled. "Ah, how kind of you, Mrs. Holt. As you now must realize, I already knew there was a problem."

I did not answer.

"Shaw wants me to kill you." Isaac's matter-of-fact tone made my blood run cold. "But I'm not sure that's necessary," he continued. "You see, it doesn't really matter what you tell people once Shaw and I have disappeared because no one is going to find us. Therefore, all I need to do is make sure no one finds you before Shaw and I have left town. I hate the thought of killing a woman."

I felt a surge of hope. Perhaps I was not going to die. Gradually, my ability to think logically was coming back, but try as I might, I could not think of a way to escape Isaac's office.

My heart skipped a beat, though, when Isaac pulled a length of cloth out of a desk drawer. My eyes must have betrayed my terror, because Isaac laughed as he walked toward me.

"I am not going to strangle you, Mrs. Holt, though I'm sure that's what Shaw would prefer. No, I am going to gag you with this so you can't alert anyone to your presence here. You can scream all you want, but no one will be able to hear you with it in your mouth. Quite a useful device."

He tied the cloth around my head and shoved the ends into

my mouth. I gagged repeatedly to the sound of his gleeful laughter. He put his hat on and turned the gas jet off. The room was swallowed by darkness.

"This is goodbye, Mrs. Holt. I am sure our paths will not cross again. Do not fret—you will only die if no one is able to find you here over the next several days."

I heard a *click* as Isaac locked the door behind him.

CHAPTER 43

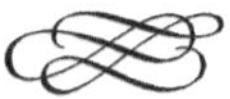

Think, I told myself. I could not give in to the panic rising in my chest. *How can I get out of here?*

I needed to take one step at a time. Thinking beyond that was overwhelming and threatened to plunge me into hysteria.

The first step was to get to Isaac's office door. I used the weight of my body to inch forward, one painful lurch at a time. With my hands and feet tied to the chair, all I could manage was short movements. It seemed like hours before I reached the door.

The next step was to unlock it. I had no idea how I was to accomplish that with my hands tied behind my back. I closed my eyes and tried to think of a solution.

My head jerked up suddenly. If I couldn't unlock the door, I could at least alert people that I was imprisoned in Isaac's office. To do that, I would simply need to break the glass in his door. Perhaps someone on the dock would hear the glass breaking.

The office was too dark to see if there were any implements I could use to accomplish the task, but it didn't matter—even if I had found something, I wouldn't be able to pick it up with my hands bound.

That left one option. I would have to break the glass using my body. Specifically, my head.

The thought of sending my head through a glass window caused my breath to catch. Since I could not breathe adequately through my mouth, I tried taking deep breaths through my nose to stem the escalating dread.

As the seconds crept by, I tried three times to hurl my head into the glass. Each time I stopped just short of actually hitting it. My fear was getting in my way. Tears pricked the corners of my eyes. I could not afford to be afraid of a bit of broken glass when my life might be at stake. Finally I closed my eyes, steeling myself. I took one long, deep breath and smashed my head into the glass.

It did not work. The confounded pane remained in place. I tried again and again, my head throbbing, until I heard a crack spread across the glass. One more assault on the pane and the glass shattered into a thousand pieces, falling in my hair, down my back, and into the chair.

I leaned back, panting from exertion. I smelled the unmistakable metallic scent of blood—my own, coming from wounds in my neck and scalp caused by the broken glass.

No one came running. I heard no shouts of alarm coming from the pier. If there were men out there, they had not heard the glass breaking. Or they didn't realize it meant trouble.

I sat still for several minutes, catching my breath. My next step was to shout, scream, and create a ruckus until someone heard me.

How long had I been in the building? It was sunny when I entered, but I wondered if it was dark by now. I had no sense of the time that had passed since I found myself trapped in the office.

I took a deep breath and screamed around the gag. It came out as a squeal, but the echoing sound was nevertheless terrifying. I continued screaming and shrieking and shouting as loudly as I could until I was hoarse. And in return, there was nothing but the sound of the waves of the bay lapping against the front of the building.

Another breath, and I repeated the process. Still, nothing.

I was exhausted. My body and brain were spent from my physical and mental exertion. I tried screaming one more time, but my voice was weaker, quieter.

The first fat tear, borne of frustration and fear, made its way down my cheek. It hung from my chin for a moment before landing on my dress. After that first tear came many, many more.

When I could cry no longer, I sat slumped in the chair, my chin resting on my chest. I wanted nothing more than to go to sleep.

My head jerked up suddenly when I heard a noise. It sounded like scratching, but I could not be sure.

Yes, there it was again, coming closer. I stiffened, straining as hard as I could to hear it. It was almost a scrabbling.

I had a chilling thought. Could Isaac or Mr. Shaw be returning? I knew Mr. Shaw wanted me dead. Isaac had offered leniency, but what would happen if he came back and found the broken glass? He would know I was trying to escape, trying to contact someone outside the building, and he might not be as lenient.

The scrabbling grew louder, and along with it, my heartbeat. I was wondering whether I should call out when I felt something heavy scurry across my feet.

There was a rat in the room with me. Despite the gag, I let out a scream that could have roused every person in Cape May.

The thought of sharing Isaac's office with a rat was more than I could endure. I started screaming again, and this time I did not stop. I screamed through the fear, the doubt, and the pain in my throat. I screamed until I thought I would go mad. If anything, I thought, my screams should keep the rat from coming near me again.

The next time I stopped for breath, I realized through the fog in my brain that rats are nocturnal. That meant it was night-time, and that meant everyone on the docks had likely gone home. How long had I been in the building?

I was bone weary. As much as I wanted to, I could not scream all night long to keep the rats at bay. I would rest for a few minutes, then try one last time before giving up.

After one final deep breath I let out a scream, as long and loud and shrill as I could manage. Finally I stopped, breathing heavily.

And I thought I heard a voice.

"Jeannine?"

It was coming from far away, but hope leapt in my heart. I found a deep new reserve of strength and I screamed again.

"She's this way!" I heard someone shout.

I continued to scream so the people outside the building could follow the sound of my voice. After several minutes, I heard a crash and the heavy sound of footsteps.

"Jeannine?"

It was Chloe, bless her! I tried calling out to her, but my words were indiscernible.

A few moments later someone was standing in the doorway to Isaac's office, a lantern held aloft. The person reached into the office and unlocked the door from the inside.

"Who is it?" I cried.

"It's me, Mrs. Holt."

The sheriff. I had never been so thankful to hear anyone's voice, even his.

"Jeannine?"

Chloe raced into the office and jerked to a stop, holding her lantern high. She cried out when she saw me.

"Jeannine! Thank God! Are you all right? What happened?

Oh my goodness, what am I saying? Don't answer my questions until we have untied you."

I almost laughed aloud. Several other men ran into the room as the sheriff used a knife to saw through the rope binding my hands and feet. One of the men used his lantern to locate the gas jet on the wall and turned it on.

As the room filled with weak light, I struggled to stand but fell back into the chair when I realized how weak my legs were. The sheriff tried to catch me as I fell but missed. I began to cry afresh, not from pain, but from relief.

Before I knew what was happening, Chloe was embracing me and exclaiming over the state of my bloodied face and neck. "You're safe, Jeannine. We're going to take you to see the doctor, then you are going home."

The sheriff ordered the men with him to stand guard outside the building so no one entered.

"What on earth happened?" Chloe gripped my hands in hers.

"I will tell you everything, but first … Sheriff?" I called. My throat ached from all my screaming.

He was at my side a moment later. "Don't worry, Mrs. Holt. We've got Isaac Campbell and Mr. Shaw."

"How did you know?" I asked in bewilderment.

"Sheriff?" came another voice. The man it belonged to walked into Isaac's office and stopped short. "Mrs. Holt, I'm so glad you're safe."

It was Caleb, Gideon's son. I stared at him, mouth hanging open.

"How did you—?" I asked.

"There will be plenty of time for questions and answers once we've gone over this building with a fine-toothed comb," the sheriff interrupted. He turned to Chloe. "Can you take Mrs. Holt to Doc Parsons? After he looks her over, take her home and I'll be along later."

Chloe helped me to stand and walk gingerly out of Isaac's

office. My feet and hands hurt, probably from the lack of circulation while I was tied so tightly to the chair.

"I don't want you to say one word until I have you in the carriage," she said. "I cannot imagine what you have been through tonight."

She knew where I had left the carriage and she led me to it. She helped me inside and I sat back against the cushions, exhausted, but filled with a sense of relief. She took the reins and drove me straight to the doctor's house.

Chloe helped me into his house and waited while he examined me and bandaged all the cuts made by the broken glass. When he pronounced me free to go home, Chloe drove me to The Chestnut Wig.

I limped into the parlor while she ran out to the summer kitchen to prepare tea. She was back a few minutes later with a tray of tea things and a bit of supper.

"Tell me everything," she said. She sat down across from me.

I told her the entire story, from the moment the bank teller told me Mr. Shaw was unavailable until the moment she found me. "And now tell me how you found me," I said.

"It was the sheriff who found you," she began. "Late this afternoon Caleb Welch went to the sheriff with a letter he had found among his father's belongings."

"He showed me the letter, too," I said.

"The sheriff was immediately suspicious. He and Caleb went directly to the bank to speak to Mr. Shaw about it. Unfortunately, the bank was already closed for the day. They went to Mr. Shaw's house, but Mr. Shaw wasn't there."

I took a sip of tea and breathed in the aroma as it soothed my throat.

"It took some time, but they finally located the bank teller at a tavern on Decatur Street. The sheriff confronted the teller and demanded to know where Mr. Shaw was. The teller claimed not to know, but he suggested the sheriff check Isaac Campbell's office on the docks. Then Caleb remembered you told him that Isaac had invested in the railroad, too."

Chloe continued. "Here at home, I was frantic with worry. I knew you would never willingly miss a night of work. I turned away all the people who came to The Chestnut Wig tonight, but not before sending one of them with a message for the sheriff. I sent the staff home. The next thing I knew, the sheriff and Caleb were at our house. The sheriff demanded to know what was going on. When I told him you were missing, Caleb informed us you had made an investment in the Camden Atlantic Railroad just as his father had done. He also recalled you saying Isaac had invested in the venture, too. That was when the sheriff realized you were very likely in danger—it seemed too coincidental that Gideon was dead, you told Caleb that Isaac had invested in the project, Isaac and the bank president were both missing and known to be friends, and you had not come home for work. I think the sheriff began to wonder if everything was connected. And because the teller had suggested he check Isaac's office, that was the first place we looked."

Chloe took a ragged breath as her eyes became bright. "When I saw your carriage near the docks, I thought I would die of fright, Jeannine. I was sure you had met a horrible end." She sniffled loudly just as there was a knock at the front door.

She answered it and admitted the sheriff, his deputy, and Caleb. They all came into the parlor and over the next hour, the sheriff asked all his questions. I related every word that I remembered from the conversation I overheard between Isaac and Mr. Shaw. The sheriff finally had all the information he needed to piece together the sequence of events that had culminated in the evening's horrors.

"And you have Isaac Campbell and Mr. Shaw in custody?" I asked.

The sheriff nodded. "They're each in a cell, waiting for me to question them about their roles in the stock certificate fraud.

Now that I have the information you provided, I can charge them both. I will take them to Cape May Court House first thing tomorrow."

My heart still pounding, I thanked him and Caleb again for all their help. It would be a long time before I cared to venture anywhere near the Cape May docks again.

CHAPTER 44

fter transporting the two fraudsters to the jail in Cape May Court House, the sheriff paid a visit to The Chestnut Wig to summarize everything that had happened. In short, Isaac had talked the bank president into joining him in a scheme that would allow them to get rich and disappear.

"Isaac purchased counterfeiting equipment several years ago and kept it hidden in his offices. Mr. Shaw would tell investors there were still shares available to fund the railroad to Absecon Island. It was a lie, of course. There were no shares left, since the railroad had met its funding goal. Once Shaw received payment from an investor, he would give the information to Isaac Campbell, who would create counterfeit stock certificates. Mr. Shaw kept all the investors' money in a safe at the bank."

"The plan would never have worked," I said. "It was only a matter of time before investors would realize their stocks were worthless."

The sheriff nodded. "Isaac and Shaw intended to split the money and leave town before anyone could discover the fraud. Isaac also sold his steamships, as I understand. From what you and Caleb have said, Gideon Welch knew something was rotten.

Isaac has admitted that Gideon approached him to discuss the issue, not realizing Isaac and Shaw were in cahoots."

He cleared his throat. "When Isaac realized Gideon had figured out their scheme, he had to do something to stop Gideon from revealing it to anyone else. He followed Gideon to The Chestnut Wig the night of the murder. His plan was to do away with Gideon after the close of business, but that fight in your dining room provided a cover for him to commit the deed right then and there."

"And it wasn't long after that," I said, "when I realized Isaac was selling his boats. I thought it was odd."

"That is correct. In fact, the catalyst for leaving town was when you asked Isaac about the sale. He started to panic, thinking you knew more about the scheme than you did, and he and Shaw were heading out of town when I caught up with them."

"Thank heaven you caught them when you did." Chloe squeezed my hand.

"Their plan was to go their separate ways, adopt new identities either out west or further south, and live off the money they swindled out of people's pockets. We were fortunate to catch them before they could dispose of the money they took from investors. All those people will get their money back." The sheriff shook his head. "Neither Isaac Campbell nor Mr. Shaw will be seeing the outside of a jail cell for a very long time."

"And Solomon Sanders can go home to his family," I said. "When will he be released, Sheriff?"

"As soon as Isaac is formally charged with Gideon's murder, Solomon will be released." His face reddened.

I didn't feel the need to remind him of his grave error in arresting Solomon for Gideon's murder. He knew he had made a mistake. I hoped he would be more circumspect the next time he was inclined to arrest a negro with scant evidence.

The Chestnut Wig remained closed for the next several

nights. I needed to rest and recuperate from my ordeal and I wanted the gossip and speculation to die down before I opened the doors again.

During that time, Solomon was released from jail as Isaac had been formally charged with murdering Gideon Welch. I did not wish to bother the happy Sanders family right after Solomon's homecoming, so I waited for him to come to The Chestnut Wig.

He arrived the following afternoon, still looking gaunt and tired but wearing a wide smile. His bruises were fading and his eye and lip were no longer swollen. He was eager to get back to work. The sight of him moved me to tears.

Life was returning to normal.

Now that Solomon was out of jail and the right men had been charged with Gideon's death and the events leading to it, my thoughts turned to hiring a new coachman. The last one had been a catastrophe.

Where to find a new one? Violet Curtis had proven herself an unreliable judge of character when she suggested hiring Benjamin. I would not ask her again.

I sat at the desk that afternoon with my chin in my hand, staring out the window. I allowed my thoughts to drift, wondering where Emeline was and hoping she had found her way to a happy situation. If it weren't for Benjamin and his horrid ...

My thoughts screeched to a halt.

Benjamin. A fugitive slave hunter. Emeline had said she and other runaways were trapped in the cellar of a large house, and Benjamin's home was too small to imprison a number of people. He had to have been working with someone as he preyed upon negroes. Whoever owned the house where Emeline was trapped was Benjamin's accomplice.

Emeline also said she did not have to run far to get to my

house from the place where she had been held captive. And she had distinctly heard a woman's voice when she was in the cellar.

The largest house nearby was around the corner and happened to be owned by a woman. A woman who knew Benjamin. A woman who suspected I harbored fugitive slaves and had suggested as much. A woman who had not bothered to hide her disdain for negroes.

Mrs. Violet Curtis.

Preposterous, I thought.

But was it? I would never learn from Benjamin who he worked with, but for my own peace of mind I needed to know who assisted him or even employed him. I needed to know if Violet Curtis was the unseen hand running a slave catching operation.

There was one way to find out.

I waited until darkness fell. I donned one of my chestnut wigs and an old black mourning gown. I did not wish Chloe to know what I was doing, so I slipped out of the house when she was in her rooms on the fourth floor.

Keeping to the shadows, I walked briskly to Violet's house. Light from a gas sconce shone in one room on the first floor and a silhouette moved behind the curtain. I knew Violet lived alone, so it was probably her. I would take that gamble.

I reached up and tousled the chestnut hair piled on my head. Strands of it fell in untidy curls around my face. I crumpled the front of my dress in my fists to make it look disheveled. Then I ran up her front steps and pounded on the door.

When she opened it, a look of shock on her face, I spoke quickly and in a low voice. "I need your help."

She drew me inside. "Of course. What is it? What's happened, Mrs. Holt?"

"One of the runaways I had trapped in my cellar has escaped. I saw her run behind your house. Her owner is coming for her tomorrow and if I can't produce her, there's no telling how he'll react."

Violet stared at me with her mouth open. "You have runaways *trapped* in your cellar?"

"Yes, of course," I answered tetchily. "Where else am I supposed to hide them while I await payment for them?"

A grin spread across Violet's face. I nearly choked with anger at the sight of it. "And all this time I thought you were *aiding* the runaways," she said. "Well, it is good to know you are one of us. Come along. We shall take a look outside. If your runaway is out there, we can throw her in my cellar with the others until her master comes for her."

We did not, of course, find a runaway behind Violet's house. I left with nothing but the answer I had come for.

THE FOLLOWING day I returned to Violet's house, this time in a regular day gown, since I did not have to pretend to hide in the shadows. She answered my knock with a smile and invited me inside.

"No, thank you. I thought I should come by and inform you that I will no longer be in the business of returning runaways to their owners."

"Why not?" She frowned.

"I did not find the girl who escaped last night. Her owner arrived this morning and when I could not produce her, he became irate. He told me he would sue me for his costs to travel here." I shook my head. "Worse, I feared he was going to harm me. I do not wish to court that kind of danger any longer."

Violet nodded slowly. "A shame. I hoped we could be business partners."

And I hoped I would never have to speak to Violet again.

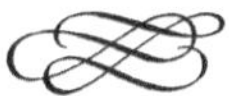

As it happened, not long after my final conversation with Violet, she was found badly beaten on the ground outside her house. Around the same time, Eliza heard at the market that a number of runaway slaves had escaped from Violet's cellar. Apparently the only person besides Violet who knew they were there was Benjamin. And since he was dead, the runaways escaped into the night without anyone being the wiser. I hope they all got to Canada safely.

I heard various rumors about how Violet came to be attacked, but I believe the most likely explanation is that one or more of the escapees managed to exact retribution from her before running away again.

Violet was disfigured in the assault, and she became a recluse. She never returned to The Chestnut Wig, and I got my wish of never having to speak to her again.

Unfortunately, she would never be punished for her actions as a slave hunter, since the federal Fugitive Slave Act encouraged such behavior.

But Violet did do me one unintended favor. She must have told the sheriff that I was selling runaways, not protecting them, because he never asked me about Emeline or any other runaway again. And since selling runaways was perfectly legal, I could not get into trouble for allegedly doing that.

For once, I know what it is like to be Chloe. I am sure word got around that I was selling runaways. And though I do not generally care what people think, I cared very much that people might think I had been selling other human beings. My staff assure me they pay no mind to such vile rumors.

In the end, though, any negative opinions that people might hold toward me work in my favor. Since that time no one has accused me of hiding and protecting fugitives, so Chloe and I are able to continue our good works with Araminta unimpeded.

It turned out that Benjamin Graham's wife knew all about her husband's shameful behavior and went so far as to actively encourage it. Under normal circumstances I would have paid Mrs. Graham a healthy sum since she lost the income her husband would have earned from his coachman position, but I felt no obligation to do that after learning about her true character.

And as for Benjamin's death, the sheriff spoke to the magistrate in Cape May Court House about my and Chloe's roles in it. The magistrate asked him to transport us to the courthouse. When Chloe and I arrived, he asked us a series of questions about the incident. Between a letter from Doc Parsons detailing my injuries that night and the testimony from us and the sheriff corroborating that information, the magistrate determined that there was insufficient evidence to charge Chloe or me with a crime.

Bert Branson paid me back in full for the money he owed The Chestnut Wig, but not before scandal engulfed him and his wife for nonpayment of debts owing to many of the most prominent people in Cape May. They were forced to move away in disgrace. I do not know where they went, and I do not care.

Lysander recovered from his head injury and it was a great

day when he returned to his still. He continues to make the finest brandies in New Jersey. He was, of course, happy for Emeline when he learned that she had finally continued on her way to safety, but I knew he would miss getting to be her friend. I don't know why I had never thought to introduce him to Eliza, but I have rectified that and they are very happy together.

The injuries from my ordeal in Isaac's office healed quickly, but the frightening memories continue in the form of nightmares, startling easily, and heart palpitations whenever I am near the Cape May piers. But I trust those symptoms will fade with time.

Business at The Chestnut Wig is as brisk as it ever was, and it continues to be the most popular gaming salon in the region. Chloe and I run the business with efficiency and have invested our profits wisely.

We are very busy, so I relish time alone. During those hours, I often find myself wondering where Emeline is. I trust that she is well and free.

THE END

AUTHOR'S NOTE

Though the events that take place in this book are fictional, they are grounded in historical fact. This is a practice I try to follow in each of my Cape May Historical Mysteries. And though I write primarily to entertain my readers, I like to think they benefit from my research as much as I do.

Take, for example, the Fugitive Slave Act (FSA), which was passed by the United States Congress as part of the Compromise of 1850. The Compromise was a series of bills passed to quiet Southern calls for secession at a pivotal moment in U.S. history. It was the kernel from which grew *Murder at the Chestnut Wig*.

In a nutshell, the federal act not only denied a slave's right to a jury trial, but provided that all slaves be returned to their southern owners, even if they managed to escape to a free state. It *compelled* citizens' assistance in apprehending these fugitive slaves and made it financially lucrative to do so.

The FSA also provided, among other things, for the imposition of a six-month jail term *and* a $1,000 fine for anyone caught harboring fugitive slaves. At the time of this writing, that was the equivalent of over $40,000 in modern currency. This is a large part of the reason Chloe is so afraid the sheriff will find out she and Jeannine are harboring Emeline.

The Fugitive Slave Act was responsible for the return of hundreds of free northern blacks to the ranks of slaves in the south, all sanctioned and encouraged by the federal government. It is a heartbreaking chapter in American history. And what's more, whereas other northern states enacted personal liberty laws to circumvent the FSA, New Jersey failed to enact such legislation, and instead actively enforced the provisions of the federal law.

I also did a good deal of research about the Underground Railroad (UGRR) in preparing to write *Murder at the Chestnut Wig*. Everyone knows the basics of the UGRR: fugitive slaves were secretly sheltered and assisted along their journey to freedom by abolitionists and others who understood slavery to be inherently evil. These people risked their own lives and property to help those less fortunate, and they should be remembered as heroes of American history. Jeannine and her late husband Daniel are fervent believers in the equality of all people, and their beliefs spawned their participation in the UGRR. Chloe did not participate in the UGRR before moving to The Chestnut Wig, but she has a good heart. She quickly understands the importance of helping fugitive slaves, even as her mind tells her it's a dangerous and risky undertaking.

And speaking of the UGRR, there's a character in this book whom many readers might recognize: Harriet Tubman.

Harriet Tubman was born Araminta Ross in 1822. She married John Tubman in 1844 and later took the first name Harriet after her mother. I used the name Araminta Ross in the story because I wanted to include a surprise for readers who were unaware of her birth name.

According to Cape May County history, Harriet Tubman spent part or all of the summer of 1852 working in Cape May. Though no one knows exactly what she did or where she worked, there have been some educated guesses made by people smarter than I. In 1852, Congress Hall was one of the premier hotels in the United States. Its size, combined with its reputation for elegance and proximity to the sea, made it a popular destination for southerners looking to escape the brutal summer heat and for northerners seeking a stylish and grand holiday destination.

Congress Hall employed a great many people in Cape May, and simple laws of probability indicate that Harriet Tubman may have worked there, too. Black women were utilized heavily as cooks and laundresses, and therefore I have given Araminta Ross the position of cook at Congress Hall. In that position, she would have worked closely with other Black women and been privy to gossip about the wealthy guests. She would also have been in the position to receive information from slaves staying at the hotel with their masters. Of special importance would have been information about fugitives headed north—where they were on their journey, when they expected to come through Cape May, and how they could be identified and assisted. Incidentally, the fight that takes place in the beginning of the book, the fight in which Gideon Welch is murdered, is based on a real fight that took place at Congress Hall between black staff and white hotel guests.

This brings me to another aspect of the story: my use of the word "negro" to describe African Americans or other Blacks. In 1852 the use of the word "negro" was common and therefore I decided to use it rather than the anachronistic "Black" or "African American." It is not my intent to insult or in any way disrespect anyone, but to show how language has evolved over the years.

The same evolution of language applies to its propriety and formality, too. For example, though the characters in the book are often referred to by their first names, in reality Jeannine and Chloe would have referred to white people as "Mr." or "Mrs." or

"Miss." This would have been especially true when one considers the class differences between Jeannine and Chloe and their well-heeled clients. To make the reading experience a bit easier, I have referred to most characters, no matter their race, by their first names. The custom of the day was to refer to free Blacks and slaves alike by their first names.

And finally, though it is not in Cape May County, I'd like to share a tidbit about the Absecon Island health spa that was referenced in the book. This was a real project, the brainchild of Dr. Jonathan Pitney, and one of the first that would bring the railroad to southern New Jersey. I have shifted the timeline of the project somewhat—in the book, the health spa is still in the investor stage. In reality, construction of the proposed railroad began in 1852 and in 1854 it began bringing visitors to the resort.

That resort is now known as Atlantic City.

I hope you have enjoyed *Murder at the Chestnut Wig* and its weaving of fact and fiction. Learning about the history of Cape May and the New Jersey shore, and sharing it with readers, continue to be the most rewarding aspects of penning this collection of mysteries.

NEWSLETTER SIGN-UP

I invite you to visit www.amymreade.com to explore my website and join my newsletter. You'll receive updates, promotions, contests, recipes, and more. As a subscriber, you'll also get access to exclusive content!

ALSO BY A.M. READE

THE CAPE MAY HISTORICAL MYSTERY COLLECTION

Cape Menace

A Traitor Among Us

The Night the Light Went Out

WRITTEN AS AMY M. READE

THE JUNIPER JUNCTION COZY HOLIDAY MYSTERY
SERIES

The Worst Noel
Dead, White, and Blue
Be My Valencrime
Ghouls' Night Out
MayDay!
Fowl Play
St. Patrick's Fray

STANDALONE BOOKS

Secrets of Hallstead House
The Ghosts of Peppernell Manor

THE MALICE SERIES

The House on Candlewick Lane
Highland Peril
Murder in Thistlecross

WRITTEN AS A. DIANNE READE

THE LIBRARIES OF THE WORLD MYSTERY SERIES

Trudy's Diary

❧

STANDALONE BOOKS

House of the Hanging Jade

ABOUT THE AUTHOR

Amy M. Reade is the *USA Today* and *Wall Street Journal* bestselling author of cozy and historical mysteries, dual time-line mysteries, and domestic suspense novels.

A former practicing attorney, Amy discovered a passion for fiction writing and has never looked back. In addition to works in several anthologies, she has so far penned eighteen novels, including standalone mysteries, the Malice Series, the Juniper Junction Cozy Holiday Mystery Series, the Libraries of the World Mystery Series, and the Cape May Historical Mystery Collection.

In addition to writing, Amy loves to read, cook, and travel. Amy lives in New Jersey and is a member of Sisters in Crime and the Alliance of Independent Authors.

You can learn more on her website at
www.amymreade.com.

BB bookbub.com/authors/amy-m-reade
g goodreads.com/amyreade

www.ingramcontent.com/pod-product-compliance
Lightning Source LLC
Chambersburg PA
CBHW061230310726
48971CB00007B/2000